The Deer in the Mirror

The Deer in the Mirror

Cary Holladay

 The Ohio State University Press • *Columbus*

Library of Congress Cataloging-in-Publication Data

Holladay, Cary C., 1958–
The deer in the mirror / Cary Holladay.
p. cm.
ISBN 978-0-8142-7002-8 (kindle) — ISBN 978-0-8142-5186-7 (pbk. : alk. paper) — ISBN 978-0-8142-9325-6 (cd)
1. American fiction—21st century. 2. Virginia—Fiction. I. Title.
PS3558.O347777D44 2013
813'.54—dc23
2013000161

Cover design by Janna Thompson-Chordas
Text design by Juliet Williams
Type set in ITC Stone Serif
Printed by Yurchak Printing

9 8 7 6 5 4 3 2 1

With love for my husband
John Bensko
and his sense of direction

and in memory of my mother
Catharine "Tas" Mitchell Holladay
writer

and my father
George Holladay
who rode a log from Rapidan to Raccoon Ford
in the flood of 1936

Contents

Acknowledgments

I am thankful to the staffs of the Museum of Culpeper History and the Orange County Historical Society for research assistance; to the University of Memphis and the National Endowment for the Arts for generous support; to Erin McGraw of The Ohio State University and to Malcolm Litchfield and his staff at The Ohio State University Press for making possible the Prize in Short Fiction; and to the editors who first published these stories, including Ben George of *Fugue;* Cheston Knapp of *Tin House;* John Easterly, the late Jeanne M. Leiby, Donna Perreault, and James Olney of *The Southern Review;* Paula Deitz and Ron Koury of *The Hudson Review;* Susan Burmeister-Brown and Linda B. Swanson-Davies of *Glimmer Train;* Christopher Stokes and Alex Taylor of *The Yalobusha Review;* R. T. Smith of *Shenandoah;* and Allan Gurganus and Kathy Pories of *New Stories from the South 2006* for suggestions both artistic and practical. Much affection to my sister Hilary Holladay and to my colleagues and students at the University of Memphis.

"Heart on a Wire" received First Prize in the 2006 *Glimmer Train* Fiction Open. "The Flood" received First Prize in the 2009 *Glimmer Train* Family Matters competition.

Acknowledgments

The stories have been previously published, some in slightly different form.

"The Flood," *Glimmer Train* 78, Spring 2011.
"The Deer in the Mirror," *Tin House* 39, Spring 2009.
"Every High Hill," *The Hudson Review* LXI: 3, Autumn 2008.
"The Runaway Stagecoach," *The Southern Review* 44: 3, Summer 2008.
"Hitching Post," *Shenandoah* 57: 3, Winter 2007.
"Heart on a Wire," *Glimmer Train* 62, Spring 2007.
"Ice Hands," *The Yalobusha Review: Literary Journal of the University of Mississippi* XII, 2007.
"The Burning," *Fugue* 28, Winter 2004–5, and *New Stories From the South: The Year's Best 2006*.
"The Days of the Peppers," *The Southern Review* 40: 4, Autumn 2004.

The Deer in the Mirror

August 1716
Morrison Plantation
James City County, Virginia

Verena Morrison Whitlow, a thirty-year-old widow, will have to share her house with another woman, for her seventeen-year-old brother Hugh is getting married. His pregnant bride, older by a good fifteen years, is abovestairs vomiting. Verena waits in the parlor with Hugh and the minister while the pendulum clock counts off the minutes and Hugh breathes through his mouth. Verena feels cold fury toward him.

The bride and her mother, a ship captain's widow, arrived last night from Norfolk. Verena's maid Sally, eighty years old and pure African, has attended the bride all day, holding her head over a basin; Verena raised the windows for fresh air.

Sweat creeps down Verena's neck. Still the bride does not appear. She's three months gone, Verena estimates. Hugh went to Norfolk in May to sell plantation goods and returned cocky and penniless. When Verena questioned him, he admitted to gambling. Two weeks ago, a letter from the woman announced her condition and imminent arrival. A postscript in another hand, probably her mother's, insinuated court consequences if Hugh failed to marry her.

In the stifling parlor, the clock strikes six.

"Let's move into the hall," Verena suggests.

The minister agrees. Hugh is silent, terrified, Verena knows, a child taking an old wife.

The central hall is cooler, and they take seats in chairs along the wall. Through a windowpane, Verena observes the broad sweep of the Chickahominy River. She loves that view. The minister's shallop, tied at the dock, bobs in shimmering light. Verena comforts herself: this time tomorrow, Hugh will be gone, off on Governor Alexander Spotswood's westward expedition. The minister will stay the night, perform a blessing of Spotswood's company, and then sail home to his six children and a wife who is ill with malaria. What might Verena send to her? Rose or barberry conserve; that's good for debility. A jar of each, if she has enough.

Since the death of Verena's father two years ago, the farm has struggled. The hemp and flax crops failed. The cattle died. The mulberry trees developed blight; the silkworms vanished. It's harder to provide for the slaves, and they've taken to running off. Hugh is little help. The Morrison plantation is the last on the road west of Williamsburg. Governor Spotswood will stop for a double purpose: to gather Hugh, who will be only so much nuisance, and, Verena expects, to propose marriage to her.

At the sound of footsteps on the stairway, Hugh rises clumsily. His bride, with her mother and Sally supporting her, descends a step and sinks. She reaches for a basin proffered by Sally. Verena and the minister avert their eyes, but Verena is aware of Hugh staring slack-jawed while the woman heaves.

The minister murmurs, "Perhaps we ought to wait until morning."

"Now," says Verena. It was she who had the banns announced in church, and never mind the haste. She picked through her mother's jewelry and found a ring to fit the woman, a pearl on an enameled band.

At last, the bride, her mother, and Sally reach the bottom of the staircase.

The woman has no one to give her away. Her father, Captain Thelaball, was a friend of Verena's father. Captain Thelaball talked of pirates, of how they lit long, slow-burning matches and stuck them in their hair and beards for the convenience of smoldering fire and for a fearsome appearance. Pirates finally murdered the old captain. Now Alexander Spotswood, who was likewise a friend of Captain Thelaball, hounds the pirates to justice. Blackbeard, the worst of all, eludes him. Alexander seems obsessed with him, and his anger disturbs Verena.

"Would you like to be seated?" she asks the bride, who looks so ill that Verena feels a stir of pity.

"Yes," the woman says, and Verena turns away from her fetid breath.

The woman lowers herself into a chair. "Oh!" she shrieks, pointing to the window. A deer peers inside.

Hugh says, "My sister's pets. She lets them into the house and gives them treats." He gives Verena a quick smile, and she remembers him as a child, clinging to her.

"You let deer inside?" hisses the bride's mother. Her face, a hog's, swings toward Verena, who ignores her.

The minister, who has witnessed an entire brace of deer in this house, clears his throat. "A charming eccentricity. Shall we begin?"

As he commences the ceremony, Verena remembers her own wedding to Thomas Whitlow. She was fifteen. Her father opened his finest wines: canary, claret, Malaga, and sherry, and there was dancing in this very hall. When Thomas died, Verena was still fifteen. Her marriage is recorded in the family Bible, where tonight she will write, *Hugh Bayly Morrison m. Lydia Frances Thelaball.*

"The ring, please," the minister says, and Hugh produces it.

The ring sticks, and the bride shoves it over her knuckle. Verena winces: her mother's pearl.

The bride's mother regards Verena with triumph in her eyes. If only the old woman knew how poor they are, despite this fine house. Of course, Verena owns her late husband's plantation, a property situated on the Blackwater River in Isle of Wight County. She keeps an overseer there and has tried without success to sell it. That farm is even less profitable than this one.

". . . man and wife," the minister says.

Hugh does not kiss his bride. After a silence, he addresses the minister. "Mint julep?"

"That would be welcome." The minister's smile, though pained, is the first in the house for some days.

Verena sends Sally for the butler, Isom, and soon there are cold pewter cups for everyone except the bride, who waves hers away. Hugh bolts his julep and reaches for another.

"I'm hungry," announces the bride's mother.

Verena gestures to the dining room, where a cold supper is ready. Hugh hurries toward it, his mother-in-law at his heels. The bride attempts to stand, then gags and vomits onto her lap.

The next morning, Verena wakes early and hears them coming—Governor Spotswood and his campaigners. Presently they arrive, sixty men and their animals making a commotion in the yard. The Governor steps down from his coach. The minister prays over the expedition and then departs, taking with him, to Verena's relief, the bride's mother.

Pale and silent, Hugh joins Verena and the Governor at breakfast. Of his bride there is no sign, and to Verena's inquiries, Hugh replies, "She's well enough." He fumbles at the sideboard for the brandy bottle.

Verena exchanges glances with the Governor—Alexander, to her. This is how marriage would feel, sharing buttered bread, small fried fish, and the intimacy of opinion. He brought oranges which came from Tangier, Morocco, where he was born to English parents. Shipments reach him often from his family holdings in that exotic place. He brought pomegranates too, and pepper, cinnamon, and cloves.

Already the day is hot, and judging from the noise outside, the men are eager to move along, yet Alexander lingers. After breakfast, he leads Verena into the parlor.

At last he says, "I would like for you to become my wife."

She has seen birds mating on the road, so impassioned they don't startle at the approach of a wagon. That's how it should be, but she doesn't feel it for him. "May I think about it?"

"Will you give me your answer when I return?"

"I will."

"There is a condition," he says. "The deer or me."

A weight descends on her heart. Oh, she has dogs and cats, but those stay outside. She loves the deer's reflections in mirrors, a glimpse of an animal's head behind her own. There's a fawn in the house at this moment, though she doesn't know where.

"They're wild animals," Alexander says. "A buck gets angry, he'll hurt you."

Is this how wedded life would be, arguments and clashing wills? In the other marriage, everything was Thomas's way, because she didn't know her own mind.

She asks, "How long will you be gone?"

"Many weeks. I won't take the coach into the mountains. We'll go on horseback." There's pleasure in his voice; he likes to be outdoors. "We'll follow the Rappahannock River, cross the Blue Ridge Mountains, and explore the Shenandoah Valley and beyond."

The enterprise holds many dangers, Verena knows: rugged terrain; the difficulties of guiding a sizable group of men, no matter how trained and eager; and hostile savages. Though the Indians are mostly gone from the East, they inhabit the frontier in large numbers. "Please be careful," she says.

Many of Alexander's men are Germans, recent immigrants. He has told her of his plans for their future. He'll establish mines and furnaces for smelting.

Everything he does is part of a larger design—as she herself would be.

The men are shooting rifles in the sultry air, wasting bullets. Dogs are yipping. Verena smells burnt powder. Alexander takes her face between his hands. His kiss surprises her, full on the mouth. He says, "You would be the Governor's lady. Mine, and that of Virginia. Does that appeal to you?"

"Such a public occupation," she says.

"Only insofar as you would like it to be. Verena, do you realize what power you have?" His grin is mischievous, an expression she hasn't seen before. "Any man would fall at your feet if you smiled, or creep off in shame if you frowned."

"Blackbeard too?"

His face grows dark. "I hear he's taken yet another wife, his fourteenth, a young girl whom he forces to lie with his companions while he watches. Does that not sicken you?"

"Good heavens." She feels more curious than sickened. "I doubt he actually marries them."

Alexander clenches his fists. "I'll kill him. I'll cut him to pieces."

His face is twisted in a snarl. Verena stifles a laugh and asks, "Is it true his flag is a devil holding an hourglass, for time running out? And a spear pointed at a heart? And his real name, what is it?"

"He's too vile to have any place in your mind." Alexander's voice rises. "He's utterly depraved, a cruel, drunken thief and coward."

"Edward something," she says. "Is that right?"

"Edward Teach. Let us say no more about him, not while we speak of marriage."

The fawn bursts into the room and knocks over a table, scattering china figurines. Alexander rises, grimacing, and steps over broken fragments.

"I'm leaving two soldiers here," he says.

Surprised, she asks, "Why?"

"Suppose there's an insurrection? Two white women on an isolated farm aren't safe."

Verena thinks of Sally and Isom and the people who work in her fields. She has never felt unsafe here. Hugh offers so little protection. It won't be any different having him gone. Last night as they finished supper, a bat flew into the dining room. Hugh shrieked louder than his bride, cowering from the bat's wavering flight, while Verena, the minister, and the bride's mother watched Isom swat the bat with a broom, scoop it off the floor, and take it out. If highwaymen burst in, or if pirates sailed upriver and seized Verena and her household, Hugh would still shriek and cower. He has always seemed childish

5

and lost. When he was barely two, their mother died giving birth to a stillborn daughter. Verena had to raise him.

"Wish me Godspeed," Alexander says, and he's out the door.

"Alexander." She follows, but he's lost to her in the throng.

His men halloo, milling and hurrying and sauntering, Negroes and Indians among them. The Germans' guttural words sound like curses. Verena's excited servants run here and there. Neighbors have arrived, seeking a word with Alexander. He is actually the lieutenant governor, though called Governor by all. The English governor, George Hamilton, the Earl of Orkney, has never visited Virginia. The Earl, it is said, spends his time among jesters and actors. He has Indians brought to him, preferring those with scarification and indelibly inked skin, and seeks to talk with them by inventing gibberish. Alexander regularly crosses the ocean to meet with the Earl and King George.

A fawn nuzzles Verena's arm. Easier to forsake a man than the beseeching wild. She wants to believe some affection for her has grown in their unknowable hearts.

Alexander is conferring with a group of others. They surround someone on the ground. Verena approaches, sensing trouble. The fallen man breathes hard, his face dark red.

Alexander tells her, "Snakebit. He's Conrad Brumback, a German. We'll have to leave him behind. Sawney sucked the poison out," and he gestures to one of the Indians.

"He can stay in the house," Verena says.

Two large men step forward, and Alexander says to Verena, "Eisley and Bingham will protect you. They'll keep watch over your farm and sleep in the barn."

One look into their faces, and rebellion ignites in Verena's heart. Their expressions are level and accusatory, as if she herself might lead an uprising. Spies, she thinks. They'll watch me, not guard me. Bingham and Eisley carry the sick man into the house.

All bustle and hurry now, though to Verena, this hot noon feels wrong for starting off. Journeys should begin in the morning. One shout from Alexander, and the men leap into formation. How fast they leave her, even at a walk. Her neighbors depart. She waves to an arm that might belong to Hugh. Well, maybe this will make a man of him.

The sky goes green and dark, but there's no rain. Verena's bergamot and columbine are trampled. Hummingbirds hover above the ruined plants. Her fowl brood in their run; her dogs on the porch rest heads on paws. A dry storm, her mother would have said.

She met Alexander five years ago when her father invited him for a visit. When he arrived, she was making pastries with nuts and cherries. He first saw her with the dough in her hands, and once the cakes were baked, she served them on a silver dish. He ate several, she remembers. That pastry-maker is the person to whom he proposed, she believes, not the stubborn deer-keeper she has become. Well, a proposal buoys a woman's spirits. *A fine man,* her father used to say of one or another of her suitors, concerned she hadn't married again.

To her surprise, Dr. Evans, the physician who has treated her family for many years, comes riding into the yard. "The Governor sent me," he says, "for the snakebitten fellow."

She leads him into the house, where Conrad Brumback lies unconscious in the parlor atop the Turkey-work carpet. Sally is bathing his face with a cloth. On his swollen arm, the bites resemble the punch marks of an awl. His prominent facial bones and dark mustache make him handsome. Verena says, "You may go, Sally."

Dr. Evans takes a bottle of turpentine from his bag and pours it into the wounds. "The poison will have to work out of his system," he explains.

If Conrad dies, Verena decides, he can be buried in the Morrison cemetery. Yet the burying ground that comes to her mind is the Whitlow plot where her husband lies—a sadder, shabbier site which dates back ninety years, to the time when the Isle of Wight was known as Warriscoyack. Thomas's grandfather is buried there, too. The stone says he was born in Dunfermline, Scotland, in 1609, the marker erected "by his Most Disconsolate Widow."

Since neither Thomas's first wife nor Verena bore Thomas any children, the long Whitlow line has ended.

"You've had hard times since your father died," the doctor says. "Hugh's learning about farming now, is he?"

"Slowly." Verena watches Conrad Brumback's impassive face. He is somewhere beyond sleep. She guesses he would agree that Hugh Morrison is a *dummkopf.*

"If what I hear is correct, the Governor will gladly help with this farm," the doctor says merrily. "Are you to marry him, Verena?"

How dare he ask her such a question in front of a stranger, even if the stranger is unconscious? She says, "My brother's wife is with child. Will you see her?"

You go into the earth when you die and are buried, and then what happens? She wonders as she takes Dr. Evans up the stairs. Lydia appears, haggard. It's the first time Verena has seen her since the nuptials. She looks as if she hasn't slept. Verena leaves Dr. Evans with her. Suppose she herself were in Lydia's position? Chrysanthemum and tansy, which she knows to be abortifacients, grow in her garden. Oh, maybe a child would be a comfort.

Her father died of a venereal disease. She believes he contracted it during a visit to England. No remedy aided, not powder of tin or asafetida or ivory filings in plantain juice. Suffering, he bathed in milk and camphor, endured tobacco clysters, and drank the water in which a smith's tools were cooled, but found no relief.

Always time running out. The hourglass, the spear pointing at the heart. Who would refuse such society, the privileges and power that would be hers, were she the Governor's wife?

Descending the stairs, she finds a small doe in the hallway. The animal passes close enough that she runs a hand along the smooth hide. It's an August afternoon, with the sun lighting up the river, and suddenly, she feels happy and hopeful. Alexander Spotswood is in part a cause of her happiness, the more so because he is away.

The sick man, Conrad: all he can do is lie in the parlor, and she in her health might go to him. Her mind stops at that, the way her feet would stop at the end of a path. She enters the parlor with apprehension. His color is normal, his breathing regular. Slowly he opens his eyes. They're a vivid blue.

She asks, "Are you better?"

"Yes." He stretches out as if he feels strength returning. "You have a fine place."

"Thank you," Verena says, glad he speaks English. She recognizes the shock of physical attraction. How would it be, with him?

"The New World," he says in wonder. "When the ship landed in Norfolk, it let the men off and took on cargo for Europe. I've never seen so much iron ore, glass, pitch, sturgeon, and bushels of, what do you call the tree that is a root, for tea?"

"Sassafras," Verena says, transfixed by his blue eyes. "Could you eat something?"

"Yes, I'm hungry."

She prepares a plate of the fruit that Alexander brought and adds ham, bread, and cheese, and takes it to him with pitchers of water and cider. She clears cards from a gaming table and sets the food down. Conrad Brumback remains on the floor for a moment. She senses he is examining the red heels of her shoes. With effort, he rises, comes to the table, and takes a seat.

When he sees the cider, he says, "I hoped for this. I saw the press this morning, and your people gave me some to drink." He looks past her and gasps, "Ah!"

She turns her head and finds the little doe in the doorway. The deer kicks her hooves together and runs. Conrad calls out in his own language. Verena recognizes one of the few German words she knows: *Liebschen*. Sweetheart.

"I told her I didn't mean to scare her," Conrad says.

Verena chuckles.

He says, "Beautiful women are at their best when they laugh. And you are very beautiful."

"How did you learn English?" she asks.

"My mother was English."

She gestures to the food. "Please eat."

She slips out of the room and closes the door behind her, embarrassed and delighted. She hears Dr. Evans's footsteps on the stairs.

"There you are, Verena," he says. "I've advised your brother's wife to drink ginger tea to soothe her stomach."

"I'll make some for her." She points to the parlor. "He's much better. I took him food. How much do I owe you?"

Dr. Evans waves his hand. "It's my pleasure to be of service."

Clearly, he assumes the Governor will pay for her family's bills.

"Thank you," she says and shows the doctor out.

She brews a pot of ginger tea and carries it to Lydia, who is lying down on a high, canopied bed. She appears older each time Verena sees her. She has plaited her long, thin hair. Her hands, reaching for a teacup, show thick veins.

She says, "Will you visit with me for a little while? I'm glad my mother is gone." Though her face is mottled, her manner is lighter, as if her mother's departure has lifted some weight from her.

Verena smiles and takes a seat in a chair beside the window. She and Lydia may become friends after all.

Lydia sips the tea gratefully. "Hugh didn't want to marry me, and I didn't want to marry him," she says. "When he came to see us, my mother served strong punch. I should have . . ."

"It'll be all right," Verena says, touched by her distress, her need to explain. Hugh may be lucky to have this forthright woman for his wife. "With Hugh away for a while, you'll have a chance to get settled."

Lydia is quiet, finishing her tea. At last she sets the cup aside and says, "I loved somebody else, a woman. My mother wanted it to stop."

Verena holds her breath.

"So it stopped," says Lydia.

That evening, Sally brushes Verena's hair. Sally's eyes are blue with cataracts.

Sally will die and her jawbone will be long like a deer's, Verena thinks. Sally announces that the slaves think Conrad Brumback died and came back to life.

"You can't believe that," Verena says. These old blacks are not Christian, though the younger ones are, quite fervently.

Sally asks, "Will you marry the Governor?"

I won't do it. And yet there would be a sense of failure if Alexander simply went away, leaving her to the river and the farm and Hugh.

"He belongs to so many others," Verena says. The kindness, the mischief on his face, come back to her, hurting her heart for a moment, but he is forty years old; his career and the world have claimed him.

"Belongs to that pirate," Sally says.

Thomas Whitlow was thirty-eight, a widower whose uncle owned land adjoining the Morrisons' plantation. Verena saw him only three times before they were married—twice at church and once when he came to visit her, or more accurately, her father. Thomas described his farm on the Blackwater River and asked for her hand. Her father was very pleased. She understood the marriage marked an enlargement of each man's fortune, and she was proud of that. *Verena Whitlow*, she whispered, and the words tasted strange.

Marriage was terrible. Thomas Whitlow forced himself on her, and when it was over, he sometimes cried. She felt little personal emotion toward him. What she did feel was a resolve not to crumble under a man's authority as she had seen other women crumble. A wife owned nothing, only what her husband allowed her. Wives were no better than slaves. The passivity of her position appalled her, and she disliked Thomas's house and the gloomy site, a two days' journey south from her father's farm. The only thing she enjoyed was the smell of tannin from nearby swamps. The only familiar person was Sally, whom Verena took with her. Thomas set Verena to keeping his agricultural accounts. It was a cold winter. She mixed her ink with brandy so it wouldn't freeze.

Scourge broke out among the sheep. They tottered and died. Verena couldn't bear to look at them. On the third morning of the sickness, Thomas stirred charcoal into their oat feed and went out among them. He came back at midday and said, "They're no better," and his face showed tears of grief. That surprised her, and she reached out to touch his hand. He ate nothing and went out again.

That afternoon, in the chilly parlor, she served tea to visitors, a wool merchant and his wife. She wanted to run away from Thomas, his dark house, and his dying animals. Those were her thoughts as Sally collected the teacups. Sally would drink the dregs, Verena knew, for the sugar. Thomas burst in, staggering. Alarmed, she thought instantly of the sheep.

"I'm sick," he said.

The visitors departed, and Verena helped him to bed. He pushed the blankets away, dirtying them with the charcoal on his hands. She felt the heat from his body on the blankets.

Five days later, he was dead. Verena hung the Whitlow coat of arms upon the door and sent two slaves as messengers, one by land and the other by water, to spread the news.

The Whitlow graveyard had once contained a small church within palisades. At Thomas's funeral, mourners stood amid the ruins. The marker erected by the *Most Disconsolate Widow* was broken, portions having been carried off by fishermen to serve as mooring stones. The entire site was washing away beneath the brackish waters of the bay. While the minister prayed, Verena pondered the fact that she could continue to live in Thomas's house. By the time the prayer ended, she had decided to return to her father's home.

She allowed her father to take charge of the Whitlow plantation. That had been the reason for the marriage, after all. Her father sent an overseer, and the overseer and his family have lived since then in Thomas's house, the rent deducted from their wages.

Thomas must have felt passion for her. "Dear Verena," he said while dying, her hand in his, and the emotion in his voice touched her heart for the second time. The first time was the day he wept for the sheep.

Once she turned sixteen, the iron band that was her wedding ring no longer fit, and she took it off. Fourteen years had to elapse and the Colony's highest official propose before she reconsidered how Thomas said, "Dear." The memory feels like an angry chaperone as she thinks of the snakebitten German in her house, in her dubious care.

The trip to England took place when Verena was eighteen and Hugh six. With their father, they visited relatives and toured museums and gardens. In London, Verena was courted by an elderly duke. Her father said, "You could do far worse, Verena." To her, the duke was absurd, with false calves tucked into tight stockings, and paint and powder upon his face. Yet men bowed to him; women curtsied and fluttered their eyelashes. The duke had a country estate—actually a castle, Verena saw as he handed her down from a carriage. Fountains and statuary surrounded her, and swans swam on a marvelous lake.

11

Inside, suits of armor and chain mail stood beside a massive staircase. The duke guided Verena and her father down to his wine cellar, serving them glass after glass. Verena stumbled as they left the cellar. The duke's hand caressed her back.

Other guests appeared, and a banquet was served: roast pheasant, cakes flaming with rum sauce, and many bottles of wine. "Do you whip your slaves?" a man asked, stroking Verena's arm. In America, he said, he'd seen blacks in a headgear of bells which rang if they tried to run away, instruments so heavy they could snap a neck.

Irish musicians played jigs and reels. Swept into a dance, Verena tried to avoid the duke, whose face turned up again and again, eyes and lips dark against his pale, wrinkled skin.

In the night, in candlelight, she woke naked. A man writhed on top of her, and she recognized the duke's cologne. She pushed him, and he slapped her across the face. She kneed him, and he buckled backwards, cursing. She jumped off the bed and ran out into the hallway.

Door after door she flung open, finding pleasure-lovers in all manner of dishabille and congress. In one room, her naked father played with two women. In another, a dozen people mounted each other. A woman clutched a bedpost while a man spanked her. Mirrors hung on the walls and the ceiling. A swan flapped its wings, filling the air with down: it was a world of ejaculate and smoke, panting and whimpering. A man grabbed her wrist, but she wrenched away.

Down the stairs at a run. She slammed into a servant bearing a tray, and they all toppled—Verena, servant, and glasses of champagne. She rolled down the steps until she landed at the metal feet of an armored soldier. Did he flip up his visor and leer at her? Didn't he?

When she, Hugh, and their father departed from England, a man on the wharf sang a ballad. She'd never known a human throat could hold a note so long. She threw coins to the man, but they fell into the oily water. The movement brought pain in her womb. Those weeks at sea, she willed it out of her, pushing bloody gobbets from her body. The issue didn't stop until she smelled the pines of the Virginia coast. She washed with salt water and welcomed the sting.

The following night, she hears a scream and sits up in bed. Another scream, and she hurries to Lydia's room. She turns the knob, but the door doesn't open.

"Lydia!" She pounds on the door, but no sound comes from inside. In a moment, a light travels up the stairs. She expects Sally, but it's Conrad, holding a lamp.

"I want to help." He points to the door and makes a pushing motion.

"Yes." Startled that he seems so much recovered, she calls, "Lydia, stand back."

Conrad sets down the lamp and puts his shoulder to the door, but it doesn't budge. Lydia must have bolted it. Conrad perspires with the effort.

Isom the butler appears, his eyes heavy with sleep. Verena sends him to fetch a ladder. "Climb to Mrs. Morrison's window," she says, "and see if she's all right."

Isom obeys, and Conrad goes too. A full moon casts generous gray light.

There is the screech of the bolt sliding back. The door swings open, and Lydia cries, "There's an animal in here, behind the curtains."

Verena lifts the drapery and finds a fawn in hiding, its eyes huge. It's the same one that was in the house when Alexander visited. Was that only yesterday morning? "Come," she says gently, reaching out. The fawn emerges, and she leads it down the stairs and lets it out. It must be hungry and thirsty, but it will find its mother, even in the night.

Only then do Bingham and Eisley materialize, bounding out of the darkness. If there were an uprising, she'd be dead before they responded.

"I don't need you," she calls, anger in her voice, and the men amble away.

Isom and Conrad Brumback come back inside. Conrad catches Verena's eye. His lips twitch, and he laughs. She finds herself laughing too. The sound rises up and down the stairway like a song. She feels the excitement of Conrad's healing self, beside her.

They laugh their way down the hall. It feels like dancing, a step for him, a turn for her, and once they're in the parlor, she puts her hands to his chest and kisses him. Because of the laughter, she feels she has known him a long time.

In silence they take off their clothes. She has on only her nightgown and dressing gown, as if this parlor were their bedroom. So strange, her parlor in darkness. Moonlight catches on the clock face and on their bodies. What a surprise: her hair is turning white down there. Beneath her hand, his heart beats feather-light. She traces the knots of snakebite on his arm. He lays her out and she uncurls beneath him.

Afterward, he says, "The Governor wants to marry you. Everyone knows."

They sit naked on the parlor carpet. She hardly knows him, yet she loves him. She says, "I haven't been with any man since my husband died."

"I'm honored," he says, "that you would choose me."

"Now you have to stay here." She makes her voice playful, but she means it. She is struck by the sudden, almost violent connection she feels to him.

"Did you say you would tell the Governor when he returns?" asks Conrad.

"I'll tell him I don't want to marry him."

"But you would be almost a queen," he says. "I can't give you anything."

All she can do is shake her head.

"I'll soon be strong enough to catch up with the others," he says.

"Don't. You need to stay and rest."

"Everything I own went with them. My broadax, pick, and spade. My other clothes."

"My brother has things that would fit you," she says, "and if they don't, I'll have Sally make new clothes."

"No, no," Conrad says with a smile in his voice. He kisses her cheek.

She feels sharp disappointment that he doesn't reach for her again. She slips on her nightgown and dressing gown, climbs the stairs, and gets back into her bed, astonished. Mere hours ago, she heard Lydia scream, and look what that led to. Her skin smells of turpentine.

The next day, he works in the blacksmith shed and fashions a lock. The metal bolt has a heart at one end, a tulip at the other. "For you," he says. She asks him to put it on the door of her room, on the inside. He does, but he makes no attempt to lie with her again.

Now that he is recovering, he sleeps in the barn with Bingham and Eisley. He works hard, repairing the weathered dock on the river, and makes the other two help. Verena goes to her fields to see to harvesting. She has got to make the farm produce, but her mind is on Conrad. He is making up the rules, and she follows. He converses with her warily and in only one spot, at the back door of her house, away from Bingham and Eisley. He is twenty-five, she learns. If she married him, she wouldn't have to share him with anyone. This appeals to her, as do his traits of caution and intelligence. And loyalty, since he spoke of rejoining the expedition.

Verena and Lydia take meals together and stroll along the river when the day's heat eases. They walk as far as a certain white oak, then turn around. More than a week has passed since Alexander's visit. He must be hundreds of miles away, in high country by now. She imagines the column of men heading into a mountain gap and disappearing forever.

14

Beside her, Lydia gestures to Conrad working on the landing. "I've never seen a stronger man."

They walk silently, though Verena believes Lydia knows what has happened.

Lydia twists a handkerchief in her hands. "Your brother and I won't be happy."

"You'll be happy once the baby comes," Verena says, "and Hugh will be proud."

Lydia asks, "If you don't marry the Governor, will Hugh be angry?"

Verena glances at her face and finds sympathy. "I imagine he would be. Having the Governor as a brother-in-law would be a great advantage. But I . . ." and she pauses.

"Don't marry him if you don't want to. Look what happens if you let somebody else choose."

Verena thinks of the heart-and-tulip lock and hopes it means Conrad wants her, that he is waiting for Alexander to return so she can refuse his proposal and accept Conrad's. She tries to feel encouraged. Yet days and nights slip by, and she can't sleep.

The Governor's Palace be damned.

It bothers her that Conrad has only one set of clothing. One morning she gathers some of Hugh's shirts and trousers and goes out to the barn. She finds him trimming his mustache, peering into a mirror balanced against a bale of hay. Gravely he puts the scissors down and faces her, his arms crossed over his chest. Bingham and Eisley are snoring in the straw. She sets the clothes on top of the hay.

He says, "I told you, I don't need more clothes."

"Talk to me," Verena whispers. Her hands tremble as she motions him outside.

There's fog this morning, and the leaves are turning yellow. She looks into Conrad's face and sees remoteness. It's not her honor or Alexander's that concerns him, she realizes, so much as his feelings for some other person whose presence she senses like a shadow.

She should have guessed before. "Is there a woman in Germany?"

"Yes," he says. "I said I would send for her. I promised."

"Do you love her? Do you want to marry her? How can you, now?"

"She's a young girl, my sweetheart." He actually smiles, as if expecting

Verena to be glad. "Her family has died. She lives with an aunt, and they're very poor. I said I would bring them here, her and her aunt."

"But you could marry me." She hates how imperious she sounds.

He pats her hand. Her mind registers that: pats her hand, when he could embrace her. "It is not even a question."

"I love you. Don't you want to be with me?"

"There was a full moon that night. It made us do what we did."

She stares at him.

He touches the corners of his lips as if from nervous habit. "You're a rich lady. I am nobody. Why do you want me?"

"I'm not rich at all. This place is . . ." She waves her arm toward the fields. Can't he see the farm is floundering?

"I don't love you."

"Then go," she says furiously. "Why do you stay here? Go away."

She heads back to the house, her head feeling as if it's on fire. She will tell Alexander yes. Yes, and they can be married right away.

Later she glimpses Conrad from her window. He moves among the trees for a little while longer, and then he is gone. Bingham and Eisley idle at the repaired dock, fishing. She keeps to her room miserably all day, looking out the window, hoping Conrad will return. How easily he departed, as if he were relieved. He *was* relieved, she realizes.

At supper, Lydia announces, "I'm going back to Norfolk."

"But you can't," Verena says, stunned. "You're married, and the baby is coming."

"The baby will be legitimate when it's born, and then Hugh can divorce me. He'll be glad," Lydia says. "He can make provision for the baby. I won't ask for much."

It's evening. They step outside to walk along the river. Lydia's broad face looks peaceful for the first time. Verena realizes she has been thinking hard.

"Are you going back to your mother's house?" Verena asks.

"I'll live with my woman friend," Lydia says. "We can take care of the baby together."

The breeze lifts their hair. Verena reminds herself that Hugh's well-being will be affected by the choices Lydia makes. "Hugh may want the child to live with him, especially if it's a son."

"He may keep the child, if it comes to that." Lydia spreads her arms. "What chance would I have in court, after all?"

"How will you and your friend survive? Who is she?"

"She's a widow. She owns a tavern. Sailors go there from round the world."

"Where will you live?"

"There are rooms above the tavern," says Lydia. "I'll work there, too."

Verena imagines drunken men and the hard, noisy labor of serving them: horrendous. She feels frightened for Lydia. "Please stay. I'll quit having deer inside. It's folly. I shouldn't risk a fawn's being away from its mother for so long. I haven't made you welcome enough."

"You've done all you could," Lydia says.

"Won't you stay at least until the baby comes?" Verena says. "Hugh is young, but he'll treat you properly. I'll see to it. Can't you see a life here, pleasant enough?"

Lydia says, "I would be so wretchedly unhappy, and so would Hugh"

"Those sailors, aren't they rough company? Fighting, causing trouble?"

"Most of them are decent, just far from home. There's a hired man who keeps order."

The river is deserted. The world feels humid and empty, as if it's both old and new. A cloudy dusk has fallen, darkening the water along the shore.

"I've done badly by Hugh," Lydia says. "I'll leave a letter for him. In a few years, he'll hardly remember me." She tugs at her pearl ring. "This was your mother's."

"Keep it, Lydia," Verena says.

"My hands are swollen. It won't come off," Lydia says, as if in apology.

They reach the oak where they usually turn around. Verena thinks this is the second honest conversation she has had today, possibly the last she'll have for the rest of her life. She has but a few moments to say the things that are true. "I fell in love with Conrad, and now he's gone."

"Will you marry the Governor?"

Verena looks across the water but sees instead a drawing room, herself receiving guests, hears Alexander's voice and children's voices. That life seems a haven of comfort and stability. With her wounded, disappointed heart, she should welcome it, but she shakes her head.

Lydia says, "Did Conrad go to join the expedition? Back to troop quarters? Go to him. I'll go with you, if you want."

"I don't know where he went," Verena says, "and he loves somebody else. He said so."

"Those two thugs out in the barn, do they know where he is?"

A mosquito stings Verena's cheek. She slaps it away. "They probably do, but I won't ask them. Conrad doesn't want me."

"Let's go back to the house," Lydia says.

I loved a man, Verena thinks, and he left; I made a friend, and she's leaving too. Conrad is the only man she ever wanted to marry, not from conviction that she should, but from desire. Those birds in the road, heedless while they coupled: will she ever know that feeling again?

Bingham and Eisley are fishing from the dock. As Verena and Lydia pass by, the men make a show of adjusting their shirts, smirking.

Why, they're wearing the garments she left at the barn. If she tells them to return the things, she'll be admitting the clothing was for Conrad. She has to pretend the clothes were meant for them, too. Their faces appear surlier than ever. She could order them to leave, but that would be a kind of surrender.

"Pay them no mind," Lydia murmurs. "You can be independent. You have a place."

Verena knows they will tell Alexander about Conrad. Maybe the news will carry on the wind. Alexander will hear it in the report of the guns his men fire to claim land for the King.

She had thought the choice was hers to make, but it isn't. Until today, this evening, she'd have said no. But with Conrad gone and her spirits sinking, she would say yes. As she heads back to the house in the dusk, Lydia a heavy shadow beside her, she knows Bingham and Eisley will be her undoing.

If she wants Alexander badly enough, she could keep vigil by the road, spend all her daylight hours watching for his return. It's too soon. He must be still out west. There has been no letter. Well, in such country, how would you get a letter out? Surely he could spare one man to ride back. Yet he had not promised her any letters.

Days pass. Bingham and Eisley fish from the dock until a chilly, stormy spell descends. When the sun breaks through, she finds the dock empty, the barn empty, Bingham and Eisley gone. She should not be shocked, but she is, her throat dry, her heart plunging. She imagines them running for the western hills, so eager to carry the news of her treachery to Alexander that they don't stop for rest or food.

To leave this farm is to disobey Alexander. He ordered them to protect her.

In the barn, the mirror Conrad used when trimming his mustache makes a brilliant mocking disk on a bale of straw where he left it. She sets the mirror on a wooden shelf with curry combs and buckets. How strange to see her eye caught in reflection among the tools.

Work consumes her. The rain has spoiled at least half the melons and corn. She pulls ears from stalks and finds worms curling in the cobs. Slaves slice open the first of the yams for her inspection: stringy and pale. At least the tobacco has survived, and the squash and pumpkins. The grapes in the arbor are sticky, fallen on the ground, rotting. She tears the remaining grapes from the trellis and piles them into baskets until her hands are blue. Three deer come close, and she feeds them. Their long necks bend as they eat.

Lydia finds her and says, "If I don't leave soon, it'll be too late for me to travel."

Verena begs, "Stay with me until Alexander comes back. And Hugh." She wipes her hands on her apron and pets the deer.

Lydia samples a grape. Her mouth puckers. "Will you help me leave? Please, Verena. Isn't there someone who could drive me, or take me away on the river?"

Verena's neck aches. Sunset blazes around them, making her stained hands look black. How lonely she will be when Lydia is gone. "All right," she says. "I'll send for a boat."

The vessel arrives the next afternoon, manned by a skilled waterman.

"I'll write you, Verena." Lydia kisses her cheek.

She feels almost too bereft to answer. Isom helps Lydia into the craft, Sally hands her a basket of food and drink, and the waterman lifts Lydia's baggage and secures it with rope. The man steers away from the dock, out toward the river's dark channel. Waving, Lydia disappears.

Another week goes by. Bingham and Eisley reappear on the dock, fishing, as if they have been there all along. Not a word passes between them and Verena. She tries not to wonder where they have been or what they have been doing. Dry weather returns. Red leaves tumble through the sky and pile up in the yard. With every wagon that passes, each cart and rider, any yelp from her dogs, she finds herself hurrying out of the house. Once at dawn, she struggles to push her arms into her dressing gown before running barefoot outside, but it's only a peddler, sleepily making his way on a mule.

Alexander has to come this way. There's no other road.

At last, on a September noon with sky as blue as the center of a flame, she hears wheels and shouting. She hurries to a window. It's the entire expedition, men and their horses as clamorous as the day they set out. She had almost forgotten them, thinking only of Alexander. The head of the column reaches the house, the men unkempt and jubilant. She searches for Conrad but can't identify him in the throng. Two figures—Bingham and Eisley—stride out of her yard and jump upon a wagon. She sinks down onto the floor and hugs her knees, her breath tight in her chest.

Sally taps her arm. "Go down to the parlor."

Verena does so, her feet numb on the stairs. Dust lifts from the road and stains the windows yellow, yet the marching men have gone quiet, or is she only imagining that? Quiet except for trudging feet and the jingle of harness.

The door opens, and a man calls, "Verena!"

It's Hugh, taller than he used to be, with sparse new whiskers making his face strangely older. His face shows no secret knowledge, only eagerness. She embraces him, and he asks, "Where's my wife?"

"She went back to Norfolk. She left a letter in your room."

Confusion spreads across his face, but Verena darts past him, out into the yard.

The column has passed except for a few desultory wagons. The Governor's coach, red and black, still approaches, bringing up the rear. Four bay horses pull it, grand animals with matched gait, the driver nestled in the box. Verena hovers beside a barberry bush and takes a deep breath. The air smells of wood smoke. She has come this far, as if her feet and not her heart have decided for her. She steps forward.

Draperies are drawn across the coach's windows, white silk curtains. The driver catches her eye and flourishes his whip. Dust rises into her face, and her ears fill with noise as the coach gathers speed. Her dogs rush toward it, snapping at the wheels. Then it's gone.

The Burning

Waugh's Ford, Virginia
Beside the Rapid Anne River
January 29, 1745

The woman is burning alive. As the fire eats her skin and muscles and nerves, her screams shake the rocks. She is chained by the neck to an iron stake, amid a pile of stones. Heavy ropes about her waist hold her fast. Her arms are tied, the wrists lashed together. Her skin flakes to ash, peels away from her body, and rises in pieces around her. Beside her, the river boils and churns from recent rains. It's already flooding. Families who live by the river will gather their things and move to higher ground, to the woods.

The woman, Rose, is a slave. She murdered her master, Peter Ryburn, by serving him poisoned milk. She has had a trial in the Court of Oyer and Terminer, where she was found guilty and ordered drawn upon a hurdle to the place of execution and there to be burnt.

While preparations were made, she was held six days in the gaol. Last night, Ryburn's son William and nephew Robert paid the keeper to go away while they raped and scourged her. She meets her death bruised and lacerated, with a broken arm.

Had the men who bound her and lit the fire—William's cousin Robert among them—anticipated the volume of her screams, they would have gagged her. They did grant her the kindness of a blindfold. Her shrieks rise and swell. The heads of the men and women gathered at the river are bells, and Rose's cries are the clapper. Children cover their ears with their hands. No men went to work this morning at the gold mine or the coal mine, though some of the planters stayed home to slog through sodden fields and tend animals, and they too hear the cries. In time, settlers thirty miles distant, all the way to the Blue Ridge Mountains, will claim they heard the woman die.

The fire takes her fast. William stands with Robert as close as they dare, the fire too loud for them to talk. The woman is a live crouching thing, her skin blackening, blood and hair exuding their own particular stench as she roasts, her limbs changing position as the smoke lifts and blows. Within the fire, tethered to the stake, she moves in a slow crawl as if stalking or hunting. She works an arm free, claws at the blindfold, and casts it from her face so it sails beyond the circle of fire. It catches William full on the cheek. He staggers, cursing, flinging the blazing cloth away, searing his fingers and palm. Through the smoke and his own pain, he sees Robert scoop a rock from the ground and hurl it toward the woman.

William is the one who will go and report to Dame Ryburn—Eileen—his father's young bride and now widow, only recently arrived from Ireland and eight months gone in pregnancy, that the execution has been accomplished. He dreads this chore. Eileen will ask for details. Beautiful, she nonetheless possesses the most expressionless face he has ever seen, and the most insatiable curiosity. You should have been there yourself, he will tell her if she presses him too much. He is surprised by how deeply the execution has troubled him. Eileen will remember forever whatever he tells her, with the same satisfaction with which she examines the jewels William's father gave her, treasures to be scrutinized and set back in their nests of velvet, inside a teakwood box, rings and bracelets that belonged to the first Mrs. Ryburn, William's mother, a woman so much older than Eileen and dead so long that Eileen has admitted confusing her with her own mother, has pictured her own mother wearing these adornments, though her mother, dead too, was poor and owned no jewelry at all.

When the burned woman is reduced to an immobile form, like melted statuary, the rain begins again. It falls on her smoking body, quelling the last flames, sizzling on the stones. The rain drives the people off, farmers and women, miners, blacks who came for their own reasons, and an Indian or two or three, for they have not entirely vanished as they are said to have done, only retreated to the darkest places of the forest, which they share with deer and bear and elk.

Rose is a knot on the boulders. A piece of bone shows through her charred leg. In death, she has twisted, woven herself into a mat of her own leather and marrow and hair.

William's face burns with a wretched heat and so does his hand, the fingers and palm that touched the blindfold she threw at him. How she writhed beneath him last night, while his cousin held her down. Now the running of the farm is up to William, in this time of damnable flood, and he is not the farmer his father was.

He turns away from the river and unties his tethered horse. Robert has already ridden away. William will go home to the splendid brick house his father built and enter the room where Eileen pours tea from a porcelain pot, hiding her condition beneath rugs and robes, the room airless from the fire she insists on day and night, believing it will drive off the fevers she fears in the strange new country. William will tell her the slave woman is dead, and she will sip her tea and look out the window at the rain falling on the bare branches of trees and the flooded pastures, the forests of tulip poplar and the gouged red clay embankments where the rain has washed away chunks of soil, carrying with it horses, cows, sheep, and an unfortunate dwelling or two, and there will begin a long war between William and Eileen over the management of the farm. Slaves predict in whispers that Eileen's baby will be born dead or deformed, a devil, but the infant that will come cannonballing out from between her legs the morning after Rose's death will be in fact superbly healthy, just small and premature, a posthumous son.

William and his wife Martha have not been blessed. Martha has not been able to bear a child. She is older than William, and now it's too late.

As he mounts his horse and turns away from the river toward the road, he spies children playing with the wooden hurdle upon which Rose was dragged. They climb on it, crashing and shrieking, and take turns pulling each other, for the object is after all a sledge, and it will be saved for use again. William wonders if the King will be notified of the poisoning and the execution. It's the sort of thing his wife might take upon herself, regarding the King as she does with a sense of duty so profound that she writes letters to him on all kinds of Orange County matters, crops and livestock, weather and politics, though William has tried to discourage her. She pours into the letters the attention she would have given their children, had they produced any. He should know of this, she will say, meaning the King, and she'll disappear into her chamber. Hours later, William will find her with a thick stack of cream vellum stationery, filled with her beautiful hand, letters ready to go to England. She's a loyal subject, ever proving her obeisance, whereas William for his part has begun to question whether the colonies might be better off with self-government.

His horse stops in the road and whickers. William slaps his legs against its sides. Rain smacks his face. His burned hand is too sore to hold the reins. The horse behaves strangely. She circles slowly, turning as if performing a maneuver that circus animals are said to do, preparing for some elaborate equine flight or trick. William cries a sharp command, flaps the reins, and kicks her side, but the animal turns back to the river, faces the execution place, pauses, and gallops toward it.

William has owned horses all his life, but he didn't know one could spring from stillness to such speed in an instant. He loses his balance, slips from the saddle, and falls to the road so hard he wonders if he has cracked his spine. Luckily, he fell clear of the horse; he wonders even as his head spins if the creature meant to throw and drag him.

For a moment he lies stunned. With difficulty he sits up, feeling every moment of his forty-seven years: the burned face and hand, the bruised spine, and the sharp dental flares that signal the onset of one of the toothaches that have beleaguered him in recent years. By nightfall, he'll be tying his jaws up in a huge handkerchief and searching his wife's cupboards for laudanum.

The crowd takes its time dispersing, people talking among themselves. Does no one see him dazed here in the mud? He jerks himself to his knees and stands, dizzy. The shouting children, the bucking sledge on its rope, blur before him. Here comes his horse, docile yet with lightning in her eyes: nothing to do but catch the bridle and climb again upon her back. He thinks the children are laughing at him; the women bending their heads toward each other and the groups of men unknotting as they leave the river front are finding fault with him and his family.

"Damn you," he says, unsteady on his horse's back. "Damn you."

A child mocks him, miming his fall—or at least that is how William interprets the youngster's swaying gait—and he leans from the saddle and cuffs the impudent face, sending the boy sprawling in the muck. The child's mother screeches, and William takes off, the horse's long, familiar strides bearing him home.

Even through the rain, he can still smell Rose and the fire. He needs a bath to wash her from his skin.

She took her secret with her: what she used in the milk. Trial and torture did not pry it out of her, nor the Ryburn men taking turns in what for William was a surprisingly pleasurable assault; his cousin Robert kept his head enough to spit some questions at her, but she did not speak, just fought with demonic strength even after Robert broke her arm above the elbow so it flapped and dangled. That was the only time she cried out.

Arsenic, people say, for arsenic can be found on every farm and in any apothecary's shop, and there are druggists in Orange and Stevensburg. Hemlock perhaps, or some roots and herbs known only to Africans, mixed in darkness and cursed in a savage tongue.

It was powdered dried foxglove that stopped Peter Ryburn's heart. That was what Rose used, and some of the other slaves know it, having discovered the concoction in a corner of the cabin where she lived alone, an arrangement created by Peter Ryburn the better to spend time with her; her two young daughters live with an old, blind slave who makes corn shuck baskets. Foxglove: a little brown flower, a little dust, and a man's heart slows and halts. The milk was tart, but that might have been because of something the cow ate, or an effect of the flood, changing the taste of the water the cattle drank from river and streams. Peter Ryburn, aged seventy-three, was hale and strong. He reeled from the table clutching his chest, his starched white napkin falling from his lap. William leaped from the table to steady him, but Peter was dead before he fell to the floor. They had been arguing, father and son, over which crops to plant in which fields, while Eileen looked from one to the other with the only real expression of pleasure William has ever observed on her lovely face.

Everyone knew Peter Ryburn's death was not natural.

All day, the day of the burning, Rose's remains lie on the stone. From high places in hills and trees, the buzzards come, dropping down to the riverside as the body cools from its fierce heat. Despite the char and ash, there is still nutrition in the deeper parts, savory to the creatures that can make a meal from carcass and offal, and these morsels they reach with their tearing beaks, flapping their wings as they jostle and balance on the boulders. Tonight, white men will come with burlap and wrap what's left. They'll bury her in the woods unmarked, for they are keeping charge of her and they don't want her grave to become a witching place for other slaves who would do as she has done.

When the birds have eaten their fill and raised their huge wings to the sky, what remains among the tossed bones is a small white stone, the size of a grape, translucent and containing a frozen human form, as if fire can freeze and preserve: Peter Ryburn's last child, a loop of flesh with discernible head, its legs a fishtail, curved within the sac. The iron stake, Rose's stake, will be pried out of the stone by slaves in the night, and for years, it will inspire plans of revenge.

Eileen will hear of the treachery of William's horse from others, as if she has an ear in the wind. That will please her, William knows, that he was thrown, humbled, that he was hurled into mud. She doesn't care about Rose, just the burning. The horse and its small mystery, the puzzle of its circling with William helpless and furious on its back, its headlong rush to the river, leaving him behind, its diffident return to its injured rider: Eileen will love that, turning it over and over in her mind as she warms herself at the fire and suckles her baby, the weight of new motherhood melting away despite the toddies and buttered shortbreads she enjoys. The servants cosset her, silently turning the blankets back, swinging the bed warmer between the cold sheets. She has no fear of them, pays them hardly any mind. They hated her husband, but so did she. She'll have the new baby and the image of William in the red mud, and such information about the execution as she decides to cherish.

William knows she heard Rose's screams, even in her rooms with the thick walls. His hand and face throb where the blindfold hit him.

Peter Ryburn was buried two Sundays ago, after church services. William and Robert sat through the night with his remains, the cousins side by side on a bench beside the coffin. It made a sound, the body did. Deep in the night, a sound, not the crude farting and moaning and sighing that the dead are known to make and which William has heard before, but a spoken phrase, a few syllables that William in his drunkenness could not make out and which the corpse would not repeat despite his entreaties. Peter Ryburn was dead when they laid him out and dead when they put him in the ground, but for a moment during those hours in between, he spoke. Robert heard it too and wept, seizing the old man's shoulders, while William slumped back on the bench. It was so like his father to have the last word. Then: sealed lips. Coins on the eyes. Gold coins from the mine Peter Ryburn owns, the mine that William's wife has described shyly in letters to the King. Words in a language the dead know, spoken as the soul crossed over. Robert, devoted nephew, sobbed out his sorrow into the whiskey and tilted the bottle to the old man's mouth. The liquor went down. Robert poured till the bottle was empty, and still the liquor never came up from the corpse's throat, and Robert cried out with hope, but William knew all along he was dead as a stone.

Eileen says make use of Rose's cabin. There is no reason it cannot be occupied by others. William directs slaves to clean it out. The blacks balk. William and Eileen stand before the cabin while the slaves study the ground, drawing their feet through the dirt. A fine mist falls.

"It built on a rattlesnake nest," a woman says at last. "We keep away."

"That's ridiculous," William cries. It hurts to speak, the bad tooth radiating needles of pain through his jaw.

"She built it her own self," the woman says, an old granny with eyes gone icy from cataracts. "You can hear them snakes, sometime. Hundreds of 'em."

Eileen stands straight and slim, as if she has not borne a child only days before. "Tear it down," she tells William.

He hates for the slaves to see her making the decisions about the running of the place, this young woman, while he stands with his face swathed and swollen, his body hurting all over from his fall from the horse. But demolish the cabin they do, once he gives the order. It's a sturdy little house, though small. Three black men knock it down, and William asks later if they saw snakes.

"Yessir," they say, but they weren't bit. A whole nest of snakes is still deep in the ground, they say, *boilin' there;* only a conjure woman would build there.

"All right. Burn the wood. Burn the ground, so if any snakes are there, they'll die," William says.

That order goes unheeded. The wood remains unburnt in a messy heap, grim and wintry. Is it then that the unraveling begins, with the slaves' disobedience while William slouches miserably in his chair in the warm house, waiting for an abscess to burst in his mouth? Eileen hearkens to the slaves' stories, their excuses: fire will bring the snakes out to multiply and swarm. Their fears have got to her.

The cabin remains a wreck of timbers. If snakes weren't there already, it's an invitation now. William holds his jaws with his hands until he can't bear it any longer and calls a doctor to pull the tooth. The long bloody root, ivory and red in the doctor's extractor, is his reward, that and the thick bitter gush of pus into his mouth.

And my husband and his cousin had congress with the condemned woman, Your Majesty, in her cell in the gaol, the night prior to her execution. I saw, for I followed them. I have learned to walk quietly, and I do not need a lantern.

Did you not call us your loyal old dominion? As you would deem an old friend. My loyal Old Dominion.

By the time the flood recedes and snow falls, William is sick. He blames Rose for the sores that fester on his genitals and thighs. Fever plagues him, only to subside and assail him again, so that he climbs out of bed to go outside in the snow and stretch out full length, clad only in his nightshirt, the heat of his body melting through the crust so that in the morning, when he creeps indoors again, his human form shows his household where he lay.

Beneath the heavy snow, the earth is packed with water. The river runs high, ice gathering at its shores in sheets and slush. It runs too fast to freeze. Those who would cut blocks of ice for summertime will have to wait.

Summer has never seemed so far off.

William asks his cousin if he too is afflicted, but Robert says no.

Why would one man contract the disease and the other be spared? William remembers the gaol cell, its cold dirt floor, the smell of mice and damp, and the strenuous climbing and conquering of her limbs. He had been with slaves before, young women whose bodies attracted him, but that was long ago, and he had not forced them. It was a game then, and they were willing. He wonders if the sickness has been in his body for a while. No, it was Rose. He's certain. The woman, the sores: she wished the illness upon him. Is it possible his father gave her the disease, and she poisoned him out of anger?

Lying in the snow, fever flaming through his body, William turns face down until at last he cools. He has never known a season of so much rain and snow, and there are still months of winter ahead. The sound of the surging river is always with him, even when he's in his chamber with draperies drawn and a pillow over his head.

He consults with his doctor and swallows bitter blue pills recommended for the malady. The medicine makes his gorge rise. One night he takes the vial of pills and buries it in the ground, digging deep beneath the snow, and afterward, sweating and thirsty, he wonders why he bothered. The sores multiply on his body. His mouth isn't healing, either. The empty socket runs with serum and stays tender, tasting foul, the edges ragged. He mixes warm water with salt, honey, and alum and gulps it, swishing it around his mouth, and that helps a little bit. Skin flakes from his burnt face and hand.

Sunshine and fresh eggs, the keys to health. His father swore by sunshine and eggs. William directs the cook to serve him eggs at every meal. The sky remains heavy, the air colder day by day. Yet he has never seen such magnificent shades of gray as the clouds during these weeks, pewter and silver, dawn and afternoon and dusk, nor does he recall the last time he thought the sky was beautiful.

He lies outside in the snow, melting it with his heat and sweat, packing snow into his mouth and around his scrotum, beneath his nightshirt and robe. Eileen loves the snow. She makes the cook prepare a dish with sugar and cream. William can't eat enough of this dessert. Snow cream and eggs are making him fat. All day he looks forward to his bed of snow at night. Even that doesn't cool him enough. Fresh snow falling at night brings him a relief that borders on joy. It covers him, but it doesn't last.

During the day, his dogs sniff the hollows where he lay, spaces where he melted through to the grass. All his life, he has had a horror of illness and weakness. He has scorned those who are frail, the lame and the infirm.

"You're getting old," Robert says.

"You're nearly as old," William answers.

To look at the two of them, William has to admit, you would no longer know they were separated by only four years. Yet these are modern times. Men live longer than they once did. William's thoughts are too disordered for him to determine how to regain his health.

He was a young man once, courting Martha who became his wife, playing hide and seek in the garden that is now mounded with snow. William's fever burns hotter than any heat of summer. Even in summer, down in the garden, there were cool spaces, shadows and dew under the boxwoods even in after-noon, and a trellis covered with blue ivy where Martha would meet him long ago, stifling her laughter, jumping out to surprise him, even frighten him.

Martha: a scurrying sound in her room, at her papers and letters all day. He is married to a sound. The ivy in the garden smelled like an old, lost world, she used to say, the sweet smell of memory. She plucked an ivy leaf and twirled it beneath his nose.

One night he awakes in panic, convinced all of his stock are dead. He bolts from his bed of snow and rushes into his house, calling for his wife, but it's Eileen who appears on the steps with a candle in her hands, a velvet dress-ing gown belted at her waist.

"The animals," he gasps. "Are they dead?" He can't remember when he last saw a sheep or a hog, a horse or a cow. The snow must have killed them weeks ago.

"They're fine," she says.

"You or my wife have seen to them, then," he says stupidly, "or the negroes."

Eileen goes to the heavy front door and pushes it closed.

William remembers something else, the stake, Rose's stake. "It was iron," he says, "so it didn't burn."

"What are you talking about?" Eileen asks.

"We should get it," William says. "Somebody should go get it. It must not become a talisman, a thing of witchcraft and," he flounders, sweat beading on his face, "a thing of evil. I'll dress and go get it."

"William," Eileen says. "You must go to bed. The stake was pulled up. It doesn't matter."

"But it does," he says, near tears.

"After a while, it'll be just an old piece of metal," she says, "and nobody will remember what it was. It'll be used for something else, or melted down, or lost."

He feels so old. He will not live as long as his father did.

"I want my wife," he says. "Tell me where she is."

"In her chamber, I suppose," Eileen says.

She stands aside, this woman Eileen, this stranger his father married, so he can climb the stairs. Sweat courses down his cheeks, and the steps are steep and hard to mount, as if he's pushing his way through a snowfall on a hill. He has not thought about his wife in days. Is that her room, the closed doorway at the end of the hall?

He turns the knob, but the door is locked. He kicks it so the hinges crack from the frame, and he shoves it open. There sits an old woman in lace cap and nightdress, frozen with horror in her chair at a writing table. She is surrounded by stacks of paper. In her hand is a dripping stick of red wax. Her gaze travels from his face to the broken door and back again.

"What are you doing?" he demands.

"Sealing my letter," Martha answers. The wax is blood-red and sweet-smelling. She blows out the flame on the taper and presses a brass implement into the daub.

"Who are you writing to?"

"The King." Martha lifts the letter to her lips and blows on the seal. "I'm writing to the King. You knew that. There's so much to tell him. Tonight I've written him about the horses in this country, how they're descended from those on shipwrecks or brought by early explorers. I explained how they grow so strong here and are well suited to the work of farms and mines."

William reaches out and takes the letter from her hands. He touches the wax, which is soft enough to show the print of his fingertip. "Where did you get this?"

"I order the paper from a shop in Philadelphia. The wax and ink I've had since we were married. My mother gave them to me in great supply. Don't you remember? Oh, William."

"Do you think the King cares about your letters?"

"I do," Martha says. "He's concerned about the colony. The people. He should know what's happening here."

William turns the letter over and reads the King's name in his wife's elegant script. "Who will deliver it for you?"

"I'll find someone traveling to a port city," she says, "who will take it to a ship's captain. I've done this many times."

"But he doesn't answer. The King."

"William, you're very ill," Martha says. "No matter what I say, you won't believe me."

●

Martha makes him lie down on her couch, and she fans the sweat from his face with a sheet of paper. Her heart, startled to triple its normal beat by his kicking in her door, has only just begun to return to normal. She takes a deep breath as William settles himself on her couch, his thick shoes leaving marks on the gray silk upholstery.

"That woman," he says, "is killing me."

"Eileen?" Martha hates the smug young woman who is the mistress of the house, mother of the heir. Martha has expected her husband to fall in love with Eileen, to divorce her, to pack her out of the house to live a pauper's life. Ever since Eileen's arrival and with greater urgency since Old Ryburn's death, Martha has been saving money in a leather bag.

"Not Eileen. Rose," he says.

"No," she says. "Rose is dead."

Martha fans his cheeks, the pores open and perspiring still. After a while, he falls asleep.

Yes, William wronged the woman Rose, but Martha must try to save him. She has watched him all these weeks since the execution, and she has hardened her heart against him, but she was with him in the days of the twirling ivy, when they were young.

He rouses in his fever and says, "Wife," then sleeps again. All night, Martha sits up on her couch with his head on her lap. This person is a ruined stranger.

Toward daybreak she dozes, then wakes to find his arms wrapped around her waist. Laboriously, she moves him aside and stands up stiffly, as if her legs are uneven. She takes a clean sheet of paper and writes, *Upriver, there is a rock in the water. Only when the rock is visible is it safe to ford the river. The place is called Raccoon Ford because of the abundance of those animals. Their meat is poor but their pelts are warm. Hunters prize the tails as decorations for their caps. Raccoons may be readily tamed and kept as pets.*

She puts the letter aside. Long ago, there was an expedition to explore the wild land to the west, across the mountains and beyond. Should not there be another? She will write and suggest it.

But first she must tend to her husband. She orders soap and hot water brought to her, and then dismisses the servant. For the first time since the early days of their marriage, and the only time without William's assistance, she removes his clothing. It's hard to do. As she peels the shirt and trousers from his body, she is saddened that his flesh is slack, muscles wasted, abdomen heavy.

Snow is falling again. The basin of hot water steams up the windows of her chamber. She'll have to concentrate and work very hard to save William. She must bring everything together in her mind, all she knows of the poison and the business in the gaol and the burning. She herself had argued, albeit only in her head, for bullets or hanging, or even exile to the West. Why burning? Barbaric. She wrote about all of it to the King, who answered with his familiar silence.

William's skin is thick and yellow. While Martha bathes him, he sleeps on, his head sometimes jerking. The sores on his groin and privates exude heat. She has guessed they were there, but these are worse than she'd expected, a rampant, livid consequence of his visit to the gaol. For a moment, her heart fails her. She dries his skin with a cloth, covers him with soft blankets, and curls herself around him, stroking his head.

Her father-in-law, Old Ryburn, drank the milk in a single swallow, smacking his lips as he set down the glass. He stood up from the table and took two strides toward the door. Wasn't a tradesman there, wanting a word with him? Or was he leaving the table in anger because he and William had been arguing? In any case, he gave a guttural cry. With one hand he gripped his throat, with the other reached high, as if grasping for something. Rose turned her head from her place at the sideboard where she was stacking plates. Turned her head so that out of the corner of her eye, she saw him fall. Martha recalls what a pretty shape Rose's cheek made, with her chin tucked into her shoulder, her face all eyelashes and stillness.

"The milk," Old Ryburn gasped. "Rose?"

It was William who caught Rose even as she tried to run, and Martha who sprang toward Old Ryburn, catching him as he fell. Eileen remained in her chair with a buttered scone in her hand. Didn't she finish it, nibbling amid the commotion? Gooseberry jam was on the table that day, and clotted cream.

Old Ryburn used to find hangings and beheadings such merry affairs. Martha has heard of his courtship of Eileen. On a visit to Ireland, his homeland, he had learned of an execution to be held some distance away, and he took the young beauty to it, with her father and brothers for company. The convict was a man who had killed his neighbor in a dispute over a hog. The scaffolding was so high, Eileen reported to her new family, that she had to shade her eyes against the sun. There was the drop of the trap and a brief wriggling of legs, a motion that disturbed her less than if a gnat had flown into her eye.

In moments the man hung limp. Eileen declared herself disappointed. They had come so far for that. Why was she not moved by the spectacle, when all around her, the crowd displayed fury and satisfaction?

Martha has guessed that for Eileen, there was no turning back from Old Ryburn then. She had agreed to marry him and was already carrying his child. Together they would make the crossing to Virginia. When she arrived, her pregnancy was evident to everyone. The day of the hanging, Old Ryburn had bought his wife-to-be a length of lace from a peddler and a tray of plum tarts, yet even then, Martha is certain, Eileen was bored, going home in the bumpy wagon, smoothing the lace out on her lap, scolding her brothers for dripping plum juice on their shirts.

Old Ryburn had drunk the entire glass of milk Rose brought to him, but in Martha's memory, the glass tips from his hand and milk spills over the table, a thick puddle spreading to the edges and dripping onto the floor. Old Ryburn was some kin by marriage to Eileen's mother. Now William must take care of Eileen and her brat forever.

And Eileen is the one who killed William's father. Martha knows this as surely as if she heard Eileen order the slave woman: *Give me some foxglove.* Eileen must have mixed it with crushed vanilla beans and sugar, then returned the compound to Rose saying, *Put this in my husband's milk when next he orders it; it is to strengthen him.*

Yet during her trial and even at the stake, Rose did not betray Eileen. Martha, with her husband sleeping heavily in her lap, considers the fact as Eileen's infant wails down the hall in its nursery. The child's attendant is one of Rose's daughters. Eileen might have murmured a promise, or what Rose took for a promise, when she accepted the compound from her mistress's hands: *I'll take an interest in the welfare of your children.* If Rose had accused her mistress in the courtroom or from the stake, who would have believed her? Rose must have known that.

Martha rolls her husband from her lap so he slumps on the bed, snoring. Her relief that he's here tonight, instead of sleeping outside in the snow, is inexpressible. She goes to her window, parts the curtains, and looks out at the night. The landscape presents an odd reversal. The snow glows like sky. The world is upside down. These weeks since Rose's execution, Martha has turned the particulars of the woman's final moments over and over in her mind. William told her very little. He arrived home from the execution in a frenzy, face scorched, clothes muddied and torn. She had to work to get the story of Rose's death from this source and that one. *No,* Rose said at her trial, when asked if she had murdered her master. *No, I didn't kill him.* Martha has heard that much. Yet surely Rose knew what substance was in the compound Eileen gave her. Rose, not Eileen, was the one who put the powder, brown and innocent as cinnamon, in Old Ryburn's milk. Rose knew. Yet she didn't tell.

A wolf howls, and Martha lets the curtain drop from her hands. She loves to hear the wolves at night, to know they are near, and herself safe in the thick walls of this house. She has seen the bloody heads brought in for bounties at the courthouse, knows the values: forty pounds of tobacco for the head of a young wolf, seventy for an old. Orange County stretches to the gigantic lakes of the north, all the way to Canada, and westward farther than she can imagine.

How many millions of wolves live within that land? Martha writes to the King. *The balance here is delicate, between the land and those who would tame it. We plow, we farm, we herd and build.*

She pauses. The King doesn't know what it's like, living here, when the balance might tip at any moment. In fifty years, this place could return entirely to savages and woods and darkness. She writes, *Do not wait. Come now. Come and visit your Old Dominion in its struggling youth, its early days from which it may rise to glory.*

The King will never come. He'll read her letter with impatience, holding it away from his weak eyes, wondering why this one subject, some old woman out in the wilderness, writes to him so eagerly, as if he would concern himself with wolves, as if he would know how it is to be alone, your only consolation a few pieces of gold in a leather sack, saved against widowhood or eviction. He cannot know, does not care, that she and her husband and their family and slaves and neighbors keep a fragile foothold. *Indians and floods,* she writes, *and crop failures and our own hatreds and greed, Your Majesty, these threaten us, yet this is the finest country.*

Beside her, William moans in his dreams. Martha writes, *My husband's cheek has healed badly from the burning blindfold the woman threw at him. It hurts him even when he sleeps.*

The Runaway Stagecoach

Vicinity of Stevensburg, Virginia
December 1808

Lewis Mundy at fifteen wants to be a stagecoach driver. He has decided this since leaving his family's small farm in Spotsylvania County at dawn and heading west toward Stevensburg, where he will serve as an apprentice to his uncle, a brick maker. To be a driver, Lewis decides, he must first develop a grand deep voice like that of Barnes, with his florid face and streaming silver hair, commander of this coach and its four enormous horses. Lewis's own voice has changed, but it is still higher and lighter than he wishes.

Barnes bawls, "Next stop, Raccoon Ford."

An old man beside Lewis shares a map, pointing to Raccoon Ford for Lewis's benefit.

The canvas shade is rolled up on the window that gives onto the driver's box, so Lewis is able to observe that a big man riding there with Barnes is waving his arms and raising some objection. Lewis hears the word *fever.*

"We always go to the Ford," Barnes insists over the din of thundering hooves, "to change horses and have a meal."

The big man hollers, "I tell you, there's fever there. Don't stop!"

Lewis watches in alarm as the big man grabs for the reins. Barnes shoves him, and the man takes a gun from his coat and with it, strikes Barnes on the head. Barnes reels and collapses from the box. The big man seizes the reins, but it's too late. Spooked, the horses bolt.

Inside, six terrified passengers tumble screaming from the benches. Lewis lands beside a pregnant woman. He gets to his knees and offers her a hand, but she waves him away with a frantic expression on her face.

An older woman who might be her mother implores, "Margaret, are you all right?"

Margaret only moans. A man named Colonel Gault tries to support her with his arm around her shoulders. Earlier, Colonel Gault performed a trick that fascinated Lewis: he took off his leg, while everyone gasped. He explained it was cork, outfitted with a boot and stocking that fit into his breeches and the stump of his knee. He'd lost his leg in the war, he said.

The coach moves too fast for anyone to regain a seat. They cling to the benches. There is only one thought in Lewis's mind: he must survive this wild, pitching run. The horses veer to the side of the road. Branches poke through the canvas shades, tearing them off with great rips. Noise from the top of the coach suggests the bags and parcels tied there are breaking loose. They bump along the roof and fly free. Lewis sees a trunk hit the ground and burst open, spilling petticoats. At least the horses seem to be back on the road. Lewis could enjoy this ride if only he knew they wouldn't crash. If one horse stumbles and falls—but he pushes the thought away.

The pregnant woman, Margaret, thrashes and clutches her belly. From beneath her clothing comes a rush of liquid.

Her mother says in dismay, "It's too soon."

A young girl, no more than fourteen, slides toward Margaret. She loosens Margaret's clothing and sets her knees up, legs apart—all as the coach bucks and sways.

Shocked, Lewis glimpses bloody garments, female flesh. He looks away.

Margaret's mother, whose elaborate hair and jewelry indicate wealth, whose scent of lavender reaches Lewis even through this confusion, watches white-faced. A rock sails through a window and hits the old man who showed Lewis a map, making his cheek bleed.

On the floor, birth is progressing.

The young girl peers under Margaret's dress and says, "I see the head. Now push."

Colonel Gault is crawling toward the front of the coach. The horses' breathing is different now, harsher. At least one of them, Lewis guesses, will have a permanently broken wind. Colonel Gault heaves himself through the window to the driver's box.

The coach leans sideways. It must be riding on two wheels. It leaves the road and hurtles through a patch of bushes. Sounds of struggle reach Lewis's ears. A shot rings out, then a sustained yell. Something flies past the window, bulk recognizable as a man. Gradually the yell grows fainter. Lewis finds himself holding the gaze of the young girl assisting in the birth. Her eyes are hazel and intelligent, like an animal's.

"Whoa! Whoa-aaah," comes Colonel Gault's voice.

The coach slows by heartbeats, and Lewis dares to breathe, to blink. Raindrops fly past the open window; no, it's spittle blown backward as the horses respond to the reins, once again feeling the bits in their sore, lathered mouths. At last, there is a kind of sinking and a dead stop. The rear of the coach slopes downward.

There is a baby among them. The young girl swabs its tiny face with her apron, and it lets out a hearty cry. A gnarled red cord stretches from the baby's middle to its mother's body. Margaret's lower parts are covered again by her clothing.

The young girl says to the older woman, "You're a grandma now, ma'am. It's a little girl." She kisses the top of the baby's head. Its eyes are open and alert, but it's quiet, as if realizing that silence and hardihood are called for. "Does anybody have a knife or scissors?"

Lewis hands the girl his knife, and she cuts the cord.

They are safe. Lewis is the first to react. He flings himself at the door but can't wrench it open. He vaults through a side window and lands hard on the ground.

And here are Colonel Gault, minus his false leg, and Barnes, alive after all, showing a few good teeth in a bloody mouth. Lewis and Barnes help the others out and lift Margaret bodily, then place her beneath a tulip poplar. Her mother eases down beside her. The young girl still holds the baby. The old man, his cheek smeared with blood, squats on his haunches. Lewis's hands are shaking, and he shoves them in his pockets.

This, then, is traveling. This is what it means to be out in the world.

Lewis and the others exclaim and sigh in tones of agitation and relief, and he feels on his own face the awe that shows on the others'. He realizes he didn't pray. He thought only to live.

The coach has halted amid trees and briars.

He asks Gault, "Where is your leg, sir?"

"When we fought, he pulled it off me. That's when I shot him," Gault says.

The coach gives a loud, rude gulp. Even as Lewis watches, the wheels sink to the axles.

"Quicksand," says Barnes. "We'd best pull her out while we can. Ladies and gentlemen, is there anything you need to save?"

The elegant woman and her daughter, Margaret, had boarded the coach in Fredericksburg with many trunks and bags. The woman says, "Everything is gone." She has only a tiny purse.

Colonel Gault says, "Your things may well be recovered, Mrs. Tinsley. People will hear of this and want to help."

Lewis asks the young girl, "What about you?"

She says, "I had one box."

"So did I," he says. The box contained his clothing, cup, tin plate, and blanket. There was something special, too—his mother's clock, the only beautiful thing she owned. She insisted he take it to her sister, Lewis's Aunt Susan, the brick maker's wife. Funny: Lewis is almost glad the clock is gone. It would have made him homesick to see it and remember his mother winding it.

The elegant woman, Mrs. Tinsley, presses a handkerchief to her eyes. "My head aches."

Gault draws a flask from his pocket. "Brandy?"

Lightning-quick, Mrs. Tinsley reaches for the flask and tilts it to her mouth for a long swallow. The young girl signals amusement to Lewis with her hazel eyes, and he grins, delighted at the small intrigue, but Barnes is calling for his help.

Together, Barnes and Lewis flank the lead horses and urge them on. The horses strain, but the coach won't move. Barnes wipes his face with his sleeve and says, "Well, she was a fine coach." He uncollars the horses, and they step nervously, whickering.

Seated on a stump, Colonel Gault smokes a pipe. It seems to Lewis that they are all under a spell. He asks Gault, "Do you want me to go and find your leg?"

A nod from the colonel, and Lewis is off like a jackrabbit.

Does he run for a long time or a short time? He will never be able to remember. Luckily the coach's trail is easy to follow, a path of wrecked brush. And here they are: cork leg and dead outlaw, not a dozen paces apart. Lewis freezes where he stands. A bobwhite calls, a summer sound, soft and sleepy on this lost winter day. The big man lies on his side, so still, with one arm reaching out as if he died crawling. A cricket springs from his black hair.

Lewis bends down and grabs the leg. It weighs almost nothing, and the kidskin boot feels soft against his fingers.

By the time he finds the others, he is panting. Gault rewards him with a coin, pulls the leg on, and stands up, whole again.

Lewis announces, "I seen him back there. He's dead."

Barnes spits a tooth on the ground. "He almost killed us all. I ain't heard about no fever at the Ford. Did any of you?"

They all shake their heads.

"Who was he?" Mrs. Tinsley asks.

"Said he was a farrier from Nansemond County," Barnes answers, "but who's to know if that's the truth?"

"His hands, though," says Colonel Gault.

"A blacksmith's hands, perhaps," concedes Barnes. "'Twas a powerful knock on my head."

Margaret rests on cloaks laid on the earth. The young girl caresses the baby as if it belongs to her. The old man calls to Lewis, "Is help on the way?"

"I didn't see anybody," Lewis says. Shame sweeps through him. Why didn't he seek a farmhouse? Is the landscape that empty, is he so stupid?

"Where are we? Would someone please tell me?" Mrs. Tinsley asks.

Barnes answers, "About seven miles past Stevensburg, I'd say, ma'am."

The women sigh and look at each other, as if the news could be better, could be worse.

The young girl brings the baby over to Lewis and says softly, "It's a beautiful day. See?"

They crane their heads toward the tall, light-filled trees. It's warm and brilliant for December, the air soft and beguiling. Afternoon now, with the day at its peak. There should be snow. There should not be this dreamy shimmering, but already, shadows gather at the woods' edge, shadows that will lengthen and grow chilly by dusk. Lewis hears water trickling, tracks the sound to its source, and finds a clean spring. Proudly he points it out.

The girl kneels and bathes the baby, cupping water in her hands and carefully sluicing it over the tiny head and limbs. She dries the baby with a corner of her apron and wraps it in her shawl. "Now hold her while I wash my hands," she says.

The baby is solid and surprisingly heavy in Lewis's arms, and the girl's shawl smells of her skin and hair. The day's arithmetic amazes Lewis. They were eight when they set out: seven passengers plus Barnes, and eight when they halted, with one dead and the newborn among them. The girl takes the baby again, and Lewis is filled with the sense that she could be his wife, the baby their own. He bends to the spring and drinks his fill. When he stands, the girl is smiling.

"Look how pretty," she whispers, stroking the baby's cheek. Why whisper? He is charmed. She asks, "Where are you headed?"

"To my uncle in Stevensburg," he says. "He's a brick maker. I'm to learn from him."

His mother arranged the apprenticeship, writing to her sister and her sister's husband. The uncle agreed and found occasion in his letter to say, *Bricks are half their weight in water till they dry*. The information seemed dire to Lewis, proof of a dreary life of hard, stupid work. Much of the work of brick making could be performed by children, his mother admitted, but firing required great skill, and masonry was an art, she insisted, and maybe his childless aunt and uncle would will the business to him some day. *Send him*, the uncle wrote. His mother held the letter for a long while, as if time itself were an envelope, hers to open. Lewis would have liked more schooling. His father was dead, and his mother had married a man who wanted Lewis out of the way. He had two boys of his own, and they were workers enough for the farm, the new husband said. Lewis's mother gave Lewis a good pair of boots that had belonged to his father. Her eyes begged him not to argue. He could not bear to tell her he wanted only the trip, not the apprenticeship.

"Are you still going?" the girl asks.

In her eyes, Lewis reads a new truth: the breakneck ride changed everything. He need not report to his uncle.

"Bricks are half their weight in water till they dry," he says, and she laughs. He feels clever, pardoned from even the responsibility of deciding. "What about you?"

"My sister lives in Raccoon Ford. She has a baby coming. I've helped her before."

"But the fever?" Lewis says.

"I hope it's not true."

Yet wasn't there conviction in the outlaw's cry? Fear stirs in Lewis's heart. He imagines the girl entering a house, calling out greetings, and finding only silence.

"Look." She points to the ground and to trees. "Persimmons. And pears. We're in an old orchard."

He takes off his jacket and gathers the fruit into it, swatting tiny wasps away. He puts a ripe persimmon in the girl's mouth, and her lips brush his finger. He wishes he could make a homestead here with her and search out more bounty: nut trees, honeycomb, pheasants, rabbit.

She says, "You looked so funny, running with that leg in your arms."

So she noticed him. He hides his gladness in a brag. "I've always been a fast runner." Her face is sublimely peaceful, as if she has waited a long time for this baby. Doesn't it need to nurse? He's not going to say anything about that.

Women know their business. They return to the others, and Lewis passes the fruit around so all may eat.

"Gather some kindling," Colonel Gault calls to Lewis. "I'll make a fire."

Glad to obey, Lewis fills his arms with sticks. Gault and Barnes will get everyone out. They can ride out if they double up. By the time Lewis delivers the wood, he has picked out the horse he wants, a claybank mare. Margaret lies very still, with her mother rubbing her head. Lewis realizes that a woman who just gave birth cannot possibly ride a horse.

Barnes returns to the coach and yanks out two bundles wedged beneath the driver's box. The first, he explains, is his own. It yields a packet of tea, a tin cup, and a kettle. The girl takes the kettle to the spring to fill it.

"And this was his'n," Barnes says. "Let's see what he's got." He tears the twine from the other bundle and lifts out cheese and sausage wrapped in paper.

Mrs. Tinsley divides the food among them and brews tea in the kettle. From her purse, she takes a few ginger cakes and adds them to the meal. Never has Lewis been served by such smooth white hands, nor has he ever been hungrier. One bite of the outlaw's sausage tells him it is made of venison. It is delicious, seasoned just right.

The coach emits a series of creaks.

"Busted," says Barnes. "She'd need oxen to drag her out."

Lewis wants to see the coach sink, yet the waste of it hurts. It is pretty, with its wheels painted red, its sides blue.

The young girl suddenly looks unhappy. Her head bends, her thin shoulders sag. Lewis observes Margaret sitting up and holding the baby to her chest. Yes, the young girl wants the baby for herself. Lewis knows this as surely as if she said so. She is considering what might happen were she to grab the infant and run. She raises her head and meets his eyes. There is anger in her face, and he knows he has guessed right.

Mrs. Tinsley says, "Margaret and I must be home by evening. We're invited to a supper party and a ball, although Margaret will be indisposed."

Margaret announces dryly, "My mother doesn't like any change of plans."

Again the young girl catches Lewis's eye and smiles.

Barnes says, "I'll ride for help. Colonel?"

"I'll go with you," says Colonel Gault.

"I will too," Lewis cries.

The old man says, "I'll stay here with the ladies."

"You'll need shelter," Gault says.

He and Barnes and Lewis cut branches from trees, and the old man fashions an arbor. They stuff leaves and brush into the spaces.

"We're off, then," says Gault.

The men choose horses. Lewis catches the claybank mare and leaps up on her back.

Barnes cautions, "We'll go no faster than a walk." He nods toward the mare and says, "Fleety's her name."

"Fleety," Lewis says, the word lovely in his mouth.

"We'll be back as soon as we can," Gault calls to the others. They make a family group, together there. "Have you a gun?" Gault asks the old fellow.

"A pistol," the old man says. "I'll keep a sharp watch."

Barnes takes a small book from his pocket and says, "I need your names and home places to make a report to the Craig brothers. They own the stage-coach line."

One by one, they respond, and Barnes scribbles in the book.

"I am Hester Tinsley, widow of Charles Tinsley, and my daughter is Marga-ret Burnett, wife of Jehu Burnett. We live in Culpeper."

The old man squares his shoulders. "Caleb Fitch, mapmaker, of Thorn-ton's Gap. Been to Richmond, trying to get back home."

"Elly," says the young girl shyly. "Elly Duffy from Petersburg."

Lewis identifies himself. He is chilled by the knowledge that Barnes is recording the names in case some further injury comes to those who will remain behind.

"James Gault," the Colonel says, "of Gault's Crossroads."

Elly tells Barnes, "Write down the baby. Write down Baby Burnett." She takes something from her pocket, wipes it with her skirt, and hands it to Lewis: his knife.

"Keep it," he says, wanting something of his to remain with her.

You looked so funny when you ran with that leg, and he tucks the image away to think about—her with the baby in her arms, watching him.

At the spring, they let the horses drink. So huge, the animals' thirst.

"Too much at once will give them colic," Barnes warns, turning his horse away from the water. Lewis lets Fleety drink a moment more. She ran so hard. He follows the men to the road, a narrow well-trod stretch, not so far after all from the sinking coach.

No one else seems to be traveling today.

Barnes says, "Now show us where he is."

Lewis leads the way. The world's gone empty. There is only this landscape of brambles and woods and sere grass. No farms or settlements or houses present themselves, no grazing animals. Lewis believes he recognizes a vase-shaped elm. Shouldn't they have found the body by now? He wishes he had taken longer to look at it, the first corpse he has ever seen.

A woodcock and its mate rise thrumming from a thicket.

"Well?" calls Barnes.

A groundhog hole looks familiar. No, Lewis can't be sure. He, who is certain of landmarks at home, whose mother calls him "my Columbus," has never been more confused. At last he points and says, "He was there, I think."

Barnes grunts. "Then where'd he go?"

They climb down from the horses and examine the ground for signs of a man dead or alive. They remount, circle around, and meet again. Still nothing.

Barnes says, "Either he ain't dead, or we've missed him. Did you see his face, boy?"

Did he? "Yes. He was lying on his side." Lewis has never had the full attention of two adults whom he respects so much. "He wasn't moving."

"Did you feel for a beating heart?" Barnes asks.

"No," Lewis says. Maybe the man was playing possum, holding his breath.

"Was there any flies on him?"

"There was a cricket on him," Lewis says.

They pause, and Lewis knows the decision about what to do next is not his to make.

Colonel Gault ventures, "Someone might have picked him up, or he's found a hiding place or another road. There's an abandoned turnpike just ahead. Let's get along."

A sense of failure washes over Lewis. The men eye the woods' edge as they proceed. The outlaw might be hurt and dying. Animals might find him and eat him up, and his bones would bleach out beneath the trees.

"'Tis the first time a baby was born in my coach," Barnes says with wonder in his voice.

The men talk of the election a week past. James Madison is to be the next President. Lewis learns that Gault knows Madison, and Gault himself plans to run for governor. He will campaign for farm reform, especially for crop rotation and the reduction of tobacco growing. Tobacco depletes the soil, he says, and Barnes nods. Gault himself plants corn, wheat, and hay in succession at his farm, he says.

At last, Gault announces, "He can't have gone too far. He was bleeding out at the shoulder where I shot him."

"If I find him," says Barnes, "I'll have his neck in my hands. The stocks, the pillory, whippings, it's all too good for him." His voice grows hoarse. "If my dog was aboard, he'd have had his throat out."

"He'll be found," says Gault. "Why, we might meet him at the tavern."

Barnes says, "He'll hang for this. Tarred first, if I have a say."

"I saw a man dunged and feathered once," says Gault. "The townsfolk were out of tar."

The men laugh, a long sound of release. Lewis feels heartened.

Gault asks Lewis, "This is a rough town, Stevensburg. Do you know the place?"

"No, sir. I've come to work for my uncle, Samuel Hornbeak. He's a brick maker," Lewis says, but bricks have nothing to do with him anymore. He could turn east, go all the way to the ocean, and take his place on a ship as a fisherman or a whaler. Yes, that's what he's meant for, a better vocation even than that of stagecoach driver.

Barnes says to Gault, "A fine report it'll make, sir, you saving us." To Lewis he says, "The Colonel lost that leg to the British," and there's pride in his voice. "Battle of Cowpens, wasn't it?"

"I was hardly older than this lad," Gault says.

A soldier's life, then, that's what is meant for Lewis. A sailor's life can't compare.

Gault says, "I once pricked my finger on a thorn and almost lost my hand. A black line ran down my arm, and I was sick all through my body. A thorn on a rosebush, it was, a rose my wife grew in our garden." He raises a hand, fingers splayed. "That was a worse time than my leg. While I was sick, my wife gave birth, and she and the infant died."

Lewis has been wishing he had tales of hardship, but Gault's story cuts through him. He can't imagine what it would be like to lose a wife. Gault rides on jauntily, then exclaims, "That party Mrs. Tinsley talked about—I was to be there too, for dinner and dancing. I had forgotten. Well! There will be other parties."

"We're nearly to Stevensburg," Barnes says. "It can't be far."

"When men fight here, it's brutish. Gouging," Gault says, turning in his saddle to Lewis. "Seems to me there's a brick maker missing both his eyes."

Lewis gasps. Gault laughs, and Lewis understands it's a joke.

"I once seen a man tear off another man's balls," says Barnes grimly, "over a woman."

"Was she beautiful?" asks Gault.

"The most beautiful woman alive," Barnes says.

"Blonde hair or dark?" asks Gault, and Barnes says yellow, then red, then admits he can't rightly remember.

Their distraction begins to feel dangerous to Lewis. He fears that the other passengers, back in the woods with the approaching shadows, will be forgotten. Yet a moment ago he'd have run off to sea. He says, "We'll have to get a wagon."

The men don't seem to hear him. Gault complains in a high falsetto, "Oh, I have a headache," and claps his hand to his forehead. Barnes brays with delight.

They reach the outskirts of town. From a public house, men call out greetings.

Gault says to Barnes, "First, a drink."

Beer, then whiskey, then cherry flip and rum punch and applejack. Gault is buying, urging Lewis to have another. Barnes's red face flashes from behind a hand of cards. Trappers fresh from the frontier throng the bar, wearing caps with wolf tail crests. Gault tells the story of the stagecoach, reenacting it. Lewis finds his own voice newly deep amid the commotion. A girl steps out from behind the bar, and soon she has him talking about whether he'd rather be a soldier or a sailor. She has good teeth, though her breath is sour. A fiddler arrives and strikes up a tune, and Lewis is glad he doesn't have to talk any more. The girl's face shows he has taken her to the ocean. She is not as pretty as Elly Duffy, but he is captain of a ship now, its sails alive with wind.

Yet something tugs at his mind, a spot of worry. He is supposed to be somewhere else. The girl wants him to dance. Drink has taken away the bad smell of her breath. The spot in his mind opens up into a picture: the people in the woods. He can see them plain as day. Elly's face merges with the face of the girl in front of him, and there's the old man standing guard, protecting the group at the edge of the forest, where anything might creep out to tear them up.

He asks the girl, "Is there fever nearby? At Raccoon Ford?"

She shakes her head. She may mean no; she might mean, *I can't hear you.*

He tells her, "I have to go." He makes his way to Gault and calls out, "Colonel!"

Gault has climbed to the top of the bar. Expertly he unfastens the boot and leg and raises it to the sound of cheers, while his face splits so wide, Lewis sees his palate shake, sees all the way to the loudest sound of all, which is Gault's laughter. Gault tosses the leg above his head and catches it behind his back. The crowd roars. As long as people applaud, Lewis sees, there is nothing else for Gault—nobody stranded in wilderness, no dwindling day.

"Sir," Lewis calls. "Colonel Gault."

Gault cups his ear, and Lewis says, "We have to go get the others."

Gault pauses, and in an instant, the cork leg becomes part of his body again, and he eases off the bar. "Yes," he says, "I'm ready."

Lewis heads to the door. He'll check on Fleety and the other horses in a field beside the tavern. Gault and Barnes can borrow a wagon, and he will go with them. Maybe they can get fresh horses and allow these to keep resting. Sunlight falls across their manes and turns the broom sedge gold. To the west, Lewis discerns blue mountains, pale as a daytime moon. He looks behind him for the colonel.

Gault is allowing the bartender to pour for him again. The girl with the pretty teeth hooks her chin over his shoulder and drinks from his cup. It's a game. The girl is good at it. Lewis should have known he had no chance with her. It's Gault's shoulder where she rests her head, Gault's thigh pressed against her body.

Where is Barnes? Lewis scans the place and finds a passageway leading to a second story. There goes Barnes with his arm around a woman's waist. Lewis recalls the driver's yearning talk about women, and panic strikes him. Barnes and Gault, heroes to him these several hours, are succumbing to desires. He had not expected this. They should be back in the forest by now.

Nausea burns in Lewis's gut, yet the clear spot comes again in his head. He shuts his eyes. If he can go deep enough inside his mind, he might find the outlaw. The spot widens, and at its center is a pool. The outlaw's face rises up from the pool, eyes and mouth enormous, and passes again before the window of the coach, slowly. Lewis discovers it's an honest face, urgent and earnest, the face of a man to whom they owe their lives. The vision brings Lewis into a shed with a glowing forge. With tongs, the man lifts out a horseshoe. He is a farrier after all, with deer meat sausage in his mouth, a lively savor of pepper and sage.

The clear space wavers in Lewis's head. Nausea washes through him again. The sweet stuff did it, the flip and the punch. The farrier's mouth is moving. Lewis listens. The man is shouting but there is no sound. Ruined baggage lies upon the ground. Finery hangs from treetops, dresses and baby clothes waving in a breeze.

Lewis opens his eyes. Those people are expecting him. He couldn't say how long was the ride from the ruined coach to this tavern, if it were one hour or many that he and Gault and Barnes traveled in the beautiful light. Margaret Tinsley Burnett, having given birth, needs a bed to lie upon. It would have started in another bed when she opened her legs and let a man in. Lewis suspects women like it as much as men. Otherwise there wouldn't be so many babies. His mother is pregnant again. He feels grateful to her for sending him away.

He leans across the bar and asks the bartender, "Is there fever about? At Raccoon Ford?"

"Aye," the man says. "They're sick and dying from it. Stay away."

Gault and the girl are busy. Lewis will have to go alone. Again he heads toward the door, but there's a huge tree coming through, carried by staggering men who cry, "Yule log!"

Women pull kettles away from an enormous fireplace, and the men wedge the log into it. Soon Lewis smells sweet burning cedar and every good supper that ever came from the hearth: roast pig and mutton, fowl basted in their own grease. Women bring out trays of oranges and oysters, and bowls of syllabub with cream floating on top. Lewis tips the cold, sweet oysters from their shells into his mouth. He peels an orange and eats the slices one by one. He has found the people he belongs among. He looks with love on the feasting crowd. Gault and Barnes slandered these folk unfairly. No one here would hurt another.

Something else is coming through the door, a trunk with shiny brass fittings, borne by men who make Lewis think of pirates. People fall upon the trunk, rifling the contents and seizing luxurious garments from the pile within. Two women fight over a lacy gown, clawing each other's arms. Droplets of blood spatter the silk. The smell of lavender reaches Lewis as if Mrs. Tinsley herself is there.

Lewis cries, "That belongs to Mrs. Tinsley. And did you find a clock?"

They don't hear him. The trunk lid falls on a woman's finger, and the woman curses.

Lightly the girl detaches herself from Gault and steps toward Lewis. She has chosen him. He can't believe his luck, but he can't go with her, can't forsake those who wait for him. He must leave right now and get a cart. Yet the girl places her hands upon his chest, and he has dreamed of holding a girl in his arms. For years it seems he has dreamed it. He draws her toward the steps where he saw Barnes take a woman.

The girl leans her head back and says, "God-awful, that leg. I couldn't, with that." Her laugh would nail ears to the pillory.

Bullets strike his chest, so he knows he became a soldier after all. He's lying on a battlefield, surrounded by others crying out, the sounds high and keening or oddly thick, purring or snoring. He didn't know the dying snored. The bullets sting, and they're wet. He sits up, dazed. Night has come, and sleet pelts through an open window above him. It's dark in this attic room, yet he makes out moving shapes. Several couples engage quietly; another makes a racket.

He is naked, and the girl is gone. He scrabbles for his clothes, pulls them on, and hollers, "Where's my boots?"

"That oughta be the name of this place," comes a wheezy male voice, followed by a woman's laugh. "Wal, it's true," the wheeze says, aggrieved.

Lewis had stuffed his warm stockings into the boots, so they are gone too. Barefoot, he runs down the steps. The log in the great hearth burns with enough light that he can make out skewed tables and jumbled crockery in the deserted room. Oyster shells give off a faint reek. His head beats with pain. He finds a mug of stale beer and gulps it down, but his tongue stays dry.

Might the people in the forest have been located and brought to the shelter of houses here or in another place? Unlikely, in the dark. Would they have come out on their own? No, they would not know which way to go, and there was only one horse remaining among them.

There cannot be many derelictions greater than leaving helpless people out in the wilderness all night.

He goes around back to piss among the empty beer barrels. It's a ragged dawn, and the ground and the road are puddled with ice. He reaches into his pocket for his handkerchief, but it's gone. His money too, and the key to his mother's clock.

At least the sleet has stopped. He finds he knows this place. His mother told him how to reach his uncle's house: *Take the road out of town going west. Go to a sycamore tree and turn north. You will see the treading pit where clay and water are mixed together. Beside it is the drying shed, and a pile of clinkers and broken bricks called bats.*

His Uncle Samuel has rheumatism, so it's Aunt Susan who hitches the mules to the wagon, all the while yelling at Lewis: "Get the bread out of the oven. There's dried peaches and boiled eggs on the table. We was expecting you yesterday."

Uncle Samuel groans from a chair beside the fire. How thin he is, with slits of eyes that bespeak heat and toil. Quick-thinking, this uncle and aunt. They listened hard, taking in all that Lewis told them. He gave a version of the story, leaving out references to time, to the long afternoon and night that he spent at the public house.

Now Uncle Samuel says, "You say there's a baby out there? Take a quilt and wrap hot bricks in it. We got plenty bricks," and he moves his legs as if they pain him. "Why are you barefoot? They wouldn't send you from home that way."

Lewis is glad to be gathering bricks, so his uncle won't see his face. He admits, "I took off my boots last night, and somebody stole them."

"A woman, you mean. You might find them on market day," Uncle Samuel gibes, "sold by the thief. You can buy them back from her."

An angry thought comes to Lewis: if it weren't for the people in the woods, he could be enjoying the memory of the girl's body beneath his own, the heat and frenzy they made together.

"Maybe she didn't take them," he says. "Maybe it was somebody else."

"Ahh," his uncle says. "Well, there's a pair of boots in the cabinet that might fit you."

Lewis opens the cabinet and finds the boots. They are big enough and won't chafe, though one has a hole at the side. He does not deserve them. "Thank you," he says.

"Yesterday you wouldn't have needed boots. It was so warm, we stomped clay till dark," says Uncle Samuel, "us and all the children in town. Now the pit's froze." He stretches toward the fire like an old cat glad for warmth.

Lewis flies about the unfamiliar house gathering what they tell him to fetch. He piles things into the wagon, and he and Aunt Susan depart. Aunt Susan drives like a madwoman, her hair whipping around her face. Lewis's mother said, *You'll know your aunt because she looks like me,* but this woman, with her blustery energy, is nothing like his gentle mother. He wonders if his mother's sister died and Uncle Samuel took another wife named Susan. She lashes the mules, shouting. He is sorry he does not have his mother's clock to give to her.

If the people in the woods are still alive, Lewis vows, he will settle in and serve his uncle, will dig clay, tend fires, carry loads too heavy for his back. Brick making may be crude, but *there is art in masonry.* His mother's words come back to him. On trips to town, his mother pointed out Flemish bond and English bond. Headers and stretchers are laid in different ways, she said, making attractive patterns that bear the weight of walls.

And if the people are dead?

Then he will have only their names.

Trees whirl past. He clings to the side of Aunt Susan's wagon. How can mules run so fast? This is nearly as bad as yesterday.

At last he hears a shot that might be a signal from the old man's gun. Aunt Susan stops the wagon, and Lewis calls out in a voice as loud as Barnes's. He picks up a scent of smoke, and through the ice-glazed trees comes a faint reply.

Aunt Susan turns in at a clearing and there they are—the travelers, the horse—and Lewis is the stunned one, counting an extra head among them. It's the outlaw, tied to the poplar tree.

Elly Duffy explains, "He crawled up to our fire. We didn't see him till he was right close, and then we was scared. Mr. Fitch was about to shoot him, but he said he was sorry. He begged."

"While I held the gun on him," Mrs. Tinsley says, "Mr. Fitch tied him up."

The old man, Mr. Fitch, says, "He'll be allowed his trial."

Is this stranger truly the man who sailed past the coach's open window? Lewis can't trust his eyes, but the clear spot in his mind opens up to say, *It is.* The man's face is bruised, and a bloody stain, bright as a sash, covers one shoulder. His scarred hands are a farrier's indeed, big as anvils and ropy with veins.

Elly says to him, "I hope you are shown mercy."

He says, "Thank you, Miss. It's mercy you've all given me."

"Where are Colonel Gault and Mr. Barnes?" Mrs. Tinsley demands of Lewis.

He hesitates and says, "I thought they might have already come for you."

Mrs. Tinsley says, "Well, young man, I think you are a diplomat."

"He means," Elly says, "they're drunk somewhere. Is that it?"

All of the rescued party throw back their heads and laugh, their voices ringing through the woods. The outlaw laughs too, a sorrowful sound. Lewis and Mr. Fitch untie him from the tree. It's lengths of wild grapevine, thick as rope, that hold him. The man's skin feels hot against Lewis's fingers, and his bloody shirt emits an odor of rot. He doesn't look nearly as large as he did yesterday. "I won't run off," he says, creeping onto the wagon, but once he is seated, Mr. Fitch binds his hands and feet again.

Margaret bundles her infant into a quilt. Mr. Fitch hops spryly up on the last horse that pulled the coach. The others pile into the wagon. Lewis stomps out their smoldering fire and takes a seat beside Elly, who holds the kettle in her lap.

"There's fever at Raccoon Ford," he says to her. "They said so in Stevensburg."

"I said so yesterday," the outlaw announces, "and if that driver had listened, none of this would've happened."

"My sister needs me," Elly says.

"Don't go," Lewis says, "please don't go."

"I must," she says. "I will," and Lewis thinks it would be fine to have a wife with such a strong spirit.

Aunt Susan declares, "Lewis, you drive. I'm wore out." She hands him the reins and scoots over.

Lewis asks Elly, "Where's the coach?"

Elly gestures toward a space of slick, grainy mud. He can make out a spar here and there, like the tips of buried masts. It's the top of the coach, so small he can hardly believe it carried them all. It is here, yet it's gone. He's looking at a grave.

Elly says, "You're wearing different boots today, worse ones. Why is that?"

When he doesn't answer, she peers into his face and gives a low hiss, as if she has figured out what happened in the night. She switches places so Lewis is beside the outlaw, who is hogging the food Aunt Susan passes around.

"Well, drive on, boy," Aunt Susan says. "What are you waiting for?"

Lewis tells the farrier, "I thought you were dead. I saw you dead."

"Oh, no, you didn't." The man shakes his head. "You don't know what you saw." With his bound hands, he takes a dried peach from a sack and puts it in his mouth.

Lewis breathes hard, as if he's been running all his days. He can barely cluck to the mules.

Every High Hill

Rapidan, Virginia
March 1885

Coleman Barbour, lamed by a fall as a young man, got married at fifty-two. His bride, Alice, grew up at a Confederate orphanage as the pet of the matrons. She would not tell her age, but Coleman guessed she was a good thirty years younger than he was. They were married in Richmond and spent their wedding night in a hotel. The next day, they traveled eighty miles northwest by train to Rapidan and arrived in the evening. In the house where Coleman had lived all his life, he and Alice took off their coats; rather, Coleman took his off and attempted to help Alice with hers, but she said the house was freezing and she would keep it on.

"This house is huge," she said, looking around, taking in the entrance hall and the many rooms branching from it. Coleman saw the house through her eyes. The stairway sweeping to the second floor had never seemed so massive.

She said, "I can't possibly take care of everything here."

He had looked forward to showing her the house. He had not anticipated complaint.

"You'll have plenty of help, Alice," he said. "I don't expect you to do everything."

"I don't intend to."

He knew he had made a mistake by giving Pearl and Edward, the couple who worked for him, two weeks' vacation. He had believed he and Alice

would enjoy having the house to themselves at first. He should have con-
sulted her. From now on, he would have to ask her about everything.

"You won't have to do very much," he said. "Just tend the children, if we
have any."

She did not blush. "Children, fine. I just don't want to fool with them all
the time."

Five minutes in the house, and he knew his marriage was folly. Alice was
beautiful, but her frown pulled her features together like a drawstring purse.

The cold house was not the first disaster: he had failed to make arrange-
ments to be met at the train depot. Luckily his friend Henry Fenton happened
to be there to pick up his brother Joe. Coleman wished he'd known Joe Fenton was aboard the train, only one car away. It would have been good to see
Joe's familiar face, to talk of crops and weather. The Fentons gave Coleman
and Alice a ride. Coleman imagined her thinking, *I'm surrounded by old men.*
The Fentons lugged her trunks to the second floor, too. That was beyond what
Coleman, with his bad leg and his cane, could do. All he could carry was
Alice's traveling valise. How strange it felt to set the valise on his bed.

He hadn't really expected it to go this far: marriage. Their courtship was
a time of ponds and water lilies, never mind that the ponds were frozen in
the back garden of the orphanage and the matrons did most of the talking
for Alice. He had noticed her as an adult only last Christmas, when she put
presents under the tree for the younger children, pretty boxes wrapped in red
paper. It was his duty, he felt, to help the orphans of that terrible war. The
orphanage was clean and orderly, yet he could never warm up to the matrons.
Steely-eyed, they took his money and pressured him to buy Confederate souvenirs from a dusty little counter in their office. Year after year, he visited. He
had cousins in Richmond, and the orphanage was just down the street. At last
he realized there weren't many orphans left. They were growing up or were
already grown. Alice was the matrons' favorite, their prize.

The courtship took a year. This past Christmas, he proposed, and now he'd
claimed her.

Here she was, shivering, asking why hadn't he had the house warm and
ready? She was exhausted, she said.

"I'm sorry," he said. "Come into the parlor, and I'll build a fire."

The parlor felt even colder than the entrance hall. He stuffed kindling
into the fireplace. Even as he held a match to the twigs, he realized that Alice
had never asked him about his own life: the fall he took at twenty-two from
a railroad bridge, the fall which cost him his chance to serve in the war, years
he spent tending the depot and running the post office in the building that

served as both. Anything that needed to be done, Coleman did it. He fixed plows, churns, and wagons. He wrote letters for people who couldn't write, letters for fathers and mothers to soldier sons. When news of his friends' deaths reached him, or reports that they were missing or captured, he grieved by working harder than ever.

"I was working before you were born, Alice," he heard himself say and discovered he'd been lecturing her in his head. "I fell off that railroad bridge before you were on this earth."

The fire drew a little, then flared. They watched the flames while a mantel clock ticked. Coleman peeked at Alice and saw not a charming bride, but a crotchety stranger.

She bit her gloves at the fingertips, pulled them off, and dropped them on the floor. Out of instinct, he picked them up and offered them to her. She threw them down again.

"What good is it, if we don't get along?" he asked. Not that the wedding night was a total disappointment; she had lain there, going along with it.

"What else was I to do but get married?" she said.

"Did other men come see you? They must have."

"Two or three."

"Well," he said, baffled, holding out his hands to the fire. "Well, then."

Thank goodness they had eaten on the train, so there was no need to worry about supper.

In the morning, a neighbor appeared, stamping her feet on the porch. Coleman hung in the door and stared at her: Mabel Stover, his sweetheart back when they were young, and a widow now.

"Are you going to let me in to meet the bride?" Mabel asked.

She breezed inside and handed him a loaf of bread wrapped in a clean towel. The bread was still warm and smelled wonderful. He leaned close to Mabel's face and said, "I've married a monster. I don't know what to do."

"Old fool," Mabel said. "We tried to tell you, all of us."

He didn't remember any such warnings. His head had been too full of Alice's perfume, of her Christmas self.

Mabel moved to the foot of the staircase and called, "Mrs. Barbour, are you up?"

"Shh," Coleman said, "don't wake her." He held out a finger and pressed it to Mabel's lips. He used to pine to kiss those lips, and now they were wrinkled and white. He tore off a chunk of bread. "I ought not to done it, Mabel," he said as he chewed. "She's a spoiled brat."

Mabel smiled. "You're all riled up. Tell me anything you want. I won't repeat it."

Women were a sea of bobbing bonnets, a league of treacherous flowers, in cahoots with each other even when they fought among themselves. Mabel, though, would keep his secrets.

Why had he not married Mabel? Why at fifty-two did he realize his mistake?

"This house is awful quiet, Coleman," Mabel said.

"Pearl and Edward went to visit her parents for two weeks." What if they were gone for good? When he went to their cabin out back, it might be empty, and well, why not, they were young, or anyway not old, and possibly itchy-footed.

Mabel said, "Will she kill you in your sleep?"

"It's bad, Mabel," he said, "real bad."

"I was at that orphanage one time." She motioned for him to follow her into the dining room, where the table was laid out all pretty with sterling silver and plates. Pearl must have done that before she left. Mabel said, "I remember those matrons selling cheap little gewgaws in their office, bored to evilness."

"That's the place," he said as Mabel urged him to sit down. He did.

"Nothing to do but fix your breakfast, and put back a plate for young miss," Mabel said.

Coleman laid his head on the table.

He felt a gentle pressure at the back of his neck: Mabel's fingertips. "I felt right bad at first, too," she said, "when I married Bob, much as I loved him. I woke up and thought, What have I done? That feeling didn't last but a day or so. I never told Bob."

Slippered feet scraped on the stairs. Mabel lifted her hands away, and Coleman raised his head. His skull weighed a thousand pounds. Alice padded into the dining room, her face wrenched into a grimace.

"Mabel," said Coleman, "meet my wife, Alice."

"You woke me up," Alice said.

"I'm sorry, honey," Mabel said with a laugh that raised goose bumps on Coleman's skin. "I bet there's eggs out in the henhouse. Why don't I go look?" She turned toward the door and stopped, pointing at a window. "It's snowing, folks, and here we thought it was spring."

＊

Rapidan had everything, Mabel told Alice, all that was bad and all that was good—fleas and stray dogs, floods that swelled the river and washed out its banks. There was quicksand, if you went far back in the woods. Relic hunters dug around on your land for bullets and such, even if you asked them not to. Hoboes from the train would snatch your clothes from the line. Gypsies would steal your child.

"That gypsy business never happened here," Coleman said, sopping up eggs with bread.

"Those are all bad things," Alice said. She was eating, too, and with appetite.

"Oh, there's mostly good things," Mabel said. "Coleman, for example. He's kept us going. He built a water pump so our wells don't run dry."

"It wasn't hard," Coleman said, but Alice cut him off.

"Where do you live?" she asked Mabel.

"Next door, but it's still right far," Mabel said. "Close enough you can borrow something if you need it, not so close I'll bother you."

Mabel's mention of floods jogged a memory in Coleman's mind. He turned to her and said, "What was it we did, first time we went walking out? Seems to me there was high water."

Mabel's smile shone like candles. "Looked for turtles, that's what we did, turtles washed out of creeks and into the fields. We found a big one stranded in the grass, and you let me have him, Coleman. He probably went for stew. My mother's turtle stew, now that was fine."

"Ugh," said Alice.

Coleman wondered if the other men who visited her were scared off by her, if the courting was no more than a glance and a word and a swift retreat.

Alice declared, "I don't like turtle soup, nor turtle stew," as if he and Mabel were the matrons at the orphans' home, who would do her bidding. She had told Coleman she was raised on white sugar and fried chicken livers. The matrons squabbled over who would get to tie ribbons in her hair. "I got good at making them fight," she'd said on the train.

He wished he could pack her off to a nanny. Mabel saw him wish it. He knew she saw, even as he dropped his gaze to his plate.

"Next door," Alice said. "You live next door. Hmm."

Mabel was country. A hick, Coleman's mother used to say, while Coleman writhed with chagrin on sweet Mabel's part. Before Mabel married Bob Stover and rose up in the world, she had lived out in the woods. Coleman's family had people to wash the clothes, clean the house, and tend the crops. Mabel's mother had only Mabel. As a girl, she was even prettier than Alice.

Had he been asleep all these years, as if the young Mabel who had spied the turtle in the flooded field had cast a spell on him and made him a wanderer in his own life? Again he remembered that terrible fall he took. It made him an old man when he was young, and now it didn't matter anymore, for what old man didn't limp? What mattered was he had married the wrong woman, and now it was too late. Could have had his old beloved, right next door all these years, could have merged his farm with her big pastures, but no, he had to go trotting off to an orphans' home to pick out the strangest woman in Virginia. Alice was a turtle, washed out of her stream. She had waited for him to find her. Better watch out, for her bite was sharp, her latching-on a fearsome thing.

Yet she must have wanted him. He wondered why.

The women cleared the table. Mabel told Alice she was lucky: Pearl and Edward would take care of things. "That's just what I was saying to him." Alice nodded toward Coleman. "I don't intend to work myself to the bone."

"You won't be able to sit idle all day," Mabel said, "but who would want to? Of course, it's more work to manage a place like this than you might think." Mabel stacked the plates, and Coleman realized with fresh admiration that she had all the skills necessary to operate a large, profitable farm. So graciously she did it, you would think her place ran itself.

Alice asked Mabel, "What would you be doing right now, if you weren't here?"

Coleman decided he had never known anybody ruder.

"I'd be out among my hens," Mabel said. "They don't like anybody but me to feed them. Bob used to say when they clucked, they were calling my name."

Out among hens, and Mabel a rich woman. Yet light of heart and sweeter than Alice would ever be. And him just beginning a new life with Alice, with wedding anniversaries ahead of them and quarrels he could feel already like storms in his chest, him losing his temper and her cool and superior, ever biting her gloves at the fingertips and drawing them off.

"Let's go up to the roof," Mabel suggested, her voice as merry as Christmas. "Come on, Coleman, we'll show Alice everything she needs to know about Rapidan."

"All right," he said, though what he really wanted was another cup of coffee and to go back to bed with a stack of newspapers, never mind if they were weeks old.

"We'll need our coats." Mabel slouched into hers and pulled on a warm hat.

Alice and Coleman followed her up the stairs, tugging on their coats and scarves. Mabel said, "I haven't been up here since, oh, when was that party your mother gave, Coleman? When we all sat out on the roof and looked at the stars?"

"Right after the war," he said, catching his breath, keeping a hand on the banister.

They went into the second-floor room his mother had used for sewing. Pearl worked in this room now. The sewing machine was closed, the basket with its needles and scissors tucked into a corner. The room smelled of light oil and clean cloth. Coleman imagined his mother's surprise at his bringing this new woman into the house. Well, sometimes she took a shine to unlikely people—a grim tinker, a lazy farmhand, a grubby woman who showed up year after year to can tomatoes. In those overlooked folks, his mother saw some spark to fan. Not that Alice was grubby or itinerant. Was it possible his mother would have liked her?

Mabel unfastened the French doors that gave onto the flat roof of the porch. When she pushed them open, frigid air and snowflakes poured in, and she laughed.

"Maybe this is a bad idea," Alice said, but Mabel took her arm and propelled her outside, with Coleman following.

"It's not snowing all that hard. You can still see a lot," Mabel said. She led Alice to the edge of the roof, where only the balustrade kept them from pitching forward.

Rapidan was a map of itself. There was the familiar configuration of river and road. The river cut into its northward bank, reminding Coleman of a mouth of uneven teeth chewing harder on one side.

"There's Henry Fenton's mill," Coleman said to Alice, pointing, "and Joe Fenton's ice and lock shop. Browning's store, and the post office and depot."

"Oh, don't get Coleman started about the post office and depot," said Mabel. "Thirty years you worked there, right?"

"But I got tired of it and wanted to concentrate on farming," he said.

A train was stopped at the station. It looked like a toy, its cars colorful amid the landscape of bare trees. As they watched, it moved down the tracks, heading south.

Gesturing through the falling snow, Mabel told Alice, "See that little cabin? Bonnie Hazlitt lives there and raises canary birds. Coleman'll get you one if you want. The Ulshes live over yonder. See the smoke rising from the hollow? Leonora Ulsh was a Nalle, marrying down."

"Chapman Ulsh is a good man," said Coleman, some egalitarian protest rising in him.

"Oh, there's still the truth of marrying up and down," Mabel said. "I married up, and I'm proud of it. I used to tease Bob Stover about marrying me. Oh, and Alice? This hill, where we live, is Gospel Hill. Baptist, Presbyterian, colored—there's churches all over it. The Episcopal church is down at the river. They get flooded and keep rebuilding. Too stubborn to move."

"On clear days, there's no better view of the mountains," Coleman said, "than from any western window in my house, Alice. Our house, I mean."

Mabel and Coleman stood silently, like parents giving their daughter a chance to absorb her lessons. Snowflakes peppered Coleman's face and caught in the women's hair. Alice moved away from Coleman and Mabel, gazing at the scene stretched all around her, river and train tracks, store and mill and houses and barns, and the patchwork fields dusted white. Alice leaned over the balustrade as if she had forgotten Coleman and Mabel were there.

Coleman wondered if she might be homesick, yet there was nobody at the orphanage that she ever mentioned with particular affection. The thought was troubling. Had her heart failed to develop in some way? Yet he had seen her give presents to the children at the orphanage and hug them too.

"She has a pretty profile," Mabel murmured, then raised her voice and called, "Be careful, Alice. Don't lean too far."

What if she fell, Coleman thought, fell and died, and it was over, that fast?

Mabel said softly, "She's older than you think. You didn't marry a girl, Coleman, you got yourself a spinster. She's thirty if she's a day."

In the snowy light, he noticed fine lines on Alice's skin and a sag under her eyes, signs of age he never saw in courtship or even yesterday on the train, while she dozed beside him, awash in the light and shadows shuttling through the windows.

"You sure, Mabel?" he said.

A blackbird winged through the powdery air, and Alice tilted her head to follow it, showing the sandy hollow of her throat.

"I'm sure," Mabel whispered. "It doesn't make any difference, does it?"

"It's a relief," he said and meant it.

A train sounded from way off. He could just make out the steam from its engine as it puffed around Clark's Mountain and snaked toward the Rapidan station. The whistle blew again, and the wheels gathered speed. This one wouldn't stop. It was a freight train, loaded.

Alice covered her ears as it passed. "I don't think I'll ever get used to that," she said.

"But you will. We all do," Mabel said. "You still hear it loud and clear, right, Coleman?"

"Loud as ever." He and Mabel were at the age where deafness could set in. He welcomed the enveloping sound of the train. He had missed it during the days spent fetching Alice down in Richmond, missed it so bad he could cry, even now.

Alice pointed to a big white house half hidden behind a stand of oaks and asked, "Is that your place, Mabel?"

"It is," Mabel said. Her sheep and cattle dotted the pastures, motionless in the spinning snow. A Bible verse edged into Coleman's mind, something from Ezekiel: *My sheep wandered through all the mountains, and upon every high hill; yea, my flock was scattered . . .* He didn't know why, but the words made him sad.

"Somebody's coming up the driveway," Alice announced.

Coleman recognized a familiar buggy, then another and another. Old friends: Carter and Delia Lyne, Henry and Fannie Fenton, and Gertrude Nalle. Their horses' bells jingled. Glad as he would be to see them, why did his heart feel so heavy?

"The news is getting around," Mabel said, as if she had planned this whole day. "I'll fix coffee."

The Lynes brought a beautiful blue and white platter. "It was my aunt's," said Delia Lyne proudly. "It's very old."

"Thank you," said Alice, running her finger along the edges as if checking for chips, then setting the platter aside. Coleman wished she had acted a little more excited about it.

The Lynes had brought a coconut, too. Coleman cracked it open with a mallet and an awl, and Delia Lyne sliced the sweet white meat for all of them to enjoy. Henry and Fannie Fenton gave Alice a silver serving spoon, a ham, and a fruitcake. Gertrude Nalle had brought her cousin, Marjorie Coad, and together they presented Alice with a set of linen sheets.

"They're not embroidered yet," Marjorie apologized. "I want to embroider a *B* on them."

"I don't care about that," said Alice, and again Coleman flinched at her rudeness, though Marjorie Coad kept smiling.

"When you start having children, I have a nice pram I'll give you," Gertrude Nalle said.

"Well," said Alice, as if thoughts of prams were not appealing.

Mabel served coffee on a silver tray, along with the fruitcake. Coleman found a bottle of wine in the gun closet, poured it into small glasses, and passed it around.

"To the bride," said Henry Fenton. "To your long and happy life together," and everyone toasted.

"We kept telling Coleman he ought to get married, Alice," said Marjorie Coad, who like Mabel was a longtime widow, her husband dead of fits the doctors couldn't cure. "All the time Coleman was courting you, we couldn't wait to meet you."

"And here I am," said Alice.

Coleman's heart sank to his toes. He pictured his heart there on the floor, something to be kicked under a chair. His courtship was madness, a neglect of his crops and stock, a single-minded chase that had as much to do with Alice being far away as it did with his being lonely, when he was perfectly all right by himself.

Yet there was something he'd glimpsed in her that attracted him, a proud shy way of standing still when the matrons praised her. Once she'd caught his eye and smiled right playful, and in that smile he saw a future. Was that a trap, set for him? He'd imagined a big family, his and Alice's children, with Christmas trees he would cut from his own fields.

"Are you tired, Coleman? Alice?" Mabel asked. "You-all had a long trip yesterday. We should be going, all of us."

He wanted to cry out, *Don't*.

"Come see us," said Fannie Fenton to Alice. "I'll give a little party for you." Fannie's face glowed; she pressed her hands together.

"Well," Alice said.

"Stay a while," Coleman begged his neighbors, but the Lynes, the Fentons, Gertrude Nalle, and Marjorie Coad disappeared in a flurry of handshakes and hugs, until only Coleman and Alice and Mabel remained, with Mabel moving toward the door.

He would rather face the Yankees again than be alone with his bride. "Mabel, could you help my wife unpack?"

She stopped in her tracks. "Why, of course. I should have thought of that myself."

The Yankees had come like a whirlwind, on such fine horses. They fired the town, burning the mill, the railroad bridge, and the store. Coleman hunkered down in the building that was both post office and depot. He had never seen a better throwing arm than belonged to the officer who hurled torches and pranced backwards on his gray horse while the fire took. Coleman ran out of the depot. Panicked, he tripped and fell.

They caught him, collared him, and dragged him to his feet.

"Looky, he's lame," one said. "You get shot, Rebel?"

"No." He recalled he'd sold a ticket for the next train to a woman who wanted to go to Warrenton. "There's a lady asleep in there," he blurted.

"Well, get her out," said the officer, tall as a thundercloud on the gray horse.

Coleman ran pell-mell back inside. "Go, Gimpy!" the Yankees yelled and laughed. His shame rose faster than the flames, shame that he forgot this stranger, this female. Gasping, he crawled through smoke to find her asleep on a bench. He lifted her onto his back. She woke up and fought him all the way out the door, a furious, flailing burden. Outside, he dumped her on the grass. She got up and shambled off. The word *hinney* came to his mind, offspring of a male horse and a female donkey. He never knew who she was or if she knew he had saved her life. Yet he used to dream about her, swapping the reality of her greasy hair and sharp elbows for beauty and kindness. Oh, it would have been fun if she'd been pretty, if she'd fallen in love with him.

By the time he hauled her to safety, the Yankees were gone, so he never got to tell them how he hurt his leg. At least they'd asked. They were dots in the distance, gone to wreak mayhem elsewhere.

He had a devil of a time getting the building repaired, with nearly every man in Rapidan gone to war. Bob Stover and Henry Fenton helped on furloughs, but Coleman did most of the work himself. A bad leg didn't mean he couldn't hammer, saw, and paint. He could even climb a ladder when he had to. The new counter, where he sold train tickets and stamps and took in mail, was never quite right. He missed the one that burned, with its long shine of elbow-worn oak.

His mother used to say, "Well, Coleman, it's up to you." Did he learn to do more, lame, than he would have with two good legs? As a child he used to get these surges of happiness for no reason except he was alive on a beautiful morning. Even during the war he sometimes had those happiness surges.

Mabel's first child was born in August of '62, the day the Battle of Cedar Mountain began. Cannon boomed and blasted seven miles away. Coleman carved a spinning top for Mabel's baby. Gleefully he tried it out on the ticket counter. He closed up at midday to ride over to Mabel's house, never mind that the cannon fire spooked his horse. He thought the reason for his cheerfulness was the toy turning out so cute. Why didn't he realize it was because he was going to see Mabel? He smelled burnt powder in the wind, yet there he was at the Stovers' door, with a top in his pocket.

So he was an old man and a new groom, trapped in his own house, wondering what to do. He climbed halfway up the stairs and paused. He would leave well enough alone. If the women were getting Alice's things unpacked, he would stay out of their way. His hand resting on the banister brought back the times he slid down it as a boy. You'd smack your behind on the newel post, but wasn't speed the whole point?

He went back down the steps, his mind still on Mabel's first baby. She died when she was only a few months old. She had a marker in the Presbyterian churchyard, a little bitty stone with a lamb carved on it.

"She loves the toy you gave her," Mabel had said, all those years ago, when she stopped by the post office. "See?" She unwrapped the blanket from the infant, and there was the top clutched in the baby's hands. "Would you like to hold her?" Mabel asked. He balanced his weight on his good leg while he reached for the baby. She weighed no more than a cat. Oh, Mabel went on to have other children, and now she was a grandmother, but he could picture the baby and Mabel as clearly as if they were right there in front of him. And to think there'd been nothing to come of Mabel's love for the baby, nothing at all.

He was crying. He sank to the bottom of the staircase and covered his face with his hands. Sobs rose up and broke in his throat with sounds he couldn't stifle.

"What's this? What?" The women's voices reached him, high chitters and running feet hurrying down the steps. There was a gentle hand on his shoulder, a firm arm around his neck, and a warm cheek against his face. It was Alice. He shook, blind from tears.

"There, there," Alice said. "Coleman, it'll be all right."

She sat and rocked with him on the bottom step. He was aware of Mabel heading in the direction of the kitchen. He blew his nose on his handkerchief and took a deep involuntary breath, as if he had been underwater and was rising to air.

"Dear, dear," Alice said, lacing her fingers through his. "I've been mean, and I'm sorry."

Moments later he smelled chocolate, opened his eyes, and found Mabel holding a cup of cocoa before him. He took it, and it warmed his hands. Stunned by giving way to feelings, *this welter* was the phrase that came to mind, he sipped and swallowed.

Mabel and Alice exchanged murmurs. The door opened with a sweep of cold air and closed with a thump. Coleman raised his head. He felt he had just waked up. He had stood on his roof in a snowstorm not five minutes ago, yet already it was night.

Mabel had departed. He saw a light bobbing out the window.

"I should drive her," he said, stirring.

"She wanted to walk," said Alice. "I made her take a lantern. I'll go check on her in the morning." She took the empty cup and saucer from him and set them on a table. "We can be happy together, Coleman. I wouldn't have married you if I didn't think so."

Her face held a still, serious expression, as if the sullen girl had vanished and a grown woman had taken her place. It seemed to Coleman that his life changed in that moment, turning in some great and permanent direction which he recognized, from the tiny buzz of hope in his heart, as inevitable. The hope would have to be enough, that and the fact Mabel still lived next door, where he could watch out for her as a neighbor and a friend.

"All right?" Alice asked.

"All right." It shouldn't be this easy, he thought—to cry like a child and have a shrewish wife turn sweet—but he would gladly accept it.

He was still sitting on the bottom step. Alice stood in front of him. "Well, one more thing, Coleman," she said. "You wish you were married to Mabel, don't you?"

He felt the nakedness of his face. "I never asked her, and she married somebody else."

"You could have asked her anytime since her husband died. Why didn't you?"

"I don't know," he said. "I never thought about it, until today."

"And now you wish you had," Alice said. "How was it you didn't know already?"

"I loved her when I was young, and then . . ." He couldn't explain. It was as if the love he felt for Mabel when they were young had gone to sleep and had awakened this morning when she stood at his door with a loaf of bread in her hands. Now he hardly knew what he felt for Mabel or Alice, either one.

For a long time they regarded each other, and he saw the intelligence in Alice's face and a sheen of hurt in her eyes. She was an orphan after all and accustomed to what that meant.

She said, "Mabel and I talked about you, about all of this, while we were upstairs. I told her I didn't think I could stay here. I didn't unpack a thing."

He shook his head, confused. A moment ago, she had said they could be happy together.

"You didn't unpack?" he said, trying to understand.

"As soon as I came downstairs this morning, I saw how you felt."

"I had to invite her in," he fumbled. "She came to wish us well."

"I want her to visit us often," Alice said. "I like her."

It was disrespectful to be seated while a woman stood. He pulled himself to his feet. The bottom of the staircase seemed an oddly suitable place for this negotiation. "When you talked with her, what did she say?"

"She likes things the way they are. She said if she ever wants to get married again, she's the one who'll do the asking."

The silence stretched out. He felt he was again reviving from that long fall off the railroad bridge, hardly knowing where he was.

Alice said, "You and I both have doubts. Do you want me to leave?"

Her face told him she would go quietly. It would be as if the marriage had never taken place. There was no blame in her gaze, only an orphan's stoicism. If he asked her to go, she would put on her coat, and he need never see her again. If he asked her to stay, then her face and form would become part of his life. Her footsteps, voice, opinions, her need for warmth and meals and sleep: he had sought those things. Had he been right or wrong? She was giving him a chance to decide all over again. As strange as it felt to be married, nothing compared to his astonishment at a woman who could offer a man that choice and mean it.

He thought about it, and he found he didn't have to think very long.

"We should have supper," he said, "and then I'd like to show you the house properly."

"Well," said Alice. She put out her hand and touched his cheek. "That's what I think, too."

She went into the kitchen, and soon he heard her working at the stove.

"Coleman," she called, "could you bring me that blue and white plate? I want to use it."

He fetched the platter the Lynes had given them. He paused, balancing it in his hands. This much felt familiar, something recalled from long ago—the turtle in the flooded field? He could manage. This was light enough.

The Flood

I. High Water

Rapidan, Virginia
April 1886

Here came something big. Twelve-year-old Gid Ulsh, in the river boiling with
flotsam, recognized the object as a hog trough. He leaned out from the boat
he shared with his father. The little craft swayed dangerously in the cold water.
The trough came close, then slipped out of reach. Gid's father waved an arm,
meaning, *Let it go.*

Gid's head filled with the shouts of other salvagers. The swollen river,
carrot-colored with the soil of pastures, poured over the mill dam. A rope was
strung across the river and tied to trees on either side. Salvagers looped their
own ropes around it to steady their boats in the current. The bridge's wooden
timbers were submerged, and the span connecting Orange County to Culpeper County was mere inches above the water. Gid saw Henry Fenton, owner
of the riverside grain mill, direct men to close the bridge. Before they could
do so, a man on horseback galloped up. Henry Fenton shook his head, but the
man leaped from his horse, took off his shirt, and draped it over the horse's
head.

Everybody was watching now, those on land and those in boats. Gid gazed upward.

The man took the bridle and led the blindfolded animal across the bridge, double-quick. Gid held his breath. So close was the bridge to the water that it appeared the bridge floated and the horse swam. When man and horse reached the Culpeper County side, the salvagers cheered. The man waved, then took the blindfold off his horse, jumped on its back, and rode away.

Gid and his father turned their attention back to salvage. The flood brought all kinds of things into Rapidan, living and dead. Carcasses caught on the submerged wall of the mill slough, jerked loose, bobbed into the channel, and disappeared around the bend. Underwater objects jolted the Ulshes' boat like whales. The danger was exciting, but the dead animals stopped Gid's pleasure: cattle, dogs, sheep, and goats.

"See there," said Gid's father. "A rabbit hutch."

They braced to try for it. Gid's father snagged it with his pole and got their boat back to shore. They hauled the hutch onto land, their shoes sopping. Gid's father stroked his earlobe, a gesture of satisfaction. The ear was notched, the result of a boyhood fight with his brother Bern, Gid's uncle. Gid peered into the hutch and saw a ball of dirty fur.

"Look at that!" Gid's father pointed at the river. A steamer trunk slid toward them, its lid askew in a crooked smile. "Stay here," his father said and shoved off again.

"You got a bunny," said a voice. An ancient woman called Sarah Nighten knelt beside Gid. She pulled the animal out and pressed Gid's hand against its tiny chest. There was its heartbeat, faint and quick. Delighted, Gid gathered it into his arms.

His brain registered a noise distinct from the rush of the river—cries of alarm. He set the rabbit back in its hutch. Something bucked in the water: a boat, overturned. Behind it, twisting through the waves, a man's arms tore at air. His father.

Gid hollered.

Two men went after his father, but their boat dumped them out, so there were three men slipping downriver faster than people could scream. The current took Gid's father speedily around the curve and out of sight. Men threw ropes to the other two, and soon they lay heaving on the banks.

Gid fought his way toward Henry Fenton and begged, "Help my papa."

Henry Fenton summoned three men to launch the biggest boat avalable. Gid felt the thrill of being helped by a powerful person. Henry Fenton directed an assistant to telegraph the miller at Raccoon Ford, five miles downriver. Other men loaded a boat into a wagon. "Ride hell for leather to the Ford," Henry Fenton said, and the men were off.

Sarah Nighten appeared, the hem of her dress sagging with mud. "This won't turn out good," she said to Gid. "When they find your daddy, don't look at him."

The phrase *hell for leather* gave Gid hope. He said, "They'll save him."

"You need to get home. Here, take t'other side of the hutch and we'll put it in your wagon," Sarah said, and they did.

"We have to get the boat," Gid said.

"Don't worry about the boat." Sarah shook the reins, and the horse moved.

At the Ulshes' cabin, people gathered, keeping watch with Gid and his mother throughout the chilly spring afternoon. Late in the day, word came that Chapman Ulsh had turned up at Raccoon Ford.

He was dead.

"No," Gid said, and "No," said his mother, Leonora Ulsh. She too believed in the powers of Henry Fenton and had expected her husband to return safely, maybe even go out and make another try for the steamer trunk, which witnesses had described to her.

At dusk, a man named Pete Grasty brought the corpse home in a wagon. Grasty called out, "I was robbed by nigras. They even robbed *him*. Took coins out of his pocket."

Gid's mother ran to the wagon, lifted the blanket, and gazed. She let the blanket fall, retreated to the porch, and said to the group, "He couldn't swim."

"Aw, Leenie," women said as she wept. "And you with a baby on the way."

Thus Gid learned he was to acquire a brother or sister. The news made him feel worse.

As the body was unloaded, it slipped out of its blanket, exposing a head with the familiar notched ear. Onlookers moaned. Gid reached the body just as Pete Grasty bundled the blanket around it. A hand fell out, and somebody on the porch guffawed. Gid placed the hand on his father's bare chest. So cold, those fingers, and he was shocked that his father was naked. He hadn't known the river would tear off clothes.

People kept coming, Gid's father's German kin: the Handiboes, Hufnagels, and Shellenbergers. They came from Lignum, Brandy Station, Mount Pony, Cedar Mountain, and Gourdvine Fork. They were farmers, tanners, and blacksmiths. Or miners: there was iron at Mine Run and gold at Vaucluse.

Out in the yard, tethered horses whinnied and pitched, churning the earth to muck.

Nobody came from Gid's mother's family. She was a Nalle, and on her mother's side a Graves, and those names carried weight. To Gid's recollection, he had never met his mother's parents. No Nalles or Graveses appeared, as if the death of Chapman Ulsh were unworthy of notice. "Oh, they know, all right," his mother cried in a ragged voice.

Gid smelled food that women were preparing, and the smoky odor of whiskey. People ate and drank in every room. When the dishes ran out, people ate from pots. Gid observed among his relatives the traits his father had condemned or championed: the Handiboes' pickley breath, the Hufnagels' hellfire stare, the Shellenbergers' speckled hands and incessant smoking.

Sarah Nighten brought Gid a prize, a roast chicken leg. He retreated to his bed to eat. It was dark. All the candles and lanterns were in the front room with the body. Cousins crowded into bed with Gid, and he soon lost the chicken leg. Other kinfolk pushed into the room and spread coats on the floor. Gid felt stifled and miserable.

The next day dawned cloudy but without rain. The grave took all morning to dig. Gid fell asleep in church; a cousin kicked his leg. When the funeral and burying were over, it was time to eat. Back at the house, the wagon driver talked about another death caused by the flood. A tree had crashed through a roof and impaled a woman in her bed.

"Who?" Gid's mother asked with tears on her cheeks.

"Old lady up the mine road," Pete Grasty said. "The tree went through her heart."

"Did you see the lady and the tree your own self?" demanded Gid's Uncle Bern.

"Naw, but . . ." Pete Grasty appealed to Gid's mother. "You believe me, Leenie?"

"Leave her alone, Pete Grasty," Uncle Bern said. "I think *you're* the one that robbed a dead man. You robbed my brother and his widow-woman," and he and Pete Grasty argued back and forth, *did not, did so,* until Uncle Bern leaped from his chair.

He raised his end of the table so plates, food, and cutlery slid off in a long, splattering clatter. Gid tasted cinnamon and blood as a dish of pear butter cut his lip. Mourners twisted away from the crash. Pete Grasty and Uncle Bern wrestled in the mess. Gid crouched and hid until the commotion was over. Eventually he fell asleep.

When he opened his eyes, evening sun shone through the window. He crawled out from the slurry of food. Sarah Nighten heaved broken dishes into a barrel.

"Where is everybody?" Gid asked. "Where's my mother?"

"Sleeping," she said. "The others, they're at the river."

"Has the water gone down?"

"Down everywhere. Fenton's got his mill running. They say you can see the rock at Raccoon Ford," Sarah said.

If you could see that rock from either bank, you could safely cross the water. What good would that do, now that his father was dead? Gid remembered the fight. "Who won?"

"Your uncle did," said Sarah. "Your mother will need looking after. Can you do that?"

"No," said Gid. There was a theatrical element in his mother's emotions that scared him.

People returned to the house, trumpeting about treasures pulled from the river. They ate leftover food, smacking their lips. By midnight Gid had had enough of snores and farts. He stood up on his bed and shouted, "Go home." He dodged a swatting hand and said, "Go home!"

They kicked him off his bed, somebody's foot on his fanny and somebody else's in the small of his back. Toppling, he saw himself as a grown man: *Go home, get out,* to neighbors and callers and kin, everybody but his own woman and kids.

When the mourners finally departed, the only food left was sauerkraut and walnuts.

Sarah Nighten haunted the riverbanks. Gid heard the stories. If she found a boy tormenting a frog or throwing fish onto the ground instead of back into the water, she'd pounce. "Eat dirt," she'd say until the boy did it.

"You don't see her till she's right on you," boys said.

She caught one of the Jouette brothers killing a snake for the fun of it, and she yanked out a chunk of his hair. The boy, a friend of Gid's, had a bald spot to prove it.

By then the flood was a couple weeks past. Gid's mother wore a brooch she'd made with his father's hair, a lock braided beneath a chip of glass. Already Pete Grasty was attempting to court her, never mind that she was pregnant, and so were other men, bringing cream and strawberries. She didn't let them stay to eat with her.

"I was meant for better," she declared, her eyes dark as watermelon seeds. She was Leonora Nalle, she reminded Gid, before she was ever Leenie Ulsh.

"We're going home," she said. "To my parents. Don't bother to pack anything."

Gid did get the rabbit hutch, and his mother drove the wagon *hell for leather* some miles away from their cabin, which after all the Ulshes did not own. They rented it from Henry Fenton.

Gid's mother pulled up to a splendid house and parked in the yard. "My mother will take care of us," she said.

Gid followed her. The columns of the porch were as thick as tree trunks, and the steps were so high they hurt his legs.

"Take off that ugly thing," was the first thing Gid's grandmother said, pointing at the hair brooch. Gid's mother unclipped it as if it were some small living horror that had dropped from the sky. She tossed the brooch onto a hallway table. Mrs. Nalle told a servant to bring tea.

The next thing she said was to Gid himself, in tones like a curse: "You look like him." The old lady's disapproval made Gid proud of the yellow hair and green eyes he'd inherited from his father, and a mouth so wide it cracked his face in two. He hoarded the practical knowledge his father had passed on: if you hear *fire,* grab a bucket and run to help. If your tooth hurts, crush a ladybug between your fingers and put the powder on the gum. He thought of those things while his grandmother glared.

"You saw Gid when he was a baby, Mother," Gid's mother protested faintly.

"All babies look alike," Mrs. Nalle said. Her hand was cold when it touched his, and the tea tasted bitter. He was glad there was food. "Frozen sultana pudding with claret sauce," his grandmother said, placing tiny portions onto plates.

It was delicious. Gid was hungry.

The Nalles' house sat so high that the cabin Gid and his parents had occupied was not even a speck in the valley below. He imagined his mother's suitors pushing open the cabin door to find her gone. Courtship of a Nalle was not for such folk as Pete Grasty. It was for Greens or Slaughters, for Pendletons and Swans. In time, those men came to the Nalles' house, sweeping their hats from their heads and talking with Leonora's tall, unsmiling father. The suitors waited endlessly while Leonora sat at her dressing table. Gid, seeing despair on a caller's face, would trot up to his mother's room to remind her about her visitor. "We've got to get you in school," she would say.

He learned not to disturb her. She slept so deeply in her own giant bed in her own huge room that when he jostled her arm, she didn't wake up. On restless nights, he went downstairs, past the brooch forgotten on the hallway table where she had flung it. He went outside, lifted his rabbit from the hutch, and hugged it. It had come from the river. It had survived.

"Papa saved you," Gid whispered, and the rabbit clutched his neck as if it knew.

Gid was sleepy during the day. "Lazy," Grandmother Nalle said. He knew what she saw when she looked at him: his father's notched ear at the top of a ladder. She was the one who had found the window open and Leonora's bed empty, the breeze of elopement stinging her face. Gid studied a family tree that hung in a hallway. His mother's name appeared on a twig. Beside it was the letter *m* and his father's name, and a word freshly inked: *Chapman Ulsh (drowned)*.

Leonora's belly swelled. She nibbled chicken from trays. Gid asked if he could pull the wishbone with her.

"Oh, yes!" She snapped the wishbone hard, as if there was something she really wanted.

Gid decided he was glad about getting a brother or sister. But events moved faster than the river in flood. Leonora died in childbirth, and the baby died too. Grandmother Nalle flew into a lasting rage which focused on Gid. He found himself ejected from his grandparents' house. He went out to get his rabbit, but its cage was padlocked. Behind him, Grandmother Nalle said, "It's mine now."

"I hate you," Gid said, and the old lady tightened her mouth, almost smiling.

Farmed out to his Ulsh kin, who were kind but overtaxed, Gid felt himself a burden, always underfoot. He wanted to live with his Uncle Bern, but he had moved to Kentucky.

In the spring of 1887, Gid ran away from the Ulsh relatives, back to the cabin where he'd lived with his parents. Luckily, Henry Fenton had not rented it out. Gid was still a child, scrounging and starving in the empty house. No corn in the crib, no potatoes in the barrel. The kitchen garden was slick with weeds and humpy with rodent burrows. No furniture. Everything was stolen. He went to the river and fished. His father's screams were still in the water.

Sarah Nighten saw him, came home with him, and stayed.

She knew all the rivers, hills, and roads. She drew maps in the dirt with sticks: here's where the Rapidan River meets the Rappahannock. Here's the way to Orange, Stevensburg, Verdiersville. She talked about an old pole road that ran from Devil's Jump to Ebenezer Church, how she'd been married in the middle of that road long ago with friends and neighbors gathered round. She was fourteen, she said. "He was a soldier."

Gid asked, "Did he fight in the war? Did he die?"

"Probably dead by now. Wasn't the war with the Yankees. It was before that. He came back and went away again, and I never saw him no more."

"Why did he leave?"

"People just go," she said. "I tried to keep him. Caught hold of his shirt, and it stretched out in my hand like taffy."

They lived on fish and wild greens. Summer came, and the river shrank to a trickle. Gid explored the mud and found a buggy wheel and a broken plow, likely remnants of the Great Flood. He excavated a battered trunk. Could it be the one that lured his father to his death? He lifted the crabbed lid and found stiff rags of clothing, but also a pair of shoes, squashed but whole. They fit. Excited, he dragged the trunk home. Sarah cleaned it up, and they used it to store their few possessions. In Gid's mind, it was a present from his father.

Henry Fenton showed up with a sack of clothing. He didn't say anything about rent, only, "My wife sends you these things. We've got boys your age."

Eagerly Gid pulled out good shirts and pants. There was a dress for Sarah. "Thank you," he said.

Henry Fenton said, "Would you like to work at the mill? I need an errand boy."

Soon Gid went about on a mule provided by Henry Fenton. Thanks to Sarah Nighten, Gid knew every road. The geography in his head never failed him.

High on the wall of the mill office was a dark line. Henry Fenton would point it out to customers, saying, "The water was all the way up to *here*." Silence always followed, and a low whistle or two, as farmers clutched hats to chests, remembering.

"Who was the man that blindfolded his horse to go across the bridge?" Gid asked.

Henry Fenton said, "I've never known. Never saw him before or since."

People were forgetting Gid's history. Some thought Sarah Nighten was his grandmother. Men at the mill and boys he fished with: Gid found that his origins remained crystal clear in the minds of some, but others forgot, as if by growing up, he had erased the child he was.

Out in the mill yard, he heard the workers' wives talking about a man who died in the flood. The women brought the noon meal to their husbands. Men and women sat apart on the banks, men eating silently, women chatting. "Name was Ulsh. Chapman Ulsh. His wife came from a rich family," a woman said. "He married a Nalle, but I don't remember her first name."

"Leonora," Gid said, but not so loud they could hear him. His mother was lost to him as soon as she took off the brooch. Unclipped that pin, unplugged her very heart.

Sarah Nighten was going blind, she announced, her vision disappearing in chunks. She drew a diagram for Gid in the dirt, separating into quadrants what she could see and what she couldn't. "It's something I caught in the woods," she said.

"I'll get a doctor for you," Gid offered.

"No. This don't get better."

Fall came, and Henry Fenton said Gid had to go to school. He could work at the mill on Saturdays. So there Gid was, back in the schoolhouse he'd attended years earlier, with boys and girls ages six to fifteen shifting about on benches. Gid's legs were newly long.

"Write a story," the teacher said.

A girl named Lottie Hawley sat beside him. She was only seven, but she could read and write better than anybody else. Though not pretty, having a deformity in one leg that caused a limp, she had a powerful presence. The teacher asked her to read her story aloud. It ended with, "Time went by, and everything changed."

Gid asked Lottie in a whisper, "What's your favorite thing to do?"

"Ride my horse," she said, "to get away from my parents. I don't like them."

"Hush, Gid," the teacher scolded. The teacher wouldn't fuss at Lottie, Gid knew, because her father was a rich man, having built up a hardware store into a big business.

That was Gid's childhood. It went by that quick, a story he could sum up in his head. People in Orange and Culpeper counties, those who hadn't forgotten, knew the parts of his life that had played out in public. *Orphan boy. Did real well. Now he's Vice-President of the Bank of Culpeper.*

II. Race Day

July 1908

A kid reporter from the *Culpeper Exponent* is covering the Merchants Association meeting. The story is his brainstorm: Secrets of Success. "And your secret, Mr. Ulsh?" he asks.

"I like to work." Gideon Ulsh, banker, attends Merchants Association meetings with the likes of Charlie Yowell, A. J. Eggborn, Barry Burgandine, and Orville Waugh, men whose ancestors' names made up the muster rolls of wars with the British, the Indians, and the Yankees. Meetings are held in the dining room of the Waverly Hotel, beneath the banner of the Culpeper Minute Men with its rattlesnake emblem. The meals are important to Gid, a bachelor. He ought to hire a cook, but he's too busy.

A. J. Eggborn, who made his fortune in steam laundries, tells the reporter, "Gid goes out to visit his customers. I don't know any other banker who does that. People like it. You'll see him on the road more than at his bank. Or hanging around at the river. That's his hobby."

The reporter is scrawling, flipping through the pages of his notebook. Gid feels embarrassed that his friends have seen him often enough at the river to joke about it. Sometimes he fishes. The water's sound and movement seem to comment on his father's life and abrupt death. To Gid, the river represents all that's lost or unfinished. It holds the stories of so many people, back to Indian times and before. Odors of sand, clay, foam, fish, salamanders, and turtles change with the seasons, and he's learned two dozen birdsongs.

"Have you seen the new water fountain at the bank?" Barry Burgandine asks the reporter. "The old pump's just for emergencies now. Or baths, if Gid could get a secretary to join him."

Grinning, Gid ducks his head. A waiter brings a platter of baked chicken and rice.

Charlie Yowell, the youngest and wildest member of the Merchants Association, says, "Put this in the paper—Gid's looking for a wife."

"Nobody'll have him," says A. J. Eggborn, "so he has to advertise."

Earnestly the reporter says, "Behind every successful man . . ."

Orville Waugh interrupts. "Is a woman who pushes him out the door every morning. Lord, don't I know it."

"Just so my woman don't push me out of bed," barks Doc Minor, who is deaf only when he wants to be.

The men eat. It's Gid the reporter wants to talk to. "Mr. Ulsh, did you have somebody in particular who helped you develop your business philosophy?"

Henry Fenton is eighty years old, spending his days in a rocking chair while his son Richard, whose clothes Gid wore as a boy, runs the mill. "Henry Fenton," Gid says. "He hired me as a messenger boy. He knew how to treat his customers. I learned all I could from him."

"Thank you, sir," the reporter says. He folds his notebook and departs.

Gid thinks he should have given credit to Sarah Nighten too. He turns to

Doc Minor. "Tell me something. What kind of an illness makes a person go blind bit by bit?"

Doc sips his iced tea. "That's a bad thing. People get it in river valleys, from the soil and from birds. Hunters, for instance. Who are we talking about?"

"Sarah Nighten."

Doc nods. "Old and gone."

Gid checks his watch as if he's late for a meeting. He isn't. He just gets the urge to be alone, and when the feeling comes over him, he can't get away fast enough. It's how he felt as a child the night his father died, surrounded by people making their maddening claims on space and time. He has departed from parties without explanation, raising his hat to a host or hostess who believes he's been called away On Business, and it's only to go home to his brick house on South East Street or to ride down to Rapidan, stand on the bridge, and watch the river flow.

"If you got to be somewhere, Gid, go ahead," says Doc. "That eye disease, now. It's one of those long, funny words." Doc taps his head. "It'll come to me."

Gid stands up from the table and hurries into the warm dusk. The hotel's screen door slaps behind him. The relief of stepping outside is enormous. A few people stroll by, but nobody tries to detain Banker Ulsh. In tall trees, cicadas tune up, and this too is a relief, for nobody can hold a conversation in all this racket.

One person catches his eye for the fact of her stillness: Lottie Hawley, all grown up, sitting in a wagon in front of the depot. Her father still owns a prosperous hardware store. The wagon is painted with an advertisement for one of the store's big sellers—*DeLaval Cream Separator and Milker*. Lottie's horse twitches its ears at flies.

Lottie is said to be a little touched. She tends to fall asleep in public, to park the emblazoned vehicle and snooze. Might she understand Gid's urge to escape from people? *DeLaval Cream Sep* he reads. *Sooner or later you will get . . . DeLaval Cream Separator and Milker*. Lottie appears to take no notice of the Negroes who gather at the depot to box with each other until the station master or sheriff breaks up the matches, at which point they'll squat on their haunches and twirl wooden tops until the official goes away. You might blink and see black men idle, and blink again, and they're all sweat and ambition.

Between Lottie and the Negroes, Gid can't make a false move.

Can't they tell he's still the boy who saw his father swept away? Whenever he goes to Raccoon Ford, calling on customers on the steep bluffs above the river, he'll think, This is where they found him. Kingfishers dive, their blue wings catching light. Just yesterday, a dog trotted up the bluff and into a house where Gid sat with an old man, working out the terms of a loan. The dog pressed her head against Gid's knee.

The old man said, "I drownded the puppies this morning. She keeps looking for 'em."

"Don't do that," Gid said. He swept the papers together and stood up.

The man said, "I can't have fifty dogs round here, Mr. Ulsh. Do I still get the money?"

Gid waited while the man scrawled his name. It seemed to take a long time.

Banker Ulsh is only Gid after all. This welling in his heart these days he doesn't understand, the way the world is brighter and louder and nearer than it's ever been, and all he can do is make his quick, polished exits. He hopes nobody sees.

But Lottie sees. A horse in a fly mask might look to be dozing, but it's alert to everything around it. She's parked among the colored men and their women, yardbirds and picnickers. Red Culpeper County dust rises around them, rich red soil for growing corn and wheat and hay, *but you got to rotate it,* farmers remind each other.

As a twelve-year-old, Lottie portrayed a Redcoat in a play about the American Revolution. She had one line, dismissing the patriots as "Fahmahs with bitchforks!" She, a girl, played a man's role, her accent so hilarious that even now, men and women her age murmur the line beneath their breath. She tossed her head when she said it. Her mother had made her a wig of rolled sheep's wool dusted with powder.

Gid at eighteen had never laughed so hard in his life.

Now Lottie stirs and speaks. "Hey, Gid. Take me to the races tomorrow."

It's the most she has said to him since childhood. She is regarded as an old maid, a figure of fun, protected only by her daddy's wealth. She is twenty-eight, and he is thirty-four.

"Just get me there, all right?" she says. "You can leave anytime you want." She lifts the reins and slaps them down.

The name of Sarah Nighten's sight-robbing disease comes back to Doc Minor as the horses thunder round the bend, Lottie Hawley's pick in the lead. Doc cups his hands and bellows into Gid's ear, "Histo. Histoplasmosis." He tips his hat to Lottie, who clutches Gid's arm.

Horses pound into the home stretch. Bettors are shouting.

The long shot, a three-year-old Arabian named Bubble-U, heads for the hole. People leap to their feet and scream so loud even deaf old Doc covers his ears. Beside Gid, Lottie's suntanned face beneath a parasol is orange as a tiger lily, one eye on him and the other on Bubble-U, a skewbald creature she'd proclaimed a champ when he was born.

She throws her parasol aside, runs to the winner's circle, and throws her arms around Bubble-U's neck. She's picked horses all her life, but people have said it's luck. This changes everything. This is the race that makes her reputation. The jockey knows who this is, the Hawley woman jumping up and down. He's glad he's high enough up that she can't kiss him, for she ain't real pretty.

III. Gizzards and Wings

Gid loans money to everybody—the Negro boxers and top-spinners, and turkey farmers who drive their flocks into town so the intersection of Main and Davis Streets is a snowfall of feathers. He loans money to rich folks so they can do more of their high and mighty things, though they don't go so far as to let Gid Ulsh marry their daughters.

Old Hawley might.

Over ham, butterbeans, and ice cream, the members of the Merchants Association talk man to man. "She was a virgin when we got started, and now she needs it twice a day," says A.J. Eggborn. The pharmacist Milton Heflin, whose name reminds Gid of a sneeze, hints at having his assistant, a Miss Suddith, up against the shelves with pills and vials clattering down. "Can't imagine doing it now without something falling on my head," Milton Heflin says as men whoop.

Lottie Hawley, though: they don't tease each other about her. Sometimes her father, Mac Hawley, attends a meeting, nodding, "How do." He keeps two coffee cups full so he doesn't have to wait for a fresh cup.

Suddenly Gid bumps into Lottie everywhere.

"How do you know so much about horses?" he asks.

"I've been watching them all my life," she says, "just like I watch people."

She knows how long a lame leg should be wrapped. Recommends adding beet pulp to the feed of those that are old or tired. When Doc Minor's mare develops founder, she suggests tincture of aconite. The horse recovers. Milton Heflin's Percheron lies in a stupid state as if dead. "It's megrims," Lottie says. "Try opium," and the animal lives.

Gid gives her a desk at the bank. People seek her advice about swaps and sales. Most days she's out at stables and pastures. Lottie Hawley, driving her wagon with the flaking paint, *DeLaval Cream Separator and Milker,* possesses some wizardry that amazes Culpeper County during the hot summer and long warm fall of 1908. Gid invests in a new buggy and a boy to drive her around. People praise her to Gid, asking how he knew. He takes the credit. He's been in business long enough to know that when you can, you oughta.

The man whose hair Sarah Nighten long ago jerked out in a clump, Davy Jouette, has a colt for sale. Jouette is a grown man with children of his own. Gid visits Jouette's farm with Lottie and Doc Minor, who wants to buy the colt, but only on Lottie's say-so.

"Is he all right?" Doc Minor asks Lottie.

It's hot for October. Jouette's wife gave them lemonade back at the house. Yellowjackets buzz and scramble over a nest in a fence post. Gid worries they'll swarm up in his face, drawn by the lemonade on his lips. Buzzards circle in the hard white sky. A line of arbor vitae grows beside the fence, the soft, fringed foliage offering hot shade and smelling of sap. The pale sky bears down on them, men and woman and horses. Lottie's hat shadows her face, and there is something sad about her mouth, Gid thinks, as if she has waked from some unhappy dream.

"Well?" Doc is asking Lottie. The men wait.

"He's more than all right," Lottie says of the colt, and money changes hands.

Gid and Lottie ride out into the woods along the Rapidan River. She has promised to show him quicksand. "There," she says, pointing to a dappled place under trees. "Don't go any closer, or you might not get out."

Gid sees only a wallow, as if animals have lain there. He hears the river and the glistening sound of insects. They're on Nalle land. His grandmother, the rabbit-thief, died and left her vast property to distant relatives. She willed him one dollar. He tells himself it doesn't matter. He's self-made, almost a rich man.

Lottie says, "We could use the saddle blankets."

She climbs down from her horse, and after a moment, so does he. He hasn't been with many women, though he had more feeling for them (a girl in Verdiersville; a young widow in Madison Mills) than for Lottie. Generally he lies in his bed too tired for loneliness except on hot nights when he remembers he's still young.

They spread out the blankets. Shadows are dark as burns on the ground. High above them in a cottonwood tree, birds stutter.

"How do they do it?" Lottie says. "How do they fly?"

Their activities are rapid and athletic. Afterward Lottie laughs. "You know what my mother's always saying? I grew up hearing *don't. Don't do that. Plenty who will.*" She clasps Gid's hand and raises it against slanting sunlight. "I used to hate my mother."

"You can't mean that," he says, the ground cold as snow beneath him.

She rises on her elbow, still naked, her small breasts showing blue veins. "Oh, the people I've hated—when they've died, it hasn't made any difference. I've lived long enough to know that." She draws a pine needle through her lips. "The good part of my life is animals. My life's a history of animals."

"It's late," he says. "We should go."

"Do you think about dying?" she says. "Your father—I remember that. And you saw it."

Gid sits up, shaken. He doesn't want to talk about his father with her.

She says, "When I die, that'll be my time, all my own. Give me a hand," and he helps her up.

He wishes they hadn't. It's a relief when a drummer starts paying attention to her. The man supplies her father with a product that speeds chickens' molting process. *Get your hens back to laying . . . fast!*

At the Merchants Association Christmas luncheon, men hail Gid with an air of constraint, offering congratulations.

"What do you mean?" Gid asks.

"Your engagement," says Charlie Yowell. "You and Miss Hawley."

Seated beside Gid, Doc Minor slides something onto the table—a card addressed to Doc and his wife. Gid opens it and reads, *Merry Christmas from Lottie Hawley and Gid Ulsh.*

The fried trout in Gid's throat sticks there. He sets his fork down and pushes back his chair. "Excuse me," he says, and Doc nods.

At the bank, Lottie is at her desk conferring with a man and a woman. Gid interrupts them to tell her, "I need to talk to you."

She follows him into his office. He closes the door. "Those cards you sent."

Lottie smiles, and the smile makes him madder.

"Why did you do that?" he asks. "People think we're getting married."

"Are you going to fire me?"

His thoughts haven't gone that far.

"You won't have to," she says. "I'm going away for a while, to have an operation."

He sits down in his chair. "Are you . . . is it a baby?"

"My leg," she says. It's been a long time since he noticed her limp. "I'm going to Richmond to have it done."

Through the glass of his office, he sees the people at her desk check their watches.

"Will it help you walk better?" Gid asks.

"The doctor says so. I just want to look nicer."

Gid's fury is gone, exhaustion in its place.

Lottie says, "Don't you want anything, Gid?"

They face each other, and it seems to Gid that customers and employees sense combat, freeze where they stand, and fix their eyes on him and Lottie. No coins jingle, no bills ruffle, the telephones go silent; the clock stops; the red bows along the tellers' windows turn gray.

"I wanted a hog trough one time," he says, "in the river."

"Go to hell, Gid." Lottie returns to her desk. Slowly the bank resumes activity. Lottie bends her head over papers, then glances up at him. Gid looks away.

The New Year begins without word from her. Customers who make inquiries at the bank are told to leave word for her.

"When is she coming back?" asks Gid's secretary, Mrs. Black. "Do you know?"

"No," he says. "I don't."

In February, Gid visits Mac Hawley at the hardware store.

"She stayed with friends in Richmond," Hawley says, "but they told me she left after the operation. I went down there and found the doctor. Lottie came through just fine, he said."

"Did she go with that fellow?" Gid asks, meaning the salesman, though he has seen the man in town since Lottie left.

"He says he don't know where she is," Hawley says. "My wife's about out of her mind."

Dread curls deep in Gid's body. It's the way he felt when his father was brought home under a blanket.

Police confront him. "What about this?" asks a detective, holding up a familiar Christmas card. "Did you have relations with her?"

"One time," Gid answers. This would be funny if it was a story somebody else was telling, say at the Waverly Hotel.

Hardware Heiress Disappears. People speculate: she must have met with some accident or evil. Might be dead. Maybe she's got amnesia and is lost in some strange city.

A colored woman who sells fried chicken at the depot insists she saw Lottie only recently. She tells a reporter, "She wanted wings and gizzards."

Lottie's mother tells the papers Lottie never ate a gizzard in her life.

"Only drumsticks," Mrs. Hawley insists. "I miss my little girl." When Lottie was a child, her mother says, her hair was so bright that butterflies clustered around her.

Yet in Gid's recollections and in the newspaper photos, Lottie's hair is black as coal.

Gid believes the fried chicken seller. He seeks her out at the depot. "I been knowing Miss Lottie all my life," the woman says. "She took the Charlottesville train."

Gid buys a ticket on the next train. He searches Charlottesville, but he doesn't find her.

To the Culpeper Exponent, Box 12

I seen your letter in the paper, the woman you describe as L. Hawley is here in Richmond, she lives on Church Hill. Send the reward and I will tell you more.

A lady frequents the race track in Charles Town, often winning considerable sums. She walks without difficulty, so if indeed she had surgery, the operation must have been successful.

Is the lady your sweet heart? Maybe your romance was not meant to be. I was engaged and then he left, I have had no word for two years. Maybe he ran off with your Miss Hawley (ha ha). I have brown hair and green eyes. I would be happy to have a letter from you.

If Miss Hawley is no longer in this world, you may yet contact her by the use of Spiri-

tual Forces. My card is enclosed. I can arrange for Private Invocation of the Dead. Fees negotiable. You can Be Lucky in Love Beyond the Grave.

Women who strike out on their own deserve what they get. My advice to you is renounce the whore and find a decent woman who has accepted Jesus Christ as her Lord and Savior. A woman like L. Hawley will never forsake the sins of the flesh and the pleasures of sucking cock and fucking.

I met Miss Hawley at Orkney Springs, where she was taking the healing waters. She recovered enough to participate in bowling and billiards. She mentioned a Christmas card incident that she seemed to regret. A good sport and not a person to be taken lightly.

Gid travels to Orkney Springs and shows pictures of Lottie to the staff and guests of the inn. Nobody remembers her, nor does the proprietor recognize her name. The typewritten letter is unsigned. Gid concludes that this, the most promising lead, was a prank played by somebody who happened to know about the Christmas cards. Could Lottie have sent the letter herself? He lies awake trying to figure it all out.

In Charles Town, West Virginia, he visits the race track and shows her picture to patrons and employees. No Lottie.

In Richmond, he goes to her friends' house, but they have nothing new to tell him. He walks the neighborhoods of Church Hill, knocks on doors, and shows the photographs, but people shake their heads. He rests on the hilltop, which is green with summer, and looks down at the James River. A scent of arbor vitae reaches him, and he recalls how sad Lottie looked that day at the Jouette farm. He has believed he understood sorrow, but perhaps he doesn't. It isn't love he feels, but if he ever finds her, he'll ask her to marry him.

Her remarks about his father's drowning come back to him. Why hasn't he thought of that before? Was she planning suicide, telling him? Horror rushes through him.

Back in Culpeper, he waits. He can feel it coming.

Late one fall day, after heavy rains, a fisherman finds a body in the Rapidan River. The news rips through town. Gid calls the sheriff's office and finds out where to go. He keeps his horse to a walk until he's out of town, then heads for Blackjack Road at a gallop.

When he finds the spot, he pulls up and tries to catch his breath. Men are loading a wrapped bundle into a wagon. To Gid's relief, Doc Minor, who is county coroner, is here too. A small crowd clusters nearby. Somebody says, "She was crazy, that's what *I* heard."

"Just bones and one boot, Gid," the sheriff says quietly. He points to a scraggly bend. "It was over there. A partial skeleton, caught in those briars."

Lottie always wore riding boots. Gid goes to Doc Minor and says, "It's Lottie, isn't it?"

Doc wipes sweat off his forehead. "Can't tell yet. I'll look it over at the morgue."

Gid's hands shake. He wants to examine the body, but he's afraid of what he would see. He feels sure he would know if it's Lottie, even if it's only her bones.

He stays until the wagon pulls away.

That evening, Doc stops by Gid's house. He says, "It's a female, but smaller and younger. Lottie's ma didn't recognize the boot."

Gid says, "She'd had leg surgery. Does that show up?"

"There's only one leg, not her lame one. But this woman's teeth are crowded. Lottie had real even teeth. Her ma showed me a picture."

Gid can remember her slow, knowing smile but not her teeth. "So it isn't?"

Doc shakes his head.

"Are you holding back, Doc?"

"You know me better than that." Doc goes to Gid's cabinet and pulls out the whiskey bottle. "Animals chewed the skin off, and the water and weather . . . oh, soon enough, we're all dust. Those bones were out there a long time, probably longer than she's been gone." He pours a drink. "All the same, Lottie's ma screamed and cried. Mac had to carry her out." He knocks the whiskey back. "Others'll turn up, from time to time. One of them might be her."

The following year, Lottie's mother dies, and the mystery briefly revives. Plainclothes police attend the funeral. Gid feels their knobby stares on his back. It's late summer, hot even in the shade of the cemetery's oaks. Old Mac Hawley weeps hard as a child, covering his face with his hands. Three years later, he too is dead.

A nephew named Ayers Hawley comes from Baltimore to take over the hardware store. He expands it and joins the Merchants Association. Gid dislikes him. Ayers Hawley hogs the conversation and criticizes the food at the Waverly Hotel.

Culpeper flourishes. An opera house is constructed, and a modern fire engine replaces the horse-drawn wagon. Talk at the Waverly Hotel is all about automobiles. Gid buys an Overland and teaches himself how to drive.

Five years after Mac Hawley's death, in the autumn of 1918, a court declares Lottie Hawley dead. Ayers Hawley lays claim to the estate and wins. Mrs. Black, Gid's secretary, circles the announcement and leaves the newspaper on his desk. Nobody remarks on it. People have other matters on their minds—war in Europe and Spanish flu at home. The ancient President of the Bank of Culpeper retires, and Gid ascends to that lofty post. He hires a commodities broker out of Washington, D.C. and assigns him to Lottie's desk, which has stood unused all these years.

Sarah Nighten vanished too, yet he imagines she lay down in the woods, wanting her bones covered by leaves. The sheer passage of time suggests Sarah couldn't possibly be alive. But Lottie could be. Gid can't shake the feeling that he is responsible. He keeps hoping he'll see her when he crosses a street or looks into a crowd. She wouldn't recognize her wagon now. Ayers Hawley painted it yellow. It holds pots of flowers outside the hardware store that ought to belong to her.

IV. Bucket Brigade

A fire breaks out one night in November 1918. Waked by shouting, Gid jumps out of bed. Flames shimmer in the western sky above the business district. Ant-like figures rush about. Church bells ring and gong. He pulls on clothes and hurries downstairs. His father's voice comes back to him: "Take a bucket," and he grabs a pail.

Outside he finds he has joined a parade. Men, women, and children fill the streets in day dress and night clothes. They're rushing toward the fire. Why not run away?

It's irresistible.

A horn blares, and a man yells, "Make way!" A fire truck barrels down the street, dogs barking and plunging alongside. Gid remembers the regular driver is down with flu and wonders who is at the wheel.

Wafers of ash waft through the hot wind. The voice of the fire rises over all the human sounds. Gid finds himself braced against a warm brick wall. The crowd flashes by like a merry-go-round. An old woman shuffles with hands held out before her. Is she blind, feeling her way toward the heat? Children stagger past. A woman darts after a toddler, her blouse open, a breast visible. A man lunges after them, and they go off together.

Gid reaches the downtown district. The opera house and Hawley's Hardware are engulfed. Firemen train their hoses upon the inferno. Gid's bank is next. The sky is a tunnel of dark blue light. The air grows cold, as if it's sucking frost from the mountains. Explosions pierce the din. A rat clatters down a gutter spout, and its shining eyes find Gid's. A dog pounces from the shadows. Growl and squeal, and both creatures vanish.

Gid draws a breath and finds he knows exactly what to do.

He hollers to citizens near him, "Form a line!" He holds his bucket high and locates the pump in the side yard of the bank. A boy follows his lead, and others join in until the line is two dozen, three dozen, fifty people strong. Buckets pile up beside the pump as fast as Gid can fill them. He passes them to willing, open hands, and a boy runs the empties back to him. Gid pumps and fills, pumps and fills, until his back and shoulders ache. If he has to, he'll empty the well.

The boy cries, "It's raining!"

Gid lifts his face to the sky. Rain splashes into his eyes, and a torrent breaks loose, soaking the buildings and putting out the fire. The bank is safe. Its walls are only charred, though nearby buildings are unrecognizable. Embers crust and flare, and piles of debris crumble and crash.

Relief pours through Gid. He wishes he had a wife at home. They would eat breakfast and go back to bed. He thinks *Lottie,* but someone else springs to mind: Mrs. Black, his secretary, a widow. Her kind face hovers in his brain, a welcome surprise. Why, he might court her. Someday he could tell her how the fire led him to thoughts of her.

Firemen coil their heavy hoses and stack them on the truck. Children run about and scatter. A photographer aims a camera, shielding it from the rain with a piece of canvas. This was not a Great Fire, but people will talk about it for a long time. Gid's helpers disperse, except for the boy who first heeded his call. Tiredly they lean against the pump. Gid coughs, the wet smoke like wool in his lungs.

Beside him the boy says, "I never been so glad to see it rain."

Gid wants to commend the child to his parents. He could hire him to run errands. Yes, he'll do that. "Whose boy are you?"

As the boy opens his mouth, the fire truck starts its engine, reverses, and bumps across the yard. Gathering speed, it rushes toward them. Gid has an instant to realize it's out of control. He pushes the boy out of the way. The truck overtakes Gid, mowing him down, knocking him out of his shoes. Wheels run over his shoulders, and a buzzing blackness pulls him in.

Is this how his father felt, wet and broken? Gid's in the river, borne along. Is that his father beside him? A notched ear rides by. Gid reaches out, but his father veers away, and fish slither between them. Gid thrashes his way out and gasps in the rain. He'll get his breath, dive down, and find his father. Yet his hands strike grass. Bewildered, he tries to crawl.

Shouts, clamor, hullabaloo. Men rush toward him, crying, "Banker Ulsh!"

For the first time in his life, he is glad to be surrounded. Men lift him up, and he's flying. The fire truck doesn't stop until it crashes into a tree, and the driver tumbles out, slipping in mud, cussing. Gid wants to laugh, but his cracked body hurts too much.

He hopes his death is years away, but suddenly it matters that people come to his funeral. Will they? From Lignum and Brandy Station, Rapidan and Jeffersonton, Oak Shade and Monumental Mills, from Vaucluse and True Blue, from Wolf Town and White Shop. He wants the Fentons to be there, and the Eggborns and Burgandines, Minors and Hufnagels, the Jouettes, Pendletons, Yowells, and Greens, the Nightens and Hawleys, if any remain, and any Ulsh kin who might wish to claim him as theirs.

Ice Hands

At first, Reed Seever enjoys harassing the woman preacher, the Reverend Lori Lyles, especially since the Admiral, the church's leading member, pays him so well to do it. Reed thinks of it as arts and crafts. He mixes corn syrup with red food coloring, and *ta-dah:* blood. He sneaks in when Lori Lyles is not at home, throws the red stuff all over her walls, and slops it onto her pastel rug. Inspired, he dips her toothbrush in the mixture and puts it back in its holder.

Lori Lyles is hardly ever home. She's out saving souls, finding people to bring to church to replace the members who decided right away they disliked her. She has offended in diverse ways: Her sermons are questions. She brought a busload of homeless people all the way from Washington, D.C. to a church picnic. These things will not be forgiven by her enemies, even though she supplied extra fried chicken.

Reed Seever is eighteen. He doesn't consider himself anybody's enemy. This is a game and he is the star. Everyone knows somebody is bothering the woman preacher, and everyone wonders who it is. Reed is a messenger, and his message is *Get out, go.* He is blood and thunder, hush and expertise, slipping in and out of her house. Lori Lyles could hire a security guard, people say. She could install a video camera. She doesn't, and the talk turns ugly. She's making it up, people say, doing these things herself.

At home, Reed freezes water in rubber gloves, then peels off the gloves. The frozen shapes look like udders. He experiments, using less water, tinting it pale blue, pinching the fingers with rubber bands, and the results thrill him: a ghost's icy hands, the fingers slender, smooth, and eerie. Is it wrong to be proud of making something so beautiful? With a sharp knife, he scores the palms, creating life lines and heart lines. He takes a bottle of his mother's nail polish and paints the tips of one hand pale pink. He makes half a dozen of the ice hands, packs them in a thermal sack, takes them to the manse, and places them in Lori Lyles's freezer.

He dumps her dresser drawers and strews garbage throughout the house. For months he has tormented a woman so gentle he could never justify it, except he's making more money than he's ever dreamed of, enough to start a life with his girlfriend, Amber, as soon as she turns eighteen, of course. Yet he has reached a point where he wants to stop bothering Lori. The money is no longer enough.

Afterward he goes to the Admiral's estate to do his regular job as a farmhand. He bush hogs all afternoon, clearing fields for the Admiral's prize cattle. At sundown, he knocks on the door of the amazing house. It's Saturday—payday. Even as he waits on the breezy, lovely porch, he knows he'll remain in the Admiral's power.

Sometimes a servant answers the door, a man Reed guesses is an actual butler, the kind of person you see in movies. There is a Mrs. Admiral, but Reed has never seen her. She must live upstairs, doing whatever rich women do.

This evening the Admiral himself welcomes Reed into the entrance hall. The walls are hung with portraits of tight-lipped people with funny hair. A marble-topped table holds a crystal vase of roses. Reed is thirsty, yet he can't ask for anything here, not even a drink of water. Smiling, the Admiral reaches for his wallet.

"Did you propose to your girlfriend yet? Buy a ring?" he asks.

How exactly the Admiral found out about Amber, Reed does not know, except there's no keeping secrets in this crossroads where only a hundred people live. The nearest town, where Reed goes to school, is five miles away.

"Not yet." He doesn't want the Admiral to know Amber is only fifteen. The Admiral could have him arrested for statutory rape. The vase of roses might contain a tiny camera that records Reed's sins but never the Admiral's.

"Your work's not over, Reed. Keep at it till our preacher lady's gone. Lock stock and barrel gone, tires squealing on the road gone." The Admiral squints. "Understand, boy. I have a direct telephone line to God. That woman's been blocking it for a whole year. Bringing a bus full of bums to the picnic. Alienating folks that have belonged to our church for generations. I want my telephone line cleared away."

Reed pictures Lori Lyles, blonde and fragile, on a wire suspended between the Admiral's house and the sky. He can hear her sweet laugh. She and Amber are friends, never mind Amber is half her age. Every Sunday evening, Amber goes to the manse and does Lori's nails, a ritual Amber started, something for Lori to look forward to.

"Do we still have a deal?" the Admiral asks.

Reed nods, looking down at the polished floor.

"Don't tell me," the Admiral says, "you haven't enjoyed this. It's every boy's dream to do a little mischief and get away with it. Lori Lyles oughta be a stripper, with a name like that."

Reed is tired. The motion of the bush hog is still in his body, and he's itching from poison ivy and mosquito bites.

"Why, if we complain too much to the bigwigs," the Admiral continues, "they'll start sending a rotten minister every time. A little country church has to be careful about complaining. You could wind up with a coon. Or a queer. No, we'll let her leave on her own, and we'll ask the bishop, real polite, to find us a nice fella like Reverend Wakefield."

Reverend Wakefield, Lori Lyles's predecessor, passed away just before a long-planned fund raiser, Celtic Day. Reed can still hear him say, "It's keltic, not seltic." Reverend Wakefield lined up cloggers and bagpipers, then died, and Celtic Day was canceled.

"We'll have our Celtic Day yet," says the Admiral.

Reed feels transparent around this man. The Admiral's mind is quick, never mind he's old enough to have spots on his hands and warts on his eyelids. He's retired CIA, plantation owner, the most powerful man in the church, in the whole community. Reed was fourteen when he started working for him. Years of labor after school and on weekends have made Reed strong, but right now, the histamines whirling around in his system have dazed him. Peppermint-sized welts rise on his skin.

"When you get ready to buy an engagement ring," the Admiral says, "go to Jerry's Jewelers in Culpeper and tell them I sent you."

"Oh. Okay."

"One more thing. Have you noticed how noisy it's gotten around here in the morning, with all those trucks from the gravel pit?"

"Yes." The trucks are loud enough to drown out the birdcalls Reed is trying to learn.

"That noise will stop," the Admiral says. "Today I bought that quarry and shut it down. When I can hear traffic way up here, this far back from the road, then it's too damn loud."

"Wow. That's cool."

The Admiral is nimble as a magician, the way he can give money to Reed and put the wallet back in his pocket. There is a lot of money in Reed's hand, so much it would make wind if he fanned the bills.

The Admiral waves toward the door, and Reed understands he is dismissed. He'll go home, take a cold bath, swallow three Benadryls, and lie down with the breeze puffing through the open windows. His father's not home. He's working construction over in Sterling and staying in a trailer on the site. Reed will drift off, then wake up and eat whatever's handy. He ought to use some of the Admiral's money to buy steaks, but he's itching too bad.

Imagine being able to buy a quarry and shut it down just to make mornings quiet.

The little house Reed shares with his father, along the bend of the river but high enough that floods don't reach it, used to quake when trucks from the granite pit snarled past. All of a sudden, no trucks. Morning silence, except for the train, which he has never minded.

Silence, and he wakes early to watch the birds.

Nothing like a river and woods for birds. He writes down their calls in a notebook he uses for school. Birds have their own phonics. *Three-eight* (vireo). *Turtle, turtle, turtle* (cardinal). The illustrated bird books, borrowed from the library, disappoint him. Those with photos tend to skimp on information, and the ones with drawings don't get colors right, especially rufousness.

His mother loves birds too. He misses her. Several months ago, she went to D.C. to visit her sister, though Reed realizes his parents have separated. Do they think he doesn't know? He worries about his mother. Just last week, a woman beside her at an IMAX theater was murdered, shot for talking.

"It was me who was talking, not her," Reed's mother told him later on the phone. "The movie was about Australia. There was a mother koala bear going up a tree with her baby on her back. Bassoon music was playing."

The murderer told police the loudmouth was sitting behind him. He mocked her voice: "Look at the baby," she'd said about the koalas. "*I* said that," Reed's mother tells him. She was babysitting her niece and nephew. Reed dislikes those whining toddlers with their sippy-cups.

"Mom, come home," Reed begged. "You almost got killed."

"Can you drive up here? Come visit me," she said.

Reed said, "Maybe I can," but his truck needs work, and his mother may as well be on the other side of the world. He doesn't go. He may never go.

Two weeks till graduation. Didn't the Admiral make his offer right after Reed's mother left? The Admiral knew Reed would be too weak to refuse. Reed is nobody, just a country boy who watches birds. The Admiral dangled bait, and Reed bit.

At first, he thinks the letters are a hoax. They appear in his locker, folded up and stuffed through the metal vent. *I am mad for you Let me know if there is any hope (signed) U.M.*

Reed Seever I want to spend time with you U.M.

Una Manchester? The math teacher and girls' soccer coach who is thought to be a dyke? Thought of gently, with the acceptance a small community grants to a few eccentrics.

It can't be her. Somebody else must be sending the notes, writing (signed) as if the whole thing is a joke. Ms. Manchester—Coach Manchester—has won all the teaching awards, hitching up her pants and accepting fruit baskets and plaques from the PTA. When asked for a speech, she'll say, "Aw, jeez, can't I just eat this pineapple?" and the crowd roars with glee.

Reed Seever you are not like anybody else I cant stop thinking about you.

Una Manchester teaches dummy math to tenth and eleventh graders. She limps from a long-ago injury. Girls and guys, too, copy her swagger, the romance of it, the gait of a sailor home from the sea. Reed has her for a study period. When she signs his hall pass, the blood creeps up in her big cheeks. She wears her hair in a mullet, short on top and long in back. He has seen women like her on highway work crews.

Yet he notices her hands are as smooth as the ice hands. Her cheekbones and lashes look feminine, never mind her low brows and acne scars. She meets his eyes, and her gaze is full of love. He has seen that look in Amber's eyes and felt it in his own.

"Hey Reed," she says, "got any gum?"

"No. Sorry." He is sure his ears are red.

Three or four soccer players run to her desk with Juicy Fruit, Chiclets, and Bazooka. "Doesn't anybody have teaberry?" she asks. The girls giggle. Coach's laughter is a honk.

Just like that, teaberry's the hot flavor among all the kids. You can get it at the Walmart up in Culpeper.

You wonder if its me. You know it is

From the end of the long hallway, he sees Ms. Manchester's brawny form at his locker. He waits until she's gone, then opens the locker.

Come to my apt. I am almost always there except when I am here. Or at away games

She lives near the school, five miles by beautiful country road from Reed's house. He has seen her working on her truck, her head beneath the hood. She is huge, bursting out of cut-offs. She has led her soccer team to state quarter-finals three years in a row, and she vows, *Next year they will be champions,* her girls will bring home the trophy. She calls it a loving cup.

Or we can meet in the empty house just let me know when

She means a sagging, one-room structure, rumored to be an early Freed-man's Bureau academy, at the back of the school lot. Reed spends a lot of time trying to figure out how old the building might be so he won't have to think about the note. Kids claim slaves were chained there. Spiny weeds spring from the dirt floor. Would Coach bring a blanket? Which one would lie on their back? He would, of course. What would they talk about after sex? He and Amber talk about school. Birds. With Coach, what else but soccer strategies?

I want to take you to parradice

He tells nobody about the notes. There is rarely any need to tell anybody anything, and nobody but Amber asks him about himself. Not even Amber knows he's the person plaguing Lori Lyles. Only the Admiral knows.

Be my loving cup Every game this year was for you

Ms. Manchester takes up space in his head that he wants to devote to Amber.

They always say it happens when your not looking for it well I wasn't and here you are

After graduation, other students will be off to James Madison or Old Dominion, George Mason or Virginia Tech. Reed won't even be going to Ger-manna Community College.

"Is something wrong, Ms. Manchester?" next year's champions ask. They wear their soccer jerseys even though the season's over, proud of rips and grass stains. They say, "You look so sad, Ms. Manchester." Coach must have a girlfriend who has broken her heart. It's all right to be gay. There are some fairly cool lezzies in school, though not on the soccer team.

Coach hulks at her desk, lumpen, marking quizzes. The girls' minds are lip gloss, halter tops, menstrual calendars. Coach Manchester's mind is a vault.

Touch me and watch me explode

He buys Lori's dogs' silence with Spam—a bluetick hound and a dachshund that eyes his ankles but never bites. Lori has nightlights all over her house, like fireflies hovering at the sockets. So: switch them around. The star-shaped one from the kitchen goes in the hallway. A shamrock moves from bathroom to bedroom. Depending on how observant a person is, they might not even notice these little changes. And why not plug in all the appliances? This is an electrical service call. Blender, Crock-Pot, toaster. Plug them in so they're ready if the owner would like to use them. The Reverend has left a pint of strawberries in the sink. He eats one, but it tastes green and bitter. He pours the berries into the blender with milk and sugar, whirls it to froth, and drinks. Much better.

He's gently creative this time, just letting her know somebody was here. He lifts a framed drawing from the wall and rehangs it upside down. Closes a door that is open: kitchen cupboard. Opens a closed one: linen cabinet. The dogs follow him through the house. In her bedroom, he tosses her pillow on the floor. It would be so easy to lift the pillow to his face, to smell it and think about her tears, but he won't.

He plucks a purple iris from a vase and drops it into her toilet, where it floats, so pretty.

Back in the kitchen, he checks her freezer, and yes, the ice hands are still there, the ghost hands glacially blue and delicate, though some of the fingertips are chipped off. The hands are scattered among bags of frozen vegetables, as if she has not even noticed they are there.

As he steps outside—so bold, now, he uses the front door, though the manse opens onto a deserted, fallow field—he hears a bird call his name: "Reed Seever, Reed Seever!"

It's Sunday. Church is over, and Lori Lyles is out on her rounds, taking home the people she brought as guests in the morning. The spring air smells of flowers and earth, with a tang of manure from neighboring farms. Reed breathes as if he's never breathed before. There's no sound except the river's chuckling as it flows around the bend, the only bird a bunting disappearing into a pine. He did not imagine a bird calling him. He heard plain as day *Reed Seever* from an avian throat, *Reed Seever* from a clever craw, *Reed Seever*.

Reed Seever I write your name over and over The weekends are so long
I have secrets and so do you I can tell

Two girls never seem to graduate: Constance and Patience. They're in study hall with Reed. They have been seniors forever. They call themselves Connie and Pattie now—Connie and Pattie whispering, dowdy, swapping recipes and passing notes in silent hysteria, their clothes the garments of older days, their faces wrinkled as seashells. Their hair, worn in buns, might be blonde, or has it gone gray? Coach Manchester and the champions pay them no mind. Reed imagines Constance and Patience back in the days when women were Biddy this and Biddy that. Bonneted and busy-tongued, that's Constance and Patience. They whisper in his dreams. They might be spell-casters, mixing potions of afterbirths and toenail clippings. They might be bakers of bread, stirrers of tallow and soap, herding animals to pasture, shooing children from yard to supper table, awake all night in a garret shared by owls. Constance and Patience: spiders and the wrapped prey of spiders, bound and sealed in a web.

They sit in study hall as if they're ever seventeen, when they must be a hundred, their gingham dresses made of homespun cloth. Their gestures are urgent, their tales only for each other. From farthest memory he dredges up surnames: Greenthorn and Heth, though which is which? Do they talk of men, of assignations and encounters? If he could get a good look at their fingertips, he would find needle pricks, for surely they stitch samplers by lamplight. Yet here they are, Biddy Greenthorn, Biddy Heth, smack dab among next year's champions, among black girls dancing in their desks, swanning their arms into the air and squealing a sorority chant: "Oop, oop." Guys look right through Constance and Patience, but isn't that the fate of frumps? This disregard is not proof that Constance and Patience don't exist. Reed could try the old trick, a leg in the aisle, but they're never close enough to trip.

The bell will ring, and these ancients will hurry off to flit about the darkening commons of a colonial hamlet, flying up and down smoky alleys while a town crier marks the hour, but they'll be back tomorrow in their corner, voices so low nobody hears them but Reed Seever, his ears attuned to birdcalls: Biddy Greenthorn and Biddy Heth inaudible, invisible, as Reed himself is invisible to everybody except Amber and now Coach with her fleshy ears and scoping gaze.

Sticks of teaberry gum turn up in his locker, sweet and musty as rambling roses.

Oh darling
Darling tell me you want me

Reverend Lori Lyles drives her beaten Pontiac all over the countryside, collecting black people and white people and the occasional Mexican, her foundlings, and never mind if they fall asleep in the pews. She goes to Lignum and True Blue, Radiant and Ruckersville, all the way to Wolf Town. She knows the way to Zion Crossroads and Syria, and the mountain roads to Sperryville. She gets to church later and later. Amber tries to cover for her, persuading the cranky organist to play extra hymns, while old established families, the Bannisters and the Talbots, consult their watches, rise in patrician disgust, and depart. Lori's followers are dwindling to a bare handful of the prosperous and influential, plus Amber, whose family is as poor as Reed's and thus who hardly counts.

Reed's at church every Sunday. It's a chance to be with Amber, to sit beside her and hold her hand. The Admiral is never there. He is boycotting the church. Reed doesn't doubt that someday soon, Lori Lyles will be gone, and the Admiral will return, gloating.

The church door is a rectangle of light in the back of the sanctuary. Every Sunday, Lori shows up eventually, shaking and pink-cheeked, her Pontiac disgorging her uncertain guests, whom she leads inside triumphantly.

"It's a glorious day," she says, "when we can welcome new friends to our church home."

Reed pictures her complicated, winding routes. What does she say to get people in the car? Do they run from the urgent young woman flinging open the passenger door and patting the seat beside her? Who are these people, rounded up like stray cats? Some are deformed or garrulous or silent, in dirty clothes, sometimes barefoot. After services she packs them back into her car, and off they go. Do they still exist for Lori when Sunday is over, when she sprawls exhausted on her sofa with Amber painting her nails for her?

"All of you know what's happening to me," she says from the pulpit, and the congregation fidgets, even the strangers. "Somebody's trying to scare me off. Breaking into my house. Well, I quit locking my door a long time ago. I'm here, and I'm not scared. My God is with me."

Afterward she lingers outside, her strays milling around the grassy yard. With Amber's hand in his, Reed says, "Can I ask you something?"

"Ask me anything." Lori's hazel eyes, with thick pale lashes, make him think of dandelions.

"How did you decide to do this?" he asks. It's easy to be friendly with her. It's some other self that goes into her house and does those things.

"You mean, did I get a call from God?" Lori says. "I did."

"What was that like?"

She says, "A low hollow sound, like a voice down a chimney. I heard it every night for a year. I knew what it was."

She reaches out and squeezes Reed's and Amber's clasped hands. Reed thinks of the ice hands, and chills tingle down his back. She says, "Sweet little folks."

Amber reaches up and hugs her, hanging on her neck, making a sound like a sob, but only for a moment. Lori pats her arm.

"Do you still hear the voice?" Reed asks.

"No," Lori says, "but I wouldn't expect to. Now I'm answering it."

A horn is blowing. They turn around to see a roughneck Lori brought to church, sitting in her Pontiac, honking. Others are running wild, men and women and kids, chasing each other and wading in the river.

"Do you need us to help you?" Amber offers.

"That's okay. You dears run along," Lori says.

In early June, the Admiral asks, "How's our Reverend doing these days?"

"She's a nice lady," Reed dares to say. "Her and my girlfriend are friends."

"I don't want to hear about nice." The Admiral's eyes make Reed think of cigarette butts. "Look, boy, it's spring. She'll be gone by blackberry season. Oh, the blackberry pies my mother used to make. You get old, you think about your mama's pies. I think about those pies more than pussy. Those vines are still out in the woods, same ones I picked as a boy. Get trapped in them, and they'll cut you to pieces."

"I know what you're doing, and whose dirty work it is," Amber tells Reed. "You're the person bothering her. Is the Admiral paying you that much?"

For a long time, he is silent. They're at his house, on his bed. He has done these things, and Amber knows, and now he will have to say.

"I'm saving up so we can buy a house. When we're married." It's the first time he's ever said *married* to her. "How did you know?"

"Maybe I've always known," Amber says. "How can you be so bad to her?"

97

"The money's for you, for us, so we can be together."

His hands are in her hair. He can never quite picture her soft, limp hair when he's away from her. She had let him draw her toward the bed like nothing was wrong. Now she pushes him away.

"How can you stand yourself?" she asks. "You're a criminal."

"Does she know? Have you told her it's me?"

"I've wanted to."

"This is for her own good," Reed says. "She'd be better off somewhere else."

"That's the Admiral talking, that son of a bitch." Amber never curses. In profile, her face is a grown-up's, with shutters across it. "Leave her alone."

"It won't be much longer."

Reed's heartbeat fills his ears. Amber will end it, and the money he has saved will feel too dirty to spend on anything. Amber could say, "You've changed," and it's true. Persecuting Lori Lyles has made him creative. He could swap her dogs for curs he whistles into his truck from fields and berms, packing the manse with starved creatures that would maul her when she opened her door. He'll see lobsters at a grocery store and imagine leaving one in her bathtub for the hell of it. The devilment is an infection in his heart.

"Amber," he says, "it'll be over soon, and I won't do anything like this again."

"You spy on the manicures."

He thinks of Amber rubbing lotion into Lori's knuckles. "I'm sorry."

"I could see doing what she's doing, some day. Being a minister."

"You're not her," he says. "Be you."

Her gaze is far-off, yet she reaches for him and unbuttons his shirt.

"Amber," he says, startled by her light hands stripping him. She's a wind lifting him off the ground. She doesn't speak the whole time, except for sighs.

Afterward she says, "Your mom and dad won't be at graduation, will they?"

"I think they've forgotten." He waits for her to say, *I'll be there*. She doesn't.

I was late to home room because Stairway to Heaven was on the radio and I sat in my car and thought of you

At the manse, a bird opens its beak, and out comes the sound of a ticking clock. Reed slips leashes on Lori's dogs. He leads them outside and into his truck. The dogs are skittish, but they settle down as he eases onto the road.

Back at his house, he plugs in a tape recorder. How to get them to bark? They are quiet, wagging their tails. Maybe a game of Frisbee? He takes them out in the yard and sets the tape recorder on the grass. He throws the Frisbee, and the dogs fly for it. He'll play the tape to Lori's answering machine, calling from the pay phone at the grocery store. Lori will recognize the voices of these warm critters that sleep on her bed. He'll return the dogs tomorrow.

The tape recorder, a 1970's model with a mildewed vinyl case, was his mother's when she was a kid. He presses a button to hear what he will be recording over. His mother's voice startles him. There is his father's voice, too, and his own. They're talking about a yard sale. He remembers that. He was about seven.

How much for this fan? A dollar?

It's all rusty. A quarter. Hey Reed, you wanna sell your old toys?

Sure. Well, I don't know.

You don't have to, honey.

He plays it again to hear the little hitch in his mother's voice when she says *dollar.* He doesn't think they sold the fan. Isn't it the same one he'll plug in tonight? It will oscillate and give off its smell of electricity and oil.

He rewinds the tape and presses *Record.* He'll record the dogs' barking right over the sound of his family's voices. He feels only a little sick.

Nice dogs. Right on cue, they bark. Reed throws the Frisbee and they fetch until the Frisbee is slick from their spit. That must be enough. He clicks off the recorder. He turns on the hose and fills a bowl for the dogs.

Freak her out, to hear her own dogs' voices on her phone. Even if she calls the sheriff—*Somebody stole my dogs*—well, the sheriff's a friend of the Admiral's, and he'll be real courtly as he writes a report, just as he wrote up the fake blood, but she'll know he's laughing at her, Sheriff Sizemore all saunter and gut, king of firehall bingo.

Reed plays the tape. The dogs have barked enough, though the tape adds a whispery rush of its own. The air's so sticky he can't breathe. The dogs push at his knees, wanting more of the game. His mother's fingers touched these keys. *Rewind. Fast forward. Stop.* She would be furious with him, no matter if he said, I'm so tired, Mom. Her anger hums in his hands.

"It's not enough, Reed. Up the ante." The Admiral jerks a thumb in the air.

"So now what?" Reed says. Why can't he stand up to this man?

"Be resourceful," the Admiral says. "My college roommate and I stapled plastic all over the walls and floor of another boy's room, then filled it with water and goldfish. I'll never forget the look on his face when he opened his door." The Admiral gives a soundless laugh. "Do you lack imagination?"

Reed shrugs, and the Admiral mocks him with a shrug surely known only among the CIA brass, the most sinister gesture Reed has ever seen.

"I have something for you." The Admiral goes to an enormous desk, opens a drawer, lifts out a device, and hands it to him.

It's heavy and cold, so shiny it reflects Reed's face.

"A stun gun," the Admiral says. "Ka-pow, and they stop in their tracks."

Reed's breath goes tight. He has used his father's hunting rifle on tin cans, but he has never shot a living thing. "How does it work? Is it loaded?"

"It's always loaded. What is it Superman uses, kryptonite? Think of it as kryptonite."

Reed goes to the desk and slides the gun onto the blotter.

The Admiral says, "Take it. Put it somewhere only you know about."

"It's too creepy," Reed says.

The Admiral minces, hand over heart. "Oh, creepy! It doesn't hurt people very bad. You could almost say the effects are momentary."

"I'm always afraid she'll come home and find me there," Reed says.

"And if she finds you, you'll kill her? Have your way with her?" The Admiral's belly-laugh would echo off a mountain. "You'd love it."

"No," Reed says, but it's the *no* of a nightmare.

The Admiral holds the weapon toward him, speaking in a falsetto. "It'll talk to you, a little voice saying, *Use me!*"

"I won't do it," Reed says. "I'm done with this, you hear me?"

Yet he finds he is holding the gun, and the Admiral is smiling. Reed takes the gun, leaves the house, and heads for the tractor shed.

There he wraps it in a horse blanket and puts it on a high shelf which holds rusty saw blades and a broken vise. He doesn't see these ordinary things as tools anymore, only as the instruments of torture they could become. The shed has always been a friendly place, unkempt and cobwebby, with vines growing through cracks. Oil stains on the cement floor make patterns like continents. Reed's heartbeat shakes the walls. He tells himself he'll never come back, but the tractor is an old friend. It waits, knowing the high grass will bring him again to its seat, to turn the familiar key.

In study hall, Reed doesn't leave when the bell rings. He stays at his desk while everybody else goes out, so only he and Coach Manchester are left. It's the last class of the last day of his last year in school. Tonight is graduation.

He picks at the hearts and obscenities carved into his chair. Finally he looks up.

Seated at her desk, Coach is a statue. For a long time, they regard each other. Outside, kids shout and skirmish. The cries fade, and he feels his life turning over like a lake when the weather changes. There will be something next, because there always is.

Reed clears his throat. "I'm in over my head," he says, "way over."

She pushes back her chair, bears her weary weight toward him until she's beside him, and crouches down so her head is level with his knees. She smells like last year's leaves. What big ears she has, big enough to hold all his secrets. Already he's a distant figure in the Admiral's fields, a farmhand who doesn't have much to say. He has already disappeared. Coach blinks, her lids making a little click.

"The thing is," he says, "I've pretty much sold my soul." He puts out his hand, and she leans her cheek into his palm. "There's this stun gun in a shed, and I don't want to hear its voice."

Coach opens her mouth, and out comes the song of a bird.

The Days of the Peppers

My mother has fallen in love. We talk about it while we feed stray cats in the parking lot of Culpeper General Hospital, where I work in the cardiac ward.

"It's silly, I know," she says, "at my age."

Cats glide out from the shadows. She has trained them to expect her every night. Pouring dry food into pie plates, she calls them by name: "Whirly, Tactic, Sylvie." Their heads move fast with gobbling motions. The chow smells mealy. "You should go back in, June," she says, glancing at her watch. "Isn't your break over?"

"I've got a few more minutes." With an effort, I add, "And it's not silly, how you feel, but he's a lot younger and sort of engaged."

"Don't I know it." She bends down and wiggles her fingers at the smallest cat, but it darts away. "Tomorrow I'll bring barbecued chicken." That's their favorite, especially if she microwaves it and gets it over here still warm. Other cats materialize, and she says softly, "Hey, Twinkie. Argyle. Polka Dot."

The lights in the parking lot make everything look like reflections on a piece of foil. My response to my mother's crush is total terror. I'm scared she's losing her mind, although it's clear she isn't. Scared these feelings will end in humiliation or some other disaster for her.

The man she loves is a human jukebox. I have to admit he is amazing. Call out the name of any golden oldie, and he'll sing it. I can see how he has caught my mother's imagination, this knobby-headed longhair with his guitar and his zillion different voices—the Beatles, the Four Tops, Don McLean, Tommy James, Looking Glass, and the Fine Young Cannibals. He sings at Culpeper's only downtown nightclub, downtown consisting of three streets and the train station.

My mother doesn't care anything about pop music. What made her fall in love with the human jukebox, whose name is Shannon Gurley, is the way he sings "Goodnight, Irene." He was born to sing that forgotten song about *I'll see you in my dreams*. People ask for it now, people who never heard it before he sang it, as he does every night, with his whole heart, and suddenly you're not in a bar anymore, *Goodnight, Irene, goodnight,* you're on a leafy street at dusk and you're young and *I'll see you in my dreams.* And in my mother's dreams, and I know this because she has told me—out here in the parking lot beside the Dumpster, with only the cats to hear us—in her dreams, it's oh, a hundred years ago, and Shannon Gurley is reaching for her on a summer night back when life was simple.

"He must have had so many women in love with him," she says. "A good-looking man like that, he must have groupies." She pauses. "He's the most wonderful person I've ever known. I've never felt this way about anybody, not even your father."

A cat rubs its head against my ankle, but I don't dare pet it, I've been scratched too many times. "Where do you expect this to go? Do you see any future in it? Mom, he's young enough to be your son, and he's living with his girlfriend."

"As a matter of fact, I called him today." She chuckles. "Woke him up about three o'clock this afternoon."

"And?" I'm sweating through my T-shirt, through my scrubs, almost through my winter coat, a pink coat my mother bought to cheer me up when my husband and I divorced.

"And, well, we talked," she says. "I told him how much I like 'Draggin' the Line.' I can never hear that song enough. Now look, you can't stay out here all night. Your patients need you. How are the sundowners?"

She has learned the lingo from me. Nurses know that when night comes, older patients may get agitated and call out the name of a loved one, usually a daughter. They'll call out from their beds, lying there with the lights off and maybe not even knowing they're in the hospital, halfway asleep and crying out a name.

"We've got three or four. They're asking for Darlene and somebody named Beety."

"How do you stand it?" A cold breeze fans across the parking lot, and she pulls her jacket tightly around her.

"As long as I don't really listen, I mean listen and count the number of times they call out, I'm okay."

My mother reaches out and touches my cheek. "You're freezing. Promise me you'll drink some hot chocolate."

"Maybe I will." There's never time to fix cocoa, and anyway, the cardiac ward is always too hot. The only snack I ever want is the orange sherbet we keep for patients, regular and sugar-free.

The cats are gone. My mother collects the pie pans from the parking lot. "Party's over," she says.

"I didn't see them leave," I say. "I never do."

She stacks the pie pans, balancing them in her hands. She baked pies all the years I was growing up, because my father and I loved them. I know how those pans feel now, sticky from the cats' busy tongues. She will take the pans home, wash them, and bring them back tomorrow night.

"My kitties," she says. "In them, I see the hand of God. The very eye of God."

"I worry about you, Mom, out here in the dark, night after night."

"You don't have to spend all your breaks checking on me."

"You can talk to me. Just know that, Mom. You can tell me things."

"It's all right. I'm just like always," she says.

For a moment, I think she means she is over her infatuation with Shannon Gurley, recovered as if from an operation or an illness that's serious but short-lived, say an episode of atrial fibrillation, and my knees go weak with relief.

Then she says, "They'll never get tame. I hoped for so long they would, but now I don't expect it. The feral ones are wildlife, really."

She hugs me and then she's gone, heading toward her car, no doubt on her way to the club. The wide navy-blue sky is edged in freezing silver. Up in the mountains, it's probably snowing.

I get caught up in the sundowners' calling. The names are probably daughters who are home exhausted or at work, worried or maybe relieved that their mother or grandfather is being taken care of by other people. I get a picture of the person being called, and sometimes it's not a person being summoned but a pet, a sweet old mutt who'd lay his head on the pillow, or a cat that would hop up and knead the covers.

There's no consoling the sundowners. When I was new to nursing, I used to pretend I was the person they were asking for. "Right here," I would say, but the trance-like calling continued, except for one old man who opened his eyes, frowned, and said, "You're not Thurla!"

I told Melissa about that. Melissa is a nurse too, working in the cardiac ward along with me. And she is Shannon Gurley's girlfriend.

And tonight it's getting to me, the calling: "Beety, Beety, Beety." I remember some kitchen towels my mother had, plain ones she embroidered with beets and carrots and radishes. My mother was the beautiful daughter of poor parents. Before she was born, her father was a minor celebrity, a pitcher on the baseball team known as the Culpeper Peppers. He played only one blazing season in the nineteen-teens. Bursitis put a stop to his career. The Peppers' field is where the hospital now stands. The Dumpster where we feed the cats, my mother has said, is where first base was. She has a picture of the team, and judging from the background of the Blue Ridge Mountains, I'd say she's exactly right. In the picture, my grandfather's wearing knickers, a jersey, and serious-looking baseball shoes, laughing so hard his eyes are shut. He was twenty-two.

My mother was so pretty that she was chosen to do a wonderful thing. In 1953, Culpeper acquired fluorescent street lights, the first such lights south of the Mason-Dixon line. To celebrate, the city spread out picnic tables all down Main Street, *the longest supper table in the world,* reads the caption in the framed newspaper clipping that hangs on my mother's bedroom wall. She got to flick the switch that turned on the lights. The grainy photo shows bountiful tables, hundreds of citizens, and the glow of the lights that to this day grace Main and Davis Streets. My mother isn't in the picture, but I know how she looked. Her black hair waved back from her heart-shaped white face; her mouth was always startled. "I look like a ghost," she says of every picture of herself.

As a child, I believed the abundance was her handiwork—the food on the tables, the excited crowd, and the lights themselves.

Her father, the Pepper, lived to see her turn on the streetlights and get married, though he died before I was born. With her looks, she could have married money, but she didn't. My father managed a dry goods store on Main Street owned by an elderly woman in Warrenton. By the time my father convinced her to call it a department store, people were already shopping at big discounters out on the highway. At last, the woman sold the building to a Chinese couple who opened a restaurant there. She hadn't offered to sell it to my father, though over the years, he'd "expressed an interest," as he put it.

He was philosophical about the sale and patronized the Chinese restaurant, which folded.

Over the years, the building has housed a pet shop, a beauty parlor, and a mobile phone store. Now it's the club where Shannon Gurley sings, the storefront windows running with steam when it gets hot inside and he's worked up the crowd with hits from the 60's, 70's, 80's, and beyond. He sounds just like WKCW, *Ohhllldees fourteen twenty on your FM dial, all the best of classic pop, rock, and soul.*

How does he remember all those songs? Melissa tells me she wakes up at night hearing *click, click, click.* It's a special pen he found at the Dollar Store, with a little flashlight inside. He writes down the titles of songs he hasn't sung in a long time, keeping them fresh in his mind.

My mother has confided that, hearing the Bee Gees while grocery shopping, she has stopped in her tracks, "overcome with love for him." I picture her pausing by boxes of pizza in the frozen food aisle, enraptured by the Bee Gees' rapid, reedy melody, which evokes for her the voice of Shannon Gurley, and I wonder if I will ever feel that way.

So I'm hearing "Beety, Beety, Beety," and I'm thinking about the dry goods store, how my father would get everything shipshape and shining every single day and greet his customers with old-fashioned courtesy. I'm back in time, remembering how my mother and I stayed up late during my high school years, eating "poor man's shrimp cocktail," as she called it, her special mixture of ketchup, horseradish, and lemon juice, with Saltines for dipping.

I've been a nurse long enough that I can think hard, can remember deeply, if I stay very quiet while working with patients' IVs and medication. When I was growing up, my mother loved to hear about my classmates' activities. She relished the story of how a football coach saved a boy's life with mouth-to-mouth resuscitation. "The breath of life," she'd say. That made me decide to be a nurse: I was at that game, on a cold November night when I was sixteen, and I saw the boy start breathing again.

Melissa comes out of a patient's room, thumps me on the arm, and says, "Well, *you're* not Thurla!" and we laugh. She gets me every time. "Here." She hands me a patient's chart. "Did your mom go to the club again?"

"She might have," I say, trying to be nonchalant. How much does Melissa know? Everything, though I haven't said a word. Melissa has seen my mother at the club lots of times. Sometimes I go too, although these days I don't know whether I should sit with Melissa or my mother, if by sitting with either one, I'm taking sides in a war for the heart of Shannon Gurley.

"Shannon's not there. He stayed home sick," Melissa says.

Even now, my mother must be making her way through the dim room, the air sour with last night's smoke, finding a tiny table with a candle on it, and slipping off her jacket, the lug soles of her oxfords holding a nugget of cat chow. She'll look toward the square of linoleum where Shannon perches on a metal stool to sing and play guitar, and she'll see it's empty. His backup singers, shadowy sidekicks, won't be there either. They won't play without him.

She'll be crushed.

The chart slips out of my hands.

Melissa picks it up and gives it back to me. "I've always thought your mother is an extraordinary person," she says. "Does she love music all that much? The kind of stuff he sings?"

"It's a new interest," I say. "She knows who Van Morrison is, and Tony, oh what was his name? 'Knock Three Times.'"

"Drop a quarter in Shannon's mouth and he turns into Neil Diamond. It's nuts, when you think about it. He made a record once, did you know that?"

"No," I say, imagining my mother scanning the club in hopes he'll stroll in, hoping he's just a little late. Does she think about my father when she is there, remembering all those years when he ran the store in that building? It smelled of floor wax and of the cloth he unfurled from enormous bolts, back in the days when women sewed.

When did I become so conscious of time, measuring my fifty years against past lives? It has to do with my mother, the way her life dazzles me, all the way from *the first fluorescent streetlights in Dixie, 1953,* to her passion for the human jukebox who sings in the building where her husband sold dishes and shoes.

"It wasn't a very good record," Melissa says. "People told Shannon they couldn't tell the difference between him and the real singers, but I could. He's talented, sure, but he's also kind of afflicted." There's something other than affection in her voice, measured and objective.

"But 'Goodnight, Irene,'" I say. "My mother really likes that one."

"That's different," Melissa says. "That song, and him. Well. Have some sherbet." She's eating some. She herself resembles sherbet, her skin and hair and pastel scrubs all the soft flavors of lemon, raspberry, and rainbow.

Like my grandfather, her great-grandfather was a Pepper. We've talked about that.

"Shortstop, right?" I ask as she licks her spoon. "Your great-granddad?"

She doesn't bat an eye. You can switch topics with her, just like that. "Till 1912." She tosses the cup and spoon into a trash can. "Then, third base. Right out there, that's hallowed ground." She waves toward the glass walls that face the parking lot, the mountains, and the highway. The glass is tinted light brown. At night, reflections make a tawny shimmer. This floor is so high that the Dumpster is just a little cube. If my mother was still out there, I would see her feeding the cats, as I have seen her so many times.

Now Melissa's talking with other nurses, explaining QT intervals. She's a great teacher. She teaches her patients too, those still awake late at night. Another sundowner tunes up, calling for "Deb," making two syllables out of it: *Dayab, Dayab, Dayab.*

I think of all the threads of conversation my mother and I have picked up and dropped over the years. I try to focus on the chart Melissa gave me.

Something explodes against the wall of windows, and we whirl toward it—Melissa and the other nurses and me. A bird has hit the glass.

Whenever that happens, it blasts the heart out of me.

"A dove," says a sharp-eyed girl named Kendra.

Sometimes the birds drop straight down, dead, into the parking lot. This one catches itself, breaking its fall with flapping wings, and disappears into the night. We've all been holding our breath, and we let it out with a sigh.

"Look," Melissa says, pointing to the glass.

The bird left its outline traced in dust. The black sky allows us to see the shape of its wings, with individual feathers brushed onto the glass as if with sand. There is the empty space where the eye would be, and the angle of the beak. No image of the feet, which were a split-second too far back on the body to register on the glass.

"A dove," says Kendra softly. "As long as it doesn't rain, it'll stay there."

Jack, my ex-husband, loved trains, the sounds of the whistles and the wheels. At night in bed, he'd say, *Listen. Pretend it's wartime and all those trains are headed to the front.* Before we got married, he made it clear he hoped for a family. I didn't want children, but I thought being married would change me; surely, after a year or so, I would crave a baby.

But I didn't. Years went by. Strangers, meeting us, felt free to demand why we didn't have kids. Jack didn't pressure me, but he got more and more involved in Civil War battle re-enactments. I used to go along to take pictures, using black and white film so the scenes looked real. Jack loved a photo of himself astride a horse on a hilltop. The shadows were just right. Man and beast appeared strong but frayed at the edges, as if they'd fought all day. "Man, that could be Jubal Early himself," said Jack. He was spending a lot on his uniforms and equipment, more than we could afford.

When we separated, he said, "I always hoped when I was old, I'd have the same wife I started out with."

"That sounds impersonal," I said. "You're not really wishing for me."

I knew he was thinking of his own parents, of his stylish mother energetic in expensive woolen clothes, a good sport, doing all of the driving.

Soon after we divorced, his mother died and then his father. He inherited their house and enough money so he could devote all of his time to re-enactments. Now when people ask about children, I say, "It wasn't in the cards." Their expressions turn sympathetic. They think I wanted them. My stomach flutters at the almost-lie.

I never see Jack. I heard he moved out to the country. The trains roll through Culpeper, lonely and determined and forgotten, each hoot the final cry of a gone world, and I picture Jack cocking his head until all that's left is the velvet hum of the vanishing wheels. Maybe he's married again. He wouldn't stay with a woman who didn't fall silent at the sound of a train. Whoever she is, she has learned that much.

So now the days are growing short. Irish coffee's half-price at the club. Silver Christmas stars are up on the light posts along Main and Davis Streets, courtesy of the fire department, and Shannon Gurley's including carols in his repertoire, leaning back his knobby head and closing his eyes as he sings about *ayn-julls*.

I went to the club last week on my night off, and there was my mother, spellbound, unaware of anybody except Shannon, who slumped on his stool crooning the Chipmunks Christmas song, *hula hoop*. The crowd was drinking beer and singing along. My mother had a cup of tea, and when I touched her arm, she looked up with sparkling eyes. Shannon Gurley finished the song and slid off his stool to take a break. My mother turned the red glass candle-holder between her fingers and said, "Why do they call this place a club? I always thought a club was something you had to join. This is just a bar, isn't it?"

Shannon loped by our table, tugging his guitar strap over his head. "Hey, Dorothy," he said to my mother. "Hi, June."

"Shannon, can you come here?" my mother said, her voice full of feeling.

He turned around. "Ma'am?"

"I want to tell you something," she said.

He ambled back to us.

"Lean down." My mother reached up, grasped his shoulder, and murmured in his ear. I smelled his scent of old denim.

"Oh, wow, Dorothy," Shannon said. "Gosh."

Then he was gone, and my mother said, "Tell me I didn't make a fool of myself."

"What did you say to him?"

"Nothing really," but she was glowing.

A little later, Melissa stopped by our table. She has known my mother for years, ever since my father went into the hospital with his own heart trouble. Back then, my mother was so grateful for her kindness.

My mother barked, "Are you and Shannon getting married?"

"Mom," I said, alarmed by the bluntness, so unlike her.

Melissa swallowed, her throat moving above the V-neck of her angora sweater. "There's foot-dragging going on, by both of us," she said. "To tell you the truth, Dorothy, I don't know if we'll ever get married."

"I just wondered," my mother said.

Melissa said, "When he's not singing, Shannon's a man of few words. I kind of wish he'd talk more."

"He does just great," my mother said. She lifted her cup of tea to her lips. It must have been cold.

I ought to insist she close up her house and move in to my apartment or to the assisted living facility where so many of her friends have gone, gracefully or in fury or resignation. Yet doesn't she have hundreds, thousands, of days left, of nights to feed stray cats in the parking lot that used to be the Peppers' field?

Melissa read my mind. She pulled another chair to the tiny table and sat down, touching my mother's hand. "Let's talk about the Peppers," she said.

I'll never forget the expression on my mother's face, how important Melissa's words were to her. She said, "Okay," and her eyes filled with tears. She blinked them back.

So Melissa talked about the Peppers, and my mother chimed in with stories of her own. I thought about pictures—the Peppers team photo, the pictures of Jack at his reenactments, my high school yearbooks with Jack's smiling face and mine, the slick pages smelling like memory itself, the edges sharp enough to slice my fingers.

I went to the bar, ordered three Irish coffees, and took them back to the table. Melissa was still talking about the Peppers, and my mother nodded the way she did when my father was sick and Melissa was gently explaining what was wrong with his heart.

We sipped the Irish coffee until Shannon came back from his break and sang again.

So what did my mother say to Shannon Gurley on the phone today, waking him up on a winter afternoon when he was sick? Did she ask him, the man of a thousand songs and few words, to meet her somewhere? To sleep with her, run away with her? I picture him sneezing and saying, "Okay, Dorothy. Wow, Dorothy. Gosh."

Melissa's at the nurses' station, yawning at a computer. The sundowners have gone quiet.

"Hey," I tell her. "You're supposed to be a night owl."

She flops her head on her arms, letting out a loud pretend snore.

"Melissa?" I say, and she looks up, reading the fear in my eyes.

"Oh, June." She rises from her chair and steps out from behind the desk. "Shannon would never hurt your mom's feelings, or take advantage. She'll be all right."

"But she's getting old," I say. One day she'll be gone, and then the sky will make me think of her forever, a wide sky on fire with sunset or blue with afternoon or pale green before a storm. She has a way of entering a room that catches at my heart. It's her uncertainty, as if she doesn't think anybody will be glad to see her.

An old man wanders into the hallway, squinting, his gown too big for him. "I can't sleep," he announces. "Don't you girls tell me to watch TV. I hate TV."

"That's okay," Melissa says, her voice so warm and cheerful that he moves closer to her. She calls him by name. She's better at that than I am, learning their names. "Come here," she says, taking his arm and leading him toward the wall of windows. "Look." She points to the outline of the dove, all dust and impact on the pane. "See that? Where that bird hit?"

"I don't see anything," the man says. "It's nighttime, is all."

"You have to kind of look past the glass, at the sky. Look beyond the window, and you'll see what's on it," says Melissa.

We wait while the old man stares.

"It's like a painting," he says at last. "That's fine, real fine."

"It'll happen again," I hear myself say. "Another bird'll hit the exact same spot. *Bam.*"

Melissa says, "You're right, June," but it's like she's talking about something else, not the bird. "All you have to do is wait."

Hitching Post

"You're different," Bruce told Jennilou. Unlike his previous girlfriends, who were talkative and sarcastic and wanted to marry stockbrokers or be stockbrokers themselves, Jennilou just wanted to read, anything from Shakespeare to cheap love stories.

That was their plan. Jennilou would read, and together they would operate a general store in the river-and-railroad village where Bruce grew up. The store was ancient, and it belonged to a glamorous old lady named Frances Swan, who would rent it to them for practically nothing. Bruce would work on his art. They would not have to depend on the store or the art, because he had a trust fund.

A few weeks after their college graduation, Jennilou and Bruce were married in the campus chapel. Even as they ate wedding cake with Bruce's parents, who were down from New York where they now lived, and with Jennilou's family and friends, Jennilou hungered for the store. During a honeymoon in the Napa Valley, she treasured the thought of the store's potbellied, coal-burning stove and of the fires she and Bruce would build in it.

Back in Virginia, they got right to work. First they threw out debris left by previous tenants—musty clothing and grimy toys. The things filled several heavy-duty plastic bags. Bruce said, "Trash service here is do-it-yourself." They drove along a rolling country road to the county landfill. To Jenny, it felt like an adventure.

Their living quarters were at the top of a flight of stairs: living room, bedroom, bathroom, and tiny kitchen. It would be wonderful, Jennilou thought, to have Bruce and their child—for she wanted a baby soon, and he didn't object—all cozy in the trading post where two hundred—or was it three hundred?—years ago, animal pelts were money. In frontier days, Bruce said, you could exchange furs and deerskins for sugar, tobacco, salt, and nails.

Shelves of dusty merchandise lined the walls.

"This is ancient. It should all go to the landfill, too," said Bruce.

"Let's keep it for a little while," Jennilou said. Somehow the boxes of cake mix and cat food appealed to her, like an unexpected inheritance.

"Nobody'll buy it," Bruce said, but he didn't throw it away.

The wooden floors were scuffed but solid. A harsh fluorescent light on the ceiling was a modern touch. The scarcity of customers surprised her. There must have been more patrons back in the early days, when this little store, along with a riverside mill that stood in ruins, was the hub of the community. Now, of course, people zipped over to Charlottesville or D.C. or Richmond or bought anything they wanted on the Internet.

Bruce grew his hair long, and Jennilou found this exciting, his great head of shaggy curls and his smell of linseed oil. In bed, she felt newly acrobatic. When he declared she was wearing him out, she laughed and kissed him.

He set up his easel and painted while she swept coal soot out of corners and arranged the wares on the shelves. It was a convenience store, really, for the last-minute item—the carton of milk, the candy bar for a traveler. Two antique-looking gas pumps sat out front, and occasionally people did buy gas. Jennilou discovered she had ambitions. She installed a coffee maker, an expensive one that was a wedding present. She flavored the coffee with spices and extracts, and it was a hit with Guy, Bruce's best friend since childhood. Guy was an artist too, a weaver. He had missed their wedding because he'd been in Peru buying fibers.

"Who lives around here?" Jennilou asked Guy.

"Who lives around here?" he said. Jennilou didn't like his habit of repeating everything she said, as if it were a joke. "Landowners. Laborers. Horse people. Orchardists."

"Oh," said Jennilou. How was it that he acted like he was more sophisticated than she was, when she was from Springfield, a nice suburb of D.C.?

"Oh," Guy echoed. He grinned at Bruce, who was at his easel, wearing a cashmere beret Jennilou had given him. The men laughed. Bruce took off the beret and threw it so it sailed to the counter. Guy caught it and put it on his head. Jennilou felt a flame of fury. She reached over to snatch the beret off Guy's head, but he grabbed her wrist. The look in his eyes was combat. She had her first enemy in this funny little place, and how odd, she was ready for a fight.

He released her wrist. "You'll do fine here," he said in a voice that made Jennilou think *silky,* a villain's voice. "I'll get the word out for you."

Whatever he did must have worked, because other artists came to the store: potters and papermakers. They filled the place up. The best seat in the house was a busted armchair beside the pot-bellied stove. People fought over that. An old wooden apple crate served as a footrest.

Jennilou posted a sign over the counter that said *Coffee 50 cents.*

Local people came in too—farmers, plain-looking women, shy teenagers, and friendly children. Mass culture, pop culture, had reached even this place. Teens' teeth clinked with tongue piercings, and they wore silver toe rings. When they bought coffee, they paid for it, unlike the artists, who ignored Jennilou's sign.

"Why are there so many artists around here?" she asked Bruce.

"They're getting away from the rat race," he answered from the armchair, taking a break from painting. "I saved you from that."

Jennilou thought she might have enjoyed the rat race for a little while, to prove she could survive in it, to show Bruce he underestimated her. She pulled the lever on the coffee machine and went steely-eyed as she made cappuccino.

When Bruce's friends weren't talking about art, they talked about real estate and the inevitability of development, of the Metro line reaching out this far within a few years.

Bruce said, "The locals will fight it. They already are."

The others turned toward him. Guy said, "I'm local, but nobody seems to remember that."

"You're a citizen of the world," said Trista, a potter with a purple streak in her hair. To Bruce, she said, "Do you mean *you'll* fight it? Don't you want us outsiders here?"

Jennilou hoped Bruce would take a stand, but he answered the way he often did, by side-stepping. "Hey, my folks retired early from the sale of their farm. They've got a pretty nice brownstone in New York."

Jennilou knew her in-laws had never really been farmers. Bruce's father was a venture capitalist.

"Well," said Guy, "it's an old, old story. We're players in a drama that's played out before. What's a little more sewage? More traffic? So what if the wildlife disappears?"

Perched on the apple crate, a vintner growled, "I could do with less deer. Damn things love grapes."

A train went by, and they all paused. They had to, because the tracks were only a hundred feet from the store. When the train was gone, Guy said, "Notice how every car says Han Jin? The Chinese own us now. They make everything we use."

"*We're* making our own stuff," Trista said. "You've got to develop wisely. That's the key. These people made a big mistake not letting Disneyland build a park over in Manassas. That cost the state of Virginia a billion dollars."

"It's a Commonwealth, actually," said Guy, "and we've got something better than Disneyland. The state prison. It used to be a county work farm. Now the inmates raise corn and cattle, and they even have a marching band."

Trista socked Guy on the shoulder, flirting. "I've heard a band and thought I was imagining it."

The vintner said, "I hear the old mill's been bought and will be turned into luxury condos with a destination restaurant. That's more like it."

Some of the others clapped. Guy shrugged.

The vintner said, "That train is a drawback. Maybe the developers can move the tracks."

"I like the train," Jennilou said, but they didn't seem to hear her.

In the moments when they had all listened to the train, she had fallen in love. She put her hand to her heart: she was that surprised. She was in love with the store, the village, the sense of being out of time. The train belonged here more than these people did, more than she did. She had thought the only passion she would ever feel was for Bruce.

"What's the point of a *marching* band at a *prison?*" Trista said. Together she and Guy went out of the store. Jennilou heard her say, "I can never tell when you're joking."

Jennilou started hearing it too—the music of the marching band. Why hadn't she noticed it before? The sounds floated on the wind, faint yet cheerful, red-white-and-blue tunes that made her think of high school football games. The band was one of the voices of this place, along with the artists' voices, noisy and hip; and the locals' peculiar speech, the way even white people said *num-bah* for number, and old people said *oot* for out. Wind and animals' sounds made yet another voice, one that called to her as she went about her chores. She would stop and listen, and there was a birdcall or the low rush of the river.

When she had a moment alone, she closed her eyes and imagined it was 1950 or 1900 or 1850 or even longer ago. She loved the wavy glass panes in the store windows and the steeped aroma of fire, cooking, and weather.

One evening, she took trash out to the garbage can and found a fox in the back yard. It raced away, its red furry body low to the ground, while her heart skipped at the sight of something so beautiful and wild.

Where did her own voice fit in? She tried to listen to herself, but words bumped around in her head. It was better to stay quiet, alert for sounds she didn't even know she was waiting for.

The store had seen so much change. It was here when rebels and Yankees fought on this very road and burned the mill. All that time, people had lived here and sold goods. They ate meals and made love in the rooms upstairs. Jennilou wondered how long she would live here and who would come after her. She didn't like knowing that one day, her voice would not be heard in the store any longer. She wouldn't leave a mark.

She read books on the lives of renowned artists. When she tried to talk with Bruce about the personalities and the craft, he said, "You don't *get* it."

She took the books back to the county library and didn't try to talk about famous artists again.

The magazines on the store's racks screamed about sex. Celebrities, as always, were leading lives of tremendous passion. Gradually, she and Bruce drifted outside of the great sphere of sensuality. Yet they'd been married only six months. It was way too soon for him to be bored. She lay awake beside him, planning and reflecting.

Her sorority sisters had called him "a big ol' teddy bear." They meant he was a fuddy-duddy. Still she'd been bowled over when he asked her out. He was prep schools and old money; he spoke with weary authority about world affairs. She understood from the expensive restaurants where they ate that he was serious about her, though she was plain except for her good skin and long hair. He informed her he was a breast man *and* a leg man; she was to wear push-up bras and short skirts. Senior year, he announced that instead of joining his father in finance, he would paint instead. He had never studied art, but Jennilou told herself that he possessed abundant talent.

She had never felt like his equal, yet weren't they partners now in marriage, in everything? She reached out to him in the dark, and he swatted her away for the third time in two weeks. He was hardly a teddy bear, more like a grizzly.

Giving up was unthinkable. She wanted a baby. She went downstairs, got a magazine, read "Men's Secret Cravings," and woke Bruce again. This time, she persisted until he gave in.

One of the artists created custom leather goods, shoes and handbags that reminded Jennilou of burritos.

"Oh, pocketbooks," Jennilou exclaimed.

"I didn't know anybody said *pocketbooks* anymore," the woman said, and something in her tone made Jennilou flinch.

A grower of artisanal tobacco produced a box of hand-rolled cigarettes. Guy flicked a lighter, and others bent toward the flame.

Guy said, "Jennilou, don't you want one?"

"I'm pregnant, I shouldn't smoke." She hadn't been to a doctor or taken a test. There was one pregnancy kit for sale, but she didn't want to use her own stock. She just knew.

"Pregnant," said Guy, exhaling smoke, tilting his head toward Bruce.

Jennilou let them all stare at her, Bruce included. She said, "From now on, everybody, please pay for your coffee." She pointed to the sign above the counter: *Coffee 50 cents.*

Bruce stepped out from behind his easel. "She's kidding. You're our friends."

"It's *not* free," Jennilou said.

The coffee drinkers set down their mugs, murmured excuses, and left together in a clump. Jennilou faced Bruce. How loud the fluorescent light buzzed now that they were alone.

"Why did you do that?" he asked. "Tell everybody before you told me?"

"I wanted to get your attention," she said. "You give so much attention to the others. Here we are, newlyweds, and we should be getting to know each other." It was the first time she'd tried to put into words the loneliness she felt.

"For gosh sakes, we know each other. You act like you're competing with them."

"Oh," she said, feeling stupid, hearing Guy echo her: *Oh.* She couldn't believe he was talking about those people when she had just said she was pregnant. "But why shouldn't they pay for the coffee?"

"Why were you so rude?"

She'd never seen him look so angry, and she was scared and a little bit thrilled. "Doesn't it bother you the way they hang around and never buy anything?"

Bruce's broad face made her think of a pie. He gestured and said, "They don't need any of this stuff." The things looked worn and pitiful: cans of tuna and ravioli with faded labels, garish packages of Santa Claus cookies now stale in January. He came toward her, and she stiffened, but he was only trying to put his arms around her, and she let him. "It's hormones," he said. "It's not really about my friends."

After a moment, she said, "Why don't you design a website for the store?"

He laughed. "So people can buy out-of-date cans of soup?"

"Can't we try?" she begged. "I want this to be a real store, like in the old days when people made a living from it." She was thinking she would like him better if he had to work.

He held her at arm's length. "You mean we should sell nails and cheese? You'll have to ease up on everybody, including yourself."

She didn't say any more about charging the artists for coffee, but she put out a jar labeled "Tips" and drew a smiley face on it. Bruce threw it away.

Photographers came to the store, and a woman whom the others introduced as a joke polisher, meaning she fine-tuned the lines delivered by a late-night TV comic. Their cell phones rang with calls from Bangkok and London and Sydney. Jennilou tried to look disinterested, though her heart was in turmoil. She wasn't quite sure why, except nobody in Bangkok would ever be calling *her*.

Frances Swan, the landlady, paid a visit, mingling with the younger people. Frances went to the refrigerator, lifted out a carton of cream, and told Jennilou, "Make sure you keep fresh cream on hand for me." Jennilou promised she would. She would have to order just enough for Frances, but not so much as to lose money.

Bruce exhibited his paintings in the store. Jennilou liked his landscapes but not his newest works, abstracts which resembled smashed spiders. Frances Swan glanced at the paintings and said, "Very cute," and after she left, Bruce fumed, "My work is not *cute!*"

"You should start an artists' co-op, Bruce," said Trista, the purple-haired potter. "We'll all bring our things to sell."

"That is a great idea," Bruce said, with a wide-eyed earnestness Jennilou was learning to distrust.

In bed that night, she said, "The art and stuff, it'll be on consignment, right? I mean, we'll keep part of the money?"

Bruce was silent. There was no deeper silence, she thought, than the silence of your own husband in a wooden building two centuries old.

"They're my friends," he said. "I won't keep any money they earn."

He hadn't said *our* friends, or *we'll* keep. She bit her lip. She had stopped her attempts to be a sexy celebrity, and Bruce hadn't seemed to notice. She couldn't believe how fast their physical life had evaporated. Maybe every couple went through this, and after the baby came, things would get better. The train rumbled by with its sweet harmonica sound, and she was asleep before the caboose rattled past.

So she stocked shelves and worried about money and whether she ought to be worrying about it. She spent too much time staring at a nest in a tree by an upstairs window. The nest contained tufts of fur woven among the twigs, straw, and bark. She never saw any birds using it and wondered if the fur smelled of a predator such as a cat or a skunk.

One day she returned from a doctor's appointment and found Bruce had made space for his friends to display their creations. Much of the store's merchandise was gone.

She asked him, "Where's all the food?"

"That old stuff. I gave it to my friends."

"You could have given it to people who really need it." She remembered things they had discarded when they cleaned out the store—sad-looking garments hanging on pegs; soiled stuffed animals; musty outdated calendars. "What happened to the last people who lived here?"

He laughed. "Frances Swan can tell you about them. She had one bunch of deadbeats after another, always with a lot of kids. She was about to close the place when my dad got in touch with her about us." He paused and said, "Be nice to my friends. Can't you do that?"

The artists brought in their goods. Jennilou examined them when she was alone. The products were attractive but priced very high, she thought. The artists were the only ones who bought them, bargaining hard and giving money directly to each other. Local people picked up the weavings, the asymmetrical clay pots, and the burrito-like shoes and set them down again.

The stock market took a dive, and Bruce's trust fund wasn't yielding much interest, yet he bought a new car and a new computer. Unexpectedly, money was tight, and he admitted it. He went to Walmart, bought hunting gear, and announced they would resell it at a profit. Jennilou tried to feel encouraged. The community, the store, his art—they shared that vision after all, didn't they, the romance of it?

She couldn't believe how hungry she was now that she was pregnant. At night she lay awake thinking about pizza. She would get up and navigate the wooden steps, feeling as if the whole village were watching, the people now and the people back when this was a trading post. She yanked open the freezer and took out a Supreme Deluxe. She heated it and ate the whole thing, her mind so full of hope and worry that sometimes she had to have a few candy bars washed down with Pepsi. Upstairs, Bruce snored. Wide awake, she organized the hunting supplies in the front window.

People exclaimed over the hunting equipment, but nothing sold except one pair of socks. Jennilou and Bruce were hard pressed to come up with the rent, and there she was, eating up the inventory and hating herself for it. In the morning, Bruce held up the cardboard circles and said, "Did a mouse eat the pizza?" They had mice in the building; they'd always known that. Frances Swan offered to let them buy poison and take it off the rent, but Jennilou wouldn't. When the baby came, he might get into it. Or—the thought hit her out of nowhere—she might take some notion to eat the poison herself.

Why would she even think that?

Guy mused, "You could turn this place into an Internet café. In most places, they're passé, but not out here."

"That's for sure. My dial-up takes forever," said Trista.

"How about an antique store or a rare book shop?" Guy said.

"Not that," said Trista. "We need a place to hang out."

What Jennilou really wanted, still, was to make the store a success, as much like an old trading post as possible. She said so to Bruce, when they were alone.

"This was never about the damn store," he said. "It's about art."

"What if we turned the coffee counter into a bar? We'd make money."

"Are you crazy?" he said. "A roadhouse. The riffraff we'd get."

"At least people would pay for liquor."

"Forget about it."

Summer passed, with the air smelling of fertilizer and Jennilou feeling heavy and hot. When she had to cool off, Bruce took her for a drive in his new car. As they passed fields of crops, he would say, "Soybeans," or "Alfalfa," hesitantly, as if guessing.

The baby arrived in September, a healthy boy. Jennilou's labor was easier than she'd expected, and she felt proud. Bruce wanted to name him Guy; she lobbied for Walter, a name from her mother's family. They fought about that. She won, yet her victory was hollow. *Walter* seemed ponderous for an infant. Couldn't she get anything right?

When customers did come by, she tried too hard. Travelers, driving out to see horse country, might stop in for a sandwich and a cold drink. She'd offer to fix them something special and end up using too much of the best food, not charging enough, and somehow scaring them off. If she got to talking about books, she'd say, "I'll go get the book and show it to you." And in the instant it took her to fly up the steps and find it, the customer would leave.

Sticks of beef jerky sold, and packages of cupcakes. She sent off for corn shuck dolls and put them on display. A woman from D.C. bought two of the dolls, and her husband bought a hunting knife, and Jennilou rejoiced as she rang up the sale. But that was all. She made rock candy from a recipe in an old cookbook, but ants collected on it overnight, so she had to throw the whole mess away.

If travelers asked to use a restroom, she let them use her own bathroom upstairs. It was too hard to say no. Sometimes people thanked her, sometimes they didn't, and after they left, she ran up and sprayed with Lysol. She asked Bruce if they could have a bathroom built downstairs for customers, but he waved her away. He neglected his painting and seemed annoyed, carrying the weight of the world on his shoulders, ignoring her in bed. The only safe topic of conversation was the baby.

She loved baby Walter more than she loved Bruce. Did all new mothers feel that way? It wasn't fair to Bruce. Yet why didn't he help more? He resented having to change the baby or give him a bottle.

The store had a pay phone out front, but nobody used it. She held the rusty receiver to her ear, plunked coins into a slot, and got a dial tone. Who did she want to call? What did she want to say? She whispered, "Help." The receiver grew warm in her hand. She said, "Bruce, what's wrong?" and listened to the dial tone go on and on.

That night, she said, "Please tell me what's the matter."

"I'm trying to do what you want," he said, "living here."

"Where would you rather be?"

"New York," he said. "I bet you wouldn't want to go."

Not so long ago, when he was planning a career in finance with his father, they had intended to make their home in New York, and that was perfectly all right with her. She thoroughly enjoyed visiting his parents and riding the subway, holding Bruce's hand. She enjoyed shows at theatres. Now she couldn't imagine leaving this place. She burst into tears.

He gave a bitter laugh and said, "I guess that's your answer."

She sputtered and reached for him. "Of course we can go to New York." Uneasily, she rested in his arms. "Would you work for your father?"

"Does it occur to you I might be serious about my art?"

"I don't know what you're serious about." The truth erupted from her mouth: "Your pictures look like dead spiders."

He set her aside as if she were an empty plate. "I knew you didn't believe in me," he said, *silkily,* she thought.

Bruce started wearing the hunting clothes himself, pricey garments by Wool-rich and Levi Strauss. He was gone a lot, "to see about a commission." Jen-nilou took on extra chores, including hauling their trash to the landfill. Bruce would do it if she nagged him, but he acted so put-upon, it was easier to do it herself. She packed the garbage bags into her hatchback—Bruce didn't want to get his new car dirty—put Walter into his car seat, and drove to the dump after the store closed for the day. In a funny way, she didn't mind. Walter was good company, cooing as they jolted along. The road was as good as a roll-ercoaster. It led to a graveled clearing with big metal hoppers. She tossed the bags into the trash bins hard, as if throwing troubles away, and drove back home with the windows down. The air smelled of wood smoke. Could she imagine her son on these roads, growing up, learning to drive? Yes, she could.

She apologized to Bruce for her remark about his work. He nodded. No more was said about moving to New York. For their second Christmas together, they economized, giving presents to the baby but not to each other. By February, they owed two months' rent.

"We've got to come up with something," she said.

"Any ideas?" Bruce said.

An inspiration came to her. "A hayride. How about it?"

She called up a farmer she had met at the post office and asked if she could rent a horse, a wagon, and hay. He said he would send a man who worked for him, and for her not to worry about paying. The farmer's name was Fenton, and Jennilou knew that family had lived here for a long time.

The offer of help—from a Fenton, no less—thrilled her. It felt like accep-tance. "Thank you," she told him.

She put out a sign to advertise the hayride, writing the date and time in big numbers. The coffee-drinkers joked, making a punch line of it: "Let's have a hayride!"

Meanwhile, Jennilou's parents drove out from Springfield, bringing play-suits and Pampers. Her father touched Walter's nose and said he was cute as a button.

"Come visit us," her mother said. "We don't get to see you enough. Bring this precious little person."

"All that traffic," Jennilou said. Couldn't her mother see how desperate she was? Bruce was conspicuously absent that day, and so were his friends. Bruce and Jennilou had not recovered from their argument or from whatever was wrong before that. She wanted to tell her mother how she would hear him laughing with his pals, probably making fun of her. Was she paranoid? If she started talking, it would be impossible to stop.

Finally her mother hugged her and said, "Nobody knows where you *are*, Jennilou. Call your friends and let them know. Send out baby announcements."

Somehow she was too proud to do that. Or too lazy. She wanted her friends to seek her out the way Bruce's friends sought him, but they didn't.

On the day of the hayride, the weather turned fiercely cold. At dusk, a man, two horses, and a wagon approached. "Whoa," the man called out, and they stopped in front of the store. The man jumped down from the wagon and hitched the horses to a post. Jennilou realized it was an actual hitching post. The wagon was piled high with hay. It smelled like summertime.

The man said, "Mr. Fenton sent me."

"See the horseys?" Jennilou asked Walter, holding him up to the huge, nodding heads. The baby beamed.

The man said, "I'm afraid something's wrong with the wagon." He inspected the wheels.

Bruce appeared on the steps, his breath a cloud of steam. "What's going on?"

"One of these wheels is about to give out," the man said. He stood up and shook Bruce's hand. "I'm Dean. Hey, I think I remember you."

Bruce said, "I finished middle school here, then I went away to high school."

"Yup," said Dean. Jennilou interpreted that to mean Bruce was a pie-face even as a kid. Bruce kept an uneasy distance from the horses, whereas Dean looked like he could rope steers.

Bruce said, "Why didn't you check the wheels before you started out?"

Dean said, "It's a real old wagon. If you've got a spare wheel, I'll fix it right now."

"We don't have any wagon wheels," Bruce said.

Jennilou realized that although people had asked about the hayride, nobody had said for sure they would come.

"Come on in and get warm, Dean," she said, wanting to make peace.

She made hot cocoa for the three of them. Dean stretched out his boots toward the potbellied stove. Nobody showed up for the hayride, and finally Bruce said he was going to bed.

"Can you give Walter his bottle and put him to bed?" Jennilou said.

Bruce looked annoyed as he picked up the baby and headed upstairs.

"I thought there would be a moon tonight," Jennilou said to Dean.

"It's a new moon," Dean said, "the kind you can't see."

"What good is a moon if you can't see it?"

Dean laughed, and the sound pleased her. She heated up more cocoa. "What kind of farm work do you do?" she asked.

"Depends on the season," he said. "Right now, we're rotating cattle from one pasture to the next. And it's a good time of year to fix fences."

"Oh. It sounds fun." She wondered where Dean slept. She pictured him in a log cabin, under a sheepskin.

He finished his cocoa. "I better go."

"Is it too dark to be on the road?" she asked.

"Nah," he said. "I've got a big lantern, and I know the way by heart."

She followed him outside. The lantern was battery-powered, of course, not the candle-lit device she had pictured. Dean said, "If it's all right with you, I'll leave the wagon here till I can come back and fix it." He hoisted himself up on the seat. "Would you unhitch it?"

As Jennilou untied the rope from the post, she felt she had stepped into a rugged pioneer life. He moved the wagon into the side yard and parked it, then untied the horses from the wagon, threw a blanket across the back of one animal, and sprang up on it.

"I could drive you home," Jennilou said, knowing Bruce would be furious.

"I've got my ride. So long."

"Okay, goodnight," she said, amazed at having a man on horseback so close to her.

He rode easily, with the other horse following. She watched until his lantern beam disappeared.

All around was cold, silent stillness. She went to the wagon, grasped the side, and hoisted herself up and over. The wagon must have been used by Mr. Fenton or his parents and grandparents. It might even have been made on their property. The hay smelled glorious, and she wriggled down in it, delighted. She pulled up the hood of her parka and was warm, never mind the frigid air. Stars burned, tiny and old. She had never gone camping, but now she knew why people liked it. When a train came by, its thrumming and rattling shook the wagon.

If only Dean were there. It had been exciting to be alone with him.

She fell asleep and drowsed awake to snowflakes on her face and a low intermittent hoot that could only be owls calling. She sensed it was almost morning; the owls had been telling each other goodnight. She climbed down from the wagon and went inside and upstairs. The baby was asleep. Bruce did not move when she slipped into bed, though she suspected he was awake. If she were with a man who could ride a horse on a dark road, what would life be like?

In the morning, the snow was thin, but the temperature hovered in the twenties. She woke up feeling terrible. Had she gotten sick from sleeping outside? No, she just felt tired, exhausted in fact, with the familiar loneliness. She fed Walter and ate cheese doodles for breakfast. Bruce was out, and she realized she didn't believe his talk of commissions. She said to Walter, "I don't believe it."

The landscape out the windows looked bleak. Garbage overflowed from the metal cans behind the store, but she couldn't bear the thought of going to the landfill. No customers came. She ran hot water in the tub, remembered a jar of bubble bath in the store, and went down and got it. As she poured the pink gel into the water, she sighed, but the sigh came out as a sob, and the baby in his crib set up a wail. She screamed, "Walter, shut up," and raised her arm.

She caught herself, horrified. He kept on crying. She sat on the closed toilet and cried too. What was the matter with her? What good was one more bath? She pulled the plug and watched the suds swirl down the drain. She couldn't stand her life one more minute. She would get away, baby or no baby.

She grabbed her coat, sped downstairs, and found Frances Swan digging around in the refrigerator.

"I asked you to keep fresh cream," said Frances. "These are all past the expiration date."

"It can't be," Jennilou heard herself say. "At least, not very far past it. It should be all right."

"I'm not going to risk it." Frances Swan stood frowning. "Speaking of dates, what about the rent?"

"We don't have the money right now. I'm sorry," Jennilou said. "I'll talk to Bruce."

"Please don't expect me to pay for cream when you're in arrears."

"Take all the cream you want."

She walked out the door and headed west. Steep ditch banks rose on both sides of the narrow road. By the time a pickup truck pulled over, she had walked two hard miles.

The driver rolled down his window. "Are you all right? Need a ride?"

It was Dean. He wore an orange vest, a hunter's vest. Her heart leaped. Maybe he had come looking for her.

"Are you okay?" He leaned across the seat and opened the passenger door. She climbed in. "It's Jenny, right?" he said. "Cold day to be out walking. Where are you headed?"

"Jennilou," she said. "Could I just sit in here for a minute?"

"Sure." He pulled the truck further to the side of the road and kept it running. The heat felt wonderful on her legs. She was glad the road was empty.

"What about your baby?" he asked. "Is somebody with him?"

Surprised, she said, "Yes," thinking maybe Frances Swan was still in the store. She swallowed hard. "There's nothing to do here, is there, other than go to the landfill or plan hayrides that don't work out?"

He rested his hands on the steering wheel. "It's great here. I don't want it to be like everywhere else. Have you seen the eastern part of the county? Big box stores and cookie-cutter houses."

He could have said, *If you don't like it, you should go.* She was glad he hadn't.

He said, "There's people you can hire to haul trash. Want some names?"

"The trash situation doesn't bother me all that much," she said.

"So what is bothering you?"

She said, "People say the Metro will be out here soon. What do you think about that?"

"I hate it. What do you think about it?"

She hoped he didn't see her as part of the sweeping tide of development. "People say you can't stop change."

"Depends on who you elect to the county board of supervisors."

She took a deep breath. "Give me your opinion about something, and don't act like I'm weird for asking." She paused. "Would a bird line its nest with the enemy's fur?"

Dean glanced at her. "What kind of bird?"

"I've never seen it. The nest is always empty."

"What kind of fur?"

"Probably cat fur, but I don't know."

Dean's high cheekbones were sunburned even in winter. "Is your husband being bad to you?"

"I slept in the wagon last night," she said, "and it was wonderful." She faced him and blurted, "I wondered what it would be like to be with you. Do you think about that? About me?"

He chuckled. "I think about it with every woman I meet. But you're . . ."

"Married? But I'm not happy," she said, "and yes, I have my baby, but I can manage him by myself." She could hardly believe her ears, but she went on. "What about you? You and me?"

"You ought to have a talk with your husband, even if he's being a jerk."

She was betraying Bruce, but she didn't care. "I heard an owl last night, and snowflakes fell on my face. It was so nice. It seemed like the kind of thing you'd like too."

He was silent.

"Well?" she said.

"I don't do things that way," he said. "I might, if I liked you enough, but I don't."

She rubbed her hands together, wondering if she felt relieved or hurt. She didn't really feel anything, except desperate.

"Can't sit here in the road all morning." Dean's voice was kind.

He turned the truck around and took her back to the store. She sprang out of the truck, wondering how much time had passed since she left Walter. She raced upstairs and found him asleep. Her hands shook as she heated a bottle in the microwave. Frances Swan would tell everybody how she ranted about cream. Frances might kick them all out, or just Jennilou, sweep her out like dirt.

And Dean. He must regard her as clingy and frantic, maybe even crazy. When—if—he came to fix the broken wagon wheel, she wouldn't bother him. She hoped she wouldn't even see him. The microwave beeped. She took out the bottle and tested a drop of milk on her wrist. Walter wrapped his hands around the bottle and sucked hungrily as she held him. Would he remember that his own mother deserted him?

Downstairs, the door jangled open with a rush of air. Bruce clumped up the stairs.

"It's freezing out there," he said. Still in his coat, he flopped down on the bed.

Jennilou set Walter in the crib, then leaned down so her face was level with Bruce's, which was flattened on his pillow. Even with her pounding heart, she thought how funny they must look. She said, "Frances Swan came by."

Bruce groaned. "She's a pain. Call her and say we can pay by the middle of the month. I'll try to get some money together."

"Do you have any commissions?"

"A few. What's wrong with you? I feel like I'm being interrogated." His face was pale. "I think I'm coming down with the flu," he said.

She straightened up. "Are you having an affair?"

"I could ask you the same thing, the way you carried on with that bumpkin last night."

"I'm sorry about that." She was sorrier than he knew, given what had happened just that morning. "Is it one of the artists? Some farmer's daughter? Is it Guy?"

"Do you want a divorce, Jennilou? Because I'm thinking that's a pretty good idea."

"Tell me who it is."

At last he said, "Trista. We've been wondering if you would figure it out."

She couldn't picture the woman's face, only her sprouting purple hair. Everything was changing faster than she had thought possible. "Do you love her?"

"No, but she loves me. She keeps saying so."

Jennilou started to say, "Oh," but caught herself. She found a can of soup in a cupboard and poured it into a pan. He was still her husband, and he was sick.

"You seem old, Jennilou," he said. "You want a boring life."

Somehow she welcomed the insult. "Walter is a baby. A quiet life is what we need right now." She ladled the hot soup into a bowl, handed it to him with a spoon, and said, "You don't feel good. It's not the time to make decisions," but the words came automatically, as if she knew she had to be polite and careful.

"I'll be okay in a few days, and then I'm going to New York," he said. "I bet you still don't want to go."

She shook her head, and the gesture felt as if he had handed her an eraser and she was wiping out every moment they had spent together. Something terrifying was lurking; she could hardly put it into words. "You won't take Walter away, will you?"

"I guess we can share custody," he said. "What will you do? Go live with your parents?"

"You're the one who's going to live with your parents," she said, so relieved about the baby that nothing else mattered. "I'll stay and run the store."

His face darkened. "This store will never make any money. You ought to look for a real job. My parents told me it was a mistake to marry you. No career skills."

"I can borrow money and do things different," she said, knowing he was right and she was being stubborn. "People will buy good, fresh food. I can bake bread and sell local vegetables. I'll advertise."

It would be so easy to go back to Springfield and depend on her parents. They would welcome her and Walter, but she wouldn't do that unless she absolutely had to, unless debts and failure piled up and swallowed her. The detritus of earlier tenants came to mind, the discarded playthings and ragged clothes.

Walter, in his crib, locked his eyes on hers, and she took heart. Without Bruce criticizing her, she could make the store succeed. She imagined it newly painted, with bushels of corn and pots of geraniums on the porch. People would say, *She was married when she came here, but he left.* After a while, Bruce would be forgotten, and it would be as if she and Walter had always lived here, a mother and son tending the store as families had done for generations.

"I'm going to do it," she said.

Bruce grunted, eating his soup. "Be my guest."

Had she known all along it would end this way? She went to check on Walter. The surprise of it all ran down her body, head to toe, so she stumbled. Then her feet steadied on the familiar floor.

Heart on a Wire

Skagway, Alaska Territory
July 8, 1898

I. Say Whiskey

In a private suite in Skagway's best brothel, Emlee McCampbell stands before a mirror and mimics her lover, Soapy Smith. Her audience consists only of her pet monkey, a tiny creature dressed in a ringmaster's scarlet coat and cap, embellished with gold braid and gold epaulets. "Here he is," Emlee says, pressing the tip of her nose toward her lips and beetling her brows. The monkey rewards her with a silent laugh, its tail jerking through a vent in its costume. "Now this," and Emlee strikes a pose, arms akimbo, head swinging to and fro: the stance of Soapy Smith overseeing his telegraph office or saloon. The monkey laughs again, gleeful, clever. A gift from Soapy, the monkey spends most of its time on her dressing table amid bottles of cologne and packets of rouge. She combs its face the way it loves, currying the surprisingly stiff fur of its cheeks and forehead. It tilts its head and closes its eyes as if to say, *More.*

She can't imagine where the monkey came from: a jungle. But what is a jungle? A hot forest, with vines tangled in the trees, but the river bluffs at home in Raccoon Ford, Culpeper County, Virginia, could be described that way too.

"Keep your hands soft," Emlee admonishes the monkey. "Put lotion on them and sleep in cotton gloves."

The monkey slaps a hand onto its head and covers its face with a palm, as if overcome with mirth. Emlee laughs until she collapses on her bed, the cherrywood bed with a brocade coverlet that matches the curtains. When a knock comes at her door, she sits up and adjusts her clothes.

"Just a minute," she calls out. "I'm not ready yet."

She looks around her room, the most beautiful she has ever had, she who left Raccoon Ford with vague plans to mine the gold fields and decided on an easier means of making money. She has never been a whore, just a woman smart enough to travel light, unburdened with shovels and picks like the miners carry or with stupid props some of the girls have brought, costumes and underwear to play out games for men. She has not been with many men, and immediately upon arriving in Skagway, she was chosen by Soapy Smith.

This is Soapy's brothel, his town. He jilted another girl, Maudie, for her. Maudie has been in Skagway for a whole year, longer than any of the other girls. She has a little set of scales for weighing gold, and a doll where she hides the dust and nuggets men have paid her. She puts the gold in a pocket beneath the doll's skirt. She allows other girls to use the scales, but there is a price—you have to talk to Maudie, or rather listen to her, indulge her in her pouts and boasts. Maudie has been known to speak of what she does as a calling, advising the other girls not to disappoint the men. We're lucky here, she'll say. We have hot baths whenever we want, and the doctor visits. And Maudie points out the French Canadian pork dish Madame makes, Maudie's favorite, ground pork cooked all day with cinnamon, salt, and pepper. Maudie urges the other girls to praise it, teaching them to stay on Madame's good side.

Maudie has ambitions: a house of her own. The girls she works with, if they're lucky, might one day work for *her.*

Maudie does not speak to Emlee, and Emlee never asks to use the scales.

Maudie is fierce about Skagway. Loyal, because it's Soapy's place. She puts down Dyea, nine miles away, and teaches the other girls that the towns are in bitter competition.

Maudie got some brooches from Soapy, ugly things, though one does contain a big yellow diamond, but she never got a monkey.

This thought makes Emlee laugh again. What Maudie does have is lots of telegrams. She receives one every few days from family in Idaho and California and from friends she hasn't heard from in years. Proudly, she brandishes the telegrams at the other girls, showing off. Emlee has never received a telegram in her life or sent one, even though her lover owns the busiest telegraph office in Skagway.

Why not send one today?

Yes, a cable to her mother back in Raccoon Ford. She can imagine her mother in their ramshackle house high on the bluff over the rapids. Her mind is a camera, feeding pictures to her. Click, and there is the rock in the middle of the river. The rule is, if you can see the rock from either side, you can safely ford the river. Click, and there's the road between Raccoon Ford and True Blue, a road she loved to walk after she finished her chores. The road belonged to her, she felt, and to the critters that lived along it, wild black boars wallowing in a swamp and bare trees full of buzzards. Would anybody else think that was beautiful, wild pigs and a vultures' roost? Well, it was. If she loved Soapy, she would tell him about all of that.

She would like to love him.

Being Soapy's girl means she has time to herself. If the other girls and their men are noisy, she can turn on her gramophone to drown out the sounds, but she has learned instead to stuff cotton in her ears and listen to the shell-like quiet of her own head. Soapy is busy all the time, running the telegraph office and saloon, owning the town and getting cuts of the business at every barbershop and laundry and grocery store, a vigorous, short man, with only one night a week for her. All those other nights, in the long hours of sun and light that are the Northwest summer, he's awake and running Skagway, making money and doing deals, while she slathers lotion on her hands, tugs the cotton gloves on her fingers, and lies down in her lovely room, furnished with a gilt-framed cheval mirror and a flowered rug. Soapy usually sends for her in the morning, dispatching one of the boys or men who work for him. Emlee is expected to dress beautifully and quickly and make her way through the muddy streets to the telegraph office. Soapy will nod to her, and she will take a seat on a high three-legged stool and read a newspaper. Soapy will have coffee brought to her, and a pastry, though he has asked her not to become plump like Maudie, who didn't know when to stop eating doughnuts. There might be a fruit tart or a feather-light roll with a pat of cold butter.

If Soapy is feeling lucky—and he is superstitious; he credits his superstitions with his success—he might take an hour off for lunch and squire Emlee to his own saloon, the Mascot, or to a restaurant, where they will eat whatever strikes Soapy's fancy. He likes rabbit and chicken. He hates the salmon that's a staple of the Alaskan diet: "It don't taste right fried." He has plans for a poultry yard, oh, plans for more deals than he has time to put together. Saturday nights he spends with Emlee. Even then, he's gone by daybreak.

Maudie has spread rumors that Soapy is married, that he has at least two wives, one down in Spokane with a whole bunch of kids, and an Indian girl out in the gold fields.

Again there is a knock on Emlee's door, louder this time.

"Hold your horses," Emlee calls out. "Got to put my shoes on."

She already has her shoes on. She has been dressed and ready for half an hour, for the fun of wearing her new clothes, all presents from Soapy. She just likes to make Soapy wait. In a minute, she will open the door and find some red-cheeked boy, full of glory at being the one to fetch her.

Her shoes are supple leather with spool heels. She'll have to be careful in the mud outside. She'll venture out into the daylight and settle inside the telegraph office, dillydallying until Soapy has time for her, and when he does, he will talk about himself, how he's a *somebody* now. Anybody who said he'd never amount to anything, well, he has shown 'em all. He'll go back to the States one day and build a big house and buy a pleasure boat and take up, why, take up golf, and give away millions of dollars to help crippled children. He is having the time of his life. He is in demand. Irons in every damn fire. Toward midnight, after they have had a late supper, a man will tap him on the shoulder, and Soapy will tell Emlee business is calling him, wait for him till he gets back, and she'll sit at the table alone and order a chocolate frappé, tingling all over with the excitement of being herself.

She has asked him, *What is your name, your real name?* And he has answered, with a noble dip of his head, *Jefferson R. Smith. The R is for Randolph. I'm a Southern boy, born to genteel folk who had fell on hard times. Georgia is my birth state, but it was in the West I made my name, in Colorado. And here in Skagway I became a uncrowned king.* The Honorable, the newspapers call him. The Honorable Soapy Smith. He has friends in High Places: Skagway's bankers and lawyers, merchants and clergymen. He is the proud owner of The Century's Most Astonishing Exhibit, the Petrified Man, a prehistoric corpse presently on loan for a handsome sum to Mr. P. T. Barnum. The carcass was discovered in a Colorado canyon, yes, a mummy, a most ancient thing, though Soapy has confided to Emlee that the Petrified Man actually consists of cement and plaster, "a inspiration of mine, planted in that there gulch."

Soapy's band, his gang, she can recognize for what it is: a bunch of rogues, rounders, and rascals, all hat-tipping polite to Emlee. She saw their like back home in Mr. Beale's general store, where she worked. Even in Raccoon Ford, there was an occasional no-good, a con artist, trying to pull a flimflam deal, counting money fast, hoping to fool her into giving more change. She caught them every time. These men, Soapy's cohorts, she would avoid if she could. They're a flock of smelly birds roosting around the Honorable, keeping up his pomp and might.

There was some bad business in the weeks before Emlee's arrival, resulting in two deaths and the involvement of a Deputy U.S. Marshall, "a unfortunate incident," Soapy has said. The town of Skagway, Emlee understands, is at war:

those for Soapy versus those against him. Soapy has spoken of this, saying there is a price on his head. His chief nemesis is named Frank Reid, a surveyor, an engineer who mapped out the town. Soapy has warned Emlee about what to do if his enemies should come for him. She is to hide under the bed or run for her life. On the nights he spends with her, he keeps a bodyguard just outside the door. "My assistants," Soapy calls his men. Emlee hates to think of a thug so close by, eavesdropping, smug, balancing on his haunches out in the hallway beside her room.

"Miss Emlee," a boy cries through the door, and she relaxes, recognizing the cracking voice of Wilmer, a sixteen-year-old kid she likes. "Mr. Smith said you was to meet him there in time to go eat. He said he's powerful hungry."

"He is?" Emlee replies. "Well, I'm not. I slept late, and I had a big breakfast. I might want to stay in today." To the monkey, she whispers, *A uncrowned king,* and the monkey's lips jerk on its teeth. That's the way people smile when their photographs are taken. She has had her picture made by a man here in Skagway, a picture of herself in a satin bodice and satin drawers, a portrait commissioned by Soapy. The photographer told her to say, "Whiskey," and she said it, and that was when he snapped the shutter.

After a pause, the boy asks through the door, "Do I have to tell Mr. Smith you ain't coming? Please, Miss Emlee, he'll get mad at me if you don't come."

"I'm just teasing." She rewards the monkey with a flaky slice of a leftover napoleon and opens the door. Wilmer, chunky and awkward, beams at her.

"Well," she says, smiling back. She steps into the hallway. It's morning, the quietest time at the house. She was the only one at the breakfast table today, other than the French Canadian couple, Madame and her husband Egide. Egide complimented Emlee on her early rising and her love of scrambled eggs. The praise was all because of Soapy.

Emlee and Wilmer make their way outside to Broadway, the town's main street. Wilmer has brought a big black umbrella which he unfurls and raises over her head.

"It's not raining," she says, startled.

"Mr. Smith said to hold the parasol over you, Miss Emlee, being it's a bright day," Wilmer says. "To keep the sun off your face."

What is it with Soapy and skin? She accepts the shade even though the umbrella knocks into people. Its prongs are perilous. They could take out an eye. At last she reaches up, grabs the umbrella, and shucks it closed.

"We're almost there," she says.

"He told me, if anything was to happen to you . . ." Wilmer says.

"It's hard to hear you, Wilmer," Emlee says. The street is always too noisy for conversation, what with reeling drunks, miners and whores and yipping dogs, and she is busy keeping her feet out of the mud surrounding the planked sidewalk.

"He said if anything was to befall you on my watch, he'd make sure I was to regret it," Wilmer says.

"Nothing's going to happen to me."

They reach the telegraph office, the doorway swarming with men and boys and more dogs. Wilmer holds the door, and she picks her way through the crowd of employees to a wooden stool in a corner. Here she'll linger until Soapy is ready for her, anywhere from a few minutes to hours. When at last he approaches her, he'll take her face in his palms and kiss her with a loud smack, to make the men nearby laugh.

From across the room, she spots him, and he dips his chin toward her as if he's at an auction, bidding on her. She smiles at him, saying, "Whiskey." Her mother would say, *You are playing your cards right, girl.* She will send her mother a telegram today. What would be important enough to say to her mother in her house above the frothy Rapidan River, thousands of miles away?

Wilmer takes his place at a long counter with other clerks, accepting messages from the miners, mostly newcomers—tenderfeet, *cheechakos,* as opposed to old-timers, seasoned year-rounders, sourdoughs—all of whom are customers at Soapy's establishments. Behind the counter on a raised platform sit the telegraphers, three extremely serious, terribly busy men at a table, a cloud of tobacco smoke floating above them like a personal thunderhead. Wilmer and the other clerks hand the messages up to them, supplicants passing letters to God, and the telegraphers in their enormous dignity accept the papers and bend to the task of tapping out the words on their machines, clack, clack, clackety. The telegraphers receive messages, too, and the clerks know better than to disturb a telegrapher who is receiving. There is no one so fixed of purpose as the telegraphers, so ceremonious and solemn, as if each telegram sent or received is a clarion call, a judgment, the most important set of words ever committed to paper.

It is magic, Emlee thinks, to send words from your mouth, your heart, to another part of the world.

Mining is hard work, and the gold-seekers—argonauts, the newspapers call them—have come so far, over land and oceans. By the tens of thousands, they have come. They talk about their journeys. Not many are getting rich. They spend their money on girls and drink and dance hall tickets, and in the expensive shops where you can get anything: bananas and grapefruit, jewelry and writing paper and gramophone records. With the money Soapy gives her, Emlee makes many purchases at a candy store, buying marzipan, divinity, pralines, and her favorites, wasps' nests, made with shredded almonds and spun sugar. She knows she will never get fat. One day, she spotted a bushel basket full of unshelled nuts and asked the proprietor if he needed somebody to crack them. "Yes," he said, "but aren't you Mr. Smith's young lady?" "What of it?" she said. "I want to crack nuts." The store owner meant, since she's Soapy's girl, she doesn't have to work. He pays her well, though she enjoys the work so much she would do it for free.

Even as a child, she loved cracking nuts. Used to find herself a mallet and a board and set to work, passing hours that way. Now she keeps the baskets of nuts under her bed and works on them whenever she wants. She's fast and skilled, able to crack the hulls so the meats stay whole. It's satisfying to know the nuts will be used in fudge and toffee, giving crunch to the sweets.

She thinks of a story she read as a child, about a bad man named Rumpelstiltskin and a girl who spun cloth into gold. She's in that story with Soapy Smith, whose first present to her was a sterling silver nutpick.

"You must have read my heart," she said, smiling, tracing the sharp pick over her thumb.

"Don't do that," Soapy said. It was then he instructed her to wear salve on her hands and to sleep in cotton gloves so her skin would stay soft and her nails grow long.

"All right," she said, holding her breath, expecting there would be more rules, more orders to follow in exchange for her suddenly easy life. That very evening, she found a pair of cotton gloves on her pillow. She put them on and held out her hands like soft white stars.

The next present was the monkey. "To keep you company," he said, "when I am gone."

Soapy himself has a pet, or something close to it—an eagle, which he houses in the backyard of his saloon in a huge cage wedged between the boughs of a spruce. Men admire the bird in Soapy's hearing, rave over it, not just drunks but sober careful men, seeking Soapy's favor. Emlee hadn't known eagles could sing, but sometimes that one does, a pretty warble. It should not be caged. She has said so to Soapy.

She hears the eagle's song and the telegraph machines in her dreams. When she cracks nuts, it's to memories of the telegraphers' taps. She doesn't understand how it is that words can travel through wires.

"Whiskey," she says again in Soapy's direction, but he's looking past her, through her. Turning, she glances out the window to see Frank Reid in the street, Frank Reid the famous surveyor, the City Engineer, Soapy's rival, his enemy, one man among how many others in Skagway who would like him run out of town. Brothel gossip has it that Frank Reid is an upstanding man.

Frank Reid wears a red plaid shirt; he is tall as a pine tree. There's a woman hanging on his arm. Maudie. They pass by the telegraph office, but Soapy stands rigid as a pointer until a clerk approaches with some question for him.

Lucky she ate that big breakfast. Never mind Wilmer's claim that Soapy spoke of being hungry. Lunch could be hours away, if Soapy eats at all. He can go for hours on no food. Emlee wishes she'd brought a book to read. Usually she can find a newspaper here. Today, though, there is nothing to do but wait.

She keeps thinking of her mother. Growing up, she was never to say anything to suggest that she or her mother would not live forever. Her mother has such a fear of death. Emlee was not to mention death or ever to reveal that the wave in her mother's hair was not natural, not to give away the secrets of the pins and rags her mother used to curl it. In her mother's mind, somehow these things go together, death and straight hair, death and exhaustion so deep you don't have the energy to curl your hair.

Her mother has told her she does not remember the names of all the men she slept with or how many. There were men before Emlee's father and men after he died, though Emlee has only known the man her mother lives with, the one they call Big Jim. Emlee's mother is living the great love of her life with Big Jim. She has said so to Emlee, that she doesn't believe any woman has ever been as happy as she is. Yet her mother's face looks more urgent than joyful, as if she is still working toward something. Emlee guesses it is marriage.

It ain't fair, her mother has said, *that we all have to die. I'll die and Jim'll die, no matter how much I love him. I could go crazy thinking about that. I don't know why the whole world ain't crazy.*

For a moment, Emlee is back in Raccoon Ford, her gaze sweeping from the bluff to the rapids the way she imagines God looking down from Heaven, only it's not the river she sees but the telegraph office in Skagway, with its dirty floors and animated men and odors of sweat and machine oil, and from the street, the reek of dung from horses and dogs, and the smell of mud itself, spongy and foul. From her own skin there's the scent of lilies of the valley from the perfume and powder she uses, cosmetics back on her dresser where the monkey waits for her in its costume of scarlet and gold, her miniature champion, craving her attention.

She was what, ten years old when she realized her mother was once a whore, that this secret had been in front of her all along, all her life, that her mother was like that and yet was still her mother, her fingers scraping the box of pins every night as she put up her hair. Not till Big Jim was asleep would she roll it up, and she woke before he did, day after day, to unwind it. *Never let 'em know it ain't your natural curl.* To Emlee, that is too hard, shortening sleep by all those hours to keep a secret. Big Jim must know by now, silent Big Jim who shares her mother's bed in the ramshackle house high over the river, Big Jim going out to hunt and check his traps, to fish in the river, coming home to lean his chin on his hands in front of the fire. As a child, Emlee pestered him with questions until her mother boxed her ears: *Leave him alone.*

Emlee wears her black hair combed back from her forehead and pinned at the nape of her neck. Her mother's curls dance around her shoulders. *Put some curl in it. That bun makes you look older than me,* her mother said. Her mother makes a dark brown dye from walnut hulls to cover the strands of gray.

A newcomer enters the telegraph office. Emlee spots them easily, anybody can, the men fresh to the Territory. She can figure out a lot about their lives back home just from the clothes they wear, the way they speak, not only their accents but the words they choose. The nearest town in the fabled Klondike is Whitehorse, a hundred and ten miles north, but the actual gold fields are five, six hundred miles from Skagway. The *cheechakos* don't know how hard it will be to reach those fields. Hell awaits them on the White Pass Trail leading out of Skagway and over the Coast Range through mountains so high they'll slice the clouds, and down to the Yukon River as far as Lake Lindeman or Lake Bennett.

Nor do the *cheechakos* know that on the shores of those lakes, they will have to build their own boats, chopping trees from the forests along the banks, woods that are receding as more and more miners chop and build. After they fashion the lumber into some lakeworthy craft and make the crossing, they must still hike far, far out into the countryside, where the easy gold is already gone, picked and blasted out of the seams and creek beds. Somehow most of the remaining gold winds up in Soapy's pockets.

So another newcomer has arrived, innocent, knowing nothing at all.

He is tall, past his youth, yet with a back so straight it makes Emlee straighten up her own posture on the miserable three-legged stool. His voice carries: "I would like to send a telegram to Devon, Pennsylvania."

Young Wilmer names a price. The man reaches in his pocket and takes out money, adding a tip for Wilmer. Emlee knows the man is sending word to his wife that he has arrived safely. She hears the name Ida, and a picture springs to mind: a wealthy, humorless woman with guitar-shaped hips, furious at her husband for leaving her with their half-grown children and a large estate to manage while he gallivants off to the gold fields. That is Ida—picking dead leaves from prize geraniums in a humid conservatory in her beautiful home, thousands of miles to the East, so far away it's already tomorrow there. Surely Ida seethes with rage. The conservatory is made of glass, oh, high walls and ceilings of glass, and Ida's fury fills all of it; her guitar hips sway among potted ferns and bump an orchid from its stand.

Emlee doesn't realize she is staring at the man until he bows to her. She drops her gaze.

She wishes she were back in her room cracking nuts or holding the monkey, so small she can barely feel its weight in her arms. It uses a potty for its business, announcing its deposits with a chirp. Tonight is bath night. She'll pour warm water into a basin, take off its clothing, shampoo its fur, and rub it dry with a towel.

She observes the newcomer, whose name, he announces, is Thaddeus Scott. He is flushed with the anticipation of his message being sent from Skagway, Alaska Territory, to Devon, Pennsylvania. Tomorrow there is bound to be a message for him from his wife, Ida of the temper and the guitar hips, begging him to send money immediately.

It never fails.

Emlee does not know why that is, that all the newcomers' relatives plead for money. *Cheechakos* come in and wire home, and the next day, they get a message in return: the loved ones are poverty-stricken. The man will hand over all he can spare and much that he can't, with a face full of worry. Even if he left the loved ones in comfortable circumstances, they're suddenly in dreadful straits, and him so far away. Do they believe their argonaut has become wealthy overnight?

She doesn't really want to know just how bad Soapy is. She has whispered to her monkey, in the calm morning light, when it is just the two of them, "He robs and kills." She knows he sends men into the fields to steal from miners and to shoot any who might resist. He is such a little man, her bowlegged Rumpelstiltskin. How does he get people to do what he wants? She is taller than he is and probably heavier, yet here she is waiting for him. An hour has passed. When he gave her the silver nutpick, he said, "You will never love me," and his eyes filled with tears.

She has been in the Territory only a few weeks, but this is the world. Her own life is just a story, a few sentences that begin with Raccoon Ford and bring her as far as the cotton gloves on her night table and this crowded telegraph office with air so smoky, she could choke. The jilted Maudie adored Soapy and still does. Emlee would give him back to her if she could, would hand over the little fellow in his black suit. Maudie has told the other girls she'll kill Emlee. Emlee keeps her nutpick in her pocket, just in case.

"Arrived safely," Thaddeus Scott says and pauses, while Wilmer, his scribe, spits tobacco juice neatly into a can. She should tell the boy not to chew, that it's bad for his teeth, but her advice would do no good. He wants to belong to the great fraternity of tobacco users. "Safely," Thaddeus Scott repeats thoughtfully.

"That's probably just enough, ain't it, sir?" Wilmer says, man to man. "Nothing more they really need to know back home."

Emlee slides off her stool and goes closer, and Thaddeus Scott notices her as he concurs with Wilmer.

Soapy Smith approaches, holding out his hand. Thaddeus Scott greets him with dignity and pleasure. Soapy takes the time to make a number of inquiries. Emlee learns that Thaddeus Scott is a Philadelphia lawyer, a bishop's son, married and the father of three boys and a daughter, and yes, he misses them. He divulges this information graciously.

Soapy personally takes over from Wilmer and says he will send the message to Mrs. Scott himself. "Think how glad your lovely wife will be," and a tear gleams in Soapy's eye. "She will save the telegram, a heirloom, and pass it down to the grandkids. This'll be well worth crossing them mountains of ice," and he squeezes Thaddeus Scott's shoulder with a hand as small as a child's. "Some don't make it back home again. And some of us decides to stay. To stay and serve the public. I do my best," Soapy says and thumps his chest. "Weak lungs. I dare not remain out in the elements. I would die in a day."

"Ah," says Thaddeus Scott.

"I will live out my old age in Florida," Soapy says, "but till then, I strive to convey these messages, sacred-like, to the loved ones back home."

"You do us a kindness," says Thaddeus Scott.

Soapy gestures to a jar labeled Sled Dog Fund. Thaddeus Scott complies by dropping a silver dollar into it, then another.

"It'll come out someday," Soapy says, and Emlee sees him through the eyes of Thaddeus Scott: Soapy Smith, a short, great creature who is rumored never to sleep, whose telegraphs connect this world *inside* to the other one, *outside*. "It'll come out someday that the dogs . . ." and Soapy's face contorts as he delivers a gigantic sneeze. Emlee and Wilmer hold their breath.

"Bless you," Thaddeus Scott says, and Soapy sneezes again.

"That the dogs," Soapy says, and his voice breaks.

"Are the real saviors," offers Thaddeus Scott, and Soapy nods, overcome.

•

Emlee is on the verge of something now, something in front of her and all around her. There is something here so close at hand that is wrong, a secret she senses, a secret known by those who work here, not by Wilmer who is all trust and fat red cheeks, but by the older clerks with narrow eyes and lines down their jaws; and known by the telegraphers, those skilled regal presences at their raised table with the machines that speak in clicks, a whole language of code traveling through wire. There are wires attached to the machines, a coil of black wires that disappear behind the table where the telegraphers preside.

And where do the wires go?

She moves away from the wooden stool and eases toward the door, feeling Soapy's eyes upon her. Even as she slips outside, she knows what she will find when she looks up toward the edges of the building and its cheap roof, with the sun in her eyes, the sun that will shine all day and most of the night. Nobody in this place can get beyond the reach of the sun.

No wires.

There are wires that come into this town and connect with other telegraph operations, two others which Soapy does not own, but there are no wires that serve this building.

She stands in the street knowing now what the men know, Soapy's confederates, their secret like diamonds hidden in a chandelier. It's all a ruse: the telegraph machines and the operators, the serious faces and the bent attentive postures. The men probably slap hands together, laughing behind closed doors, laughing till they grip their middles and gasp for breath. Damnation, ol' Soap has fooled a town, a whole Territory, and his friends are in on the joke. They're the cast of a play that affords them endless pleasure, their audience the ones who give them money, who believe their words go out to *Dear Wife I am here stop I am safe.*

So that is why a miner new to town receives a telegram the day after he sends one, a message from home asking funds be wired immediately, directly, for *I am hungry, I must have money please.* Signed by the one to whom he sent the missive only the day before: *Arrived safely.* Never mind if the adventurer left behind a fat bank account or a wife with a fortune of her own. *Send money now.* The telegrams have reached men at the house where Emlee lives. She has seen the shock on their faces. *Send money right away,* and there is the name of the wife or the sweetheart or perhaps Mother or Father or Sister, *I must have money,* the daughter or the son. And on the flat crumpled yellow sheet, there is the address of home, and the man will pull on his britches and shirt and tear out of a girl's room, down the steps, and into the street, panting by the time he reaches the telegraph office, which is open night and day. They are all losing track of time, night and day, and he slides bank notes from his wallet or shakes gold dust and nuggets from his pockets, or he rushes to pawn his valuables, anything to get the money needed by Wife or Father or Sister back home.

Emlee wants to run.

But she can't. She has to push open the door, go back inside, and climb again onto the high stool, arranging her beautiful dress around her legs. Soapy whirls to face her from across the room, as if she has called his name and aimed a gun at his head, and she sees in his face that he knows. She looks away, thinking he can't possibly. He can't know, but he's striding toward her. She hops off the stool on rubbery legs, but he's there before she can take a step, he's gripping her arm and saying, "We'll go to Mort's," and she's scared to look him in the eye. She puts her mind on the fried chicken at Mort's, a restaurant formerly owned by a man Soapy is rumored to have had killed. It's managed by a Soapy ally, and she can't remember if Mort is the dead victim or the living henchman. Fried chicken and a plate of sliced tomatoes—Soapy will season his tomatoes with sugar and salt, for he is a Georgia boy.

"We'll go to the barber first, then Mort's. We'll go in just a minute," he says as Wilmer approaches him on some matter of commerce that makes the boy feel important, for this is real to him. "Sit down, honey," Soapy tells Emlee, and she does.

She'll say that to the monkey while they face her mirror: *Sit down, honey,* as she loops a strand of pearls around its neck, lustrous pearls Soapy gave her, though whether or not they are real, she doesn't know or care. No wires, so why should the pearls be real? *Sit down, honey,* and the monkey will gather the necklace in its little hand and slip a pearl between its teeth.

II. Games of Chance

"Can't he talk?" she asked her mother, about Big Jim. Oh, he could talk, he just didn't say much. "Can he hear?" She knew he could hear. She would clap her hands behind his head to make him jump.

He was always there, Big Jim, all her life, his chin on his hands in front of the fire, the fire stoked with wood he chopped. They ate the fish he caught.

He trapped animals with pretty fur and sold the pelts. She used to cry about the animals. But he was not cruel. His face resting on his hands showed he was working something out, something hard and troubling.

So couldn't he talk? Her mother said, "Plenty, just not to you, Miss Nosey. He'll talk when he's ready. You'll learn to appreciate a man who don't talk your ear off. Beware of them with ready tongues."

Such thick hair he had, Big Jim, but there was an empty patch on the back of his head where no hair grew, the skull showing pale and rocky. She put his story together from what she heard at the mill and at the store. *A Yankee soldier. Shot in the head at Cedar Mountain, August of '62. He don't know who he is. Don't remember nothing, not even his own name. Was a young boy then in a blue uniform. Head half gone, you could see his brains. Shouldn't have lived, but he did. Just no memory, no more.*

"Your mama got him at the poorhouse," an old man at the store told her in front of others. She was ten years old, and the man was awful. He handed her a gumdrop. "Your mama likes men. Time she met Big Jim, she'd had herself every kind but a Yankee without a name."

She threw the gumdrop at the old man's face, and it bounced off his nose. He cursed her, and she flung herself out of the store and ran home. There was her mother, washing clothes in a pot in the backyard. Big Jim was down on the riverbank, fishing. From where she stood, she could see the wind lifting his black hair off his head. It had some gray in it.

She asked her mother was it true what people said about Big Jim?

Her mother cried. Yes, it was true. Big Jim had fought for the North, been give up for dead, had woke up in a ditch just before gravediggers covered him over with dirt, and been brought to the poorhouse in Culpeper, where he'd lived for nigh onto eighteen years, till 1880. That was when Emlee's mother, who'd heard of the no-name, no-memory Yankee, gave in to curiosity and went to see him, taking for kindness's sake a pan of cornbread and a jar of jam. Wiping her eyes, Emlee's mother told the story with pride. Blackberry jam, that's what it was, and real good except for big seeds she hadn't took the time to strain out. And some roasted okra kernels, which to her mind make better coffee than coffee does, though there's many would disagree. She blew her nose, recollecting.

So she gave the cornbread to the poorhouse matron who was mean as a snake, and the woman said this didn't rise right, don't you know how to make cornbread? And of the okra seeds: what's this mess in this little bag here? Emlee's mother had almost left right then, but this big good-looking man stepped onto the porch and took the cornbread from the matron's hand

and said, "Thank you, ma'am," like she, Emlee's mother, was a fine lady and not just a woman with a baby that everybody acted like wasn't no good.

Right away, she fell in love.

It was August, eighteen years after his head got shot partly off. He'd been living at the poorhouse all that time, paying his way by fixing things not just there but at people's houses, to earn money, and paying rent at the poorhouse, only person ever to pay, none of the others paid for their keep, the others was too looney or too pitiful to ever have the notion. So Emlee's mother took to visiting him. She could not stay away. She was already regarded as, if not disgraced, as a wayward woman though she had not done nothing to deserve that, she had only had too many men interested in her, and the one who was Emlee's father had not made a honest woman of her but turned tail and ran when he learned he was to be a father.

Big Jim was the staying kind. She could tell. She could not believe he had not gotten married in all those years.

The worst part was the many women who came to see him, never mind it was years after the war. Northern women were still finding out about a Yankee soldier who did not remember his name or nothing else. These Northern women came to Culpeper and made their way to the poorhouse to see if he was their missing, assumed dead, husband or brother or sweetheart. She would be in his room—she blushed a little—well, reading or something, and these women would just barge in; the poorhouse matron didn't like her and wouldn't give her no privacy. Emlee's mother bristled, remembering. He was real polite to the women and answered their questions best he could. Sometimes there was two or three together, a woman and her daughter and her mother, or a woman and her sister, out searching for their lost beloved. A woman from Illinois came back three times, said it was almost her Luke but not quite. Asked him all kinds of questions. Did he remember their dairy farm and their little boy twins and the birthmark on her back? "I about fainted at that, Emlee. She pulled her dress off her shoulder and showed him."

Finally the Illinois woman decided he wasn't hers. "He didn't belong to none of them. Thank God," said Emlee's mother. "You were just a baby then, Em. I used to leave you downstairs with the poorhouse cook while I visited with him. Jim's the best man I ever knowed, better than your father. Maybe you don't want to hear that but it's true."

"Why don't you marry him?" Emlee asked.

"Oh, truth is, he just won't. He's afraid he's already married even though he can't remember. Times I think he remembers more than he's tellin'. Nothing like a war to give a man a chance to get away from things he don't like.

Some of the women came to see him, was rich. One from Massachusetts, she had rings on her hands and a picture of her husband in a gold locket around her neck. She opened it and showed it to me. It wasn't him, and she said so. She sat and visited like we was friends, and Jim sat there whittling. School children used to come look at him, the man without no memory, like he was a show. Oh Emlee, if it was him in the locket around that stranger's neck, I'd a-had to run her off."

"Don't he remember anything at all?" Emlee asked.

"He remembers soldiers hanging their clothes out the highest window in the Culpeper courthouse after the battle was over. Soldiers hanging out clothes after washing out the dirt and blood."

Her mother was quiet for a long time, stirring the family's clothes in the wash pot. A couple of geese came pecking around. "Way I figure it, he was a officer," she said. "Fine looking man like that, he'd get ahead fast. They could still come after him, the people in his family, whoever they are. Or the government. To claim a Yankee officer and take him home. Well, he *is* home."

"Mama," said Emlee and hugged her mother.

"You don't know how awful that was, the war and the years right after," her mother said. "You wasn't born till 1877. The age you are now, I was that age the year the war started. Look at him down there." She laid her stirring stick aside and put her hands on Emlee's shoulders. "Now what do you suppose he's thinkin'?"

Mother and daughter gazed down from the steep bluff to the riverbank where Big Jim was fishing. It was too far for him to hear them even if they shouted.

"I love just watching him," her mother said.

Big Jim drew the fishing line out of the water and cast it in again.

"I been with him so long," her mother said. "Look how he reaches that line so high out the water and throws it in again. He could do that with my heart if he wanted to. I used to read him lists of names trying to get him to hear his own. I'd go through the Bible and pick 'em out from Amos to Zacharias. He listened, but didn't none of 'em ring a bell. They'd been calling him Mike at the poorhouse, but that's a Yankee name, and besides, he don't look like a Mike. 'You look like a Jim to me,' I said."

For a long time, Emlee and her mother observed him while he fished.

"I don't want to stay here forever, Mama," Emlee said.

"What do you know about what you want? You're ten years old," her mother said and ruffled Emlee's hair. The breeze from the river fanned their faces.

Emlee lived in fear of a flood. People talked about floods that had already happened, how they washed away the stores and mills and houses. But their house was up so high.

Her mother read her mind. "We're safe," she said. "Nothing bad'll happen to us."

Lost in thought, she's unaware of Soapy approaching until he squeezes her arm. She jumps, hoping he has not read *No wires* in her eyes, after all.

She swallows. "I want to send a message to my mother."

He bobs his head solemnly, as if she has instructed him to telegraph the president. With a sweep of his arm, he summons Wilmer, who hurries across the room, tripping, stumbling, and sprawling at Soapy's feet. Soapy helps the boy off the floor.

"Yes, sir, Mr. Smith?" Wilmer dusts off his trousers.

"Miss Emlee would like to send word to her mother in Raccoon Ford, Virginia, a lady by the name of . . .?" Soapy prompts her.

"Zada McCampbell," Emlee says, and the sweetness of her mother's name catches in her throat.

Will she ever get back to the Ford? Some of the girls in the house where she lives have gone crazy, it is said, from homesickness. They have left in the middle of the night with strangers or on their own, striking out, taking nothing, last seen running out of town.

"Zada McCampbell," Soapy says. Wilmer writes the name down as Emlee spells it out for him. Soapy puts out a finger and touches a tear on Emlee's cheek. She hadn't known she was crying. Just one tear, and Soapy caught it. "Pretty girl," he says.

Crack the whip: a game she played as a child. It left her breathless. Why remember that now? She remembers it as Soapy and Wilmer wait, Wilmer scratching a pimple on his face.

"What do you want to say to your mother?" Soapy asks, his voice gentle.

Frank Reid appears at the window behind him, and Emlee observes Reid and Maudie loom close. They must have recognized Soapy from the back. Emlee freezes. With his fingers, Frank Reid pulls out his nostrils and the sides of his mouth, pushing out his tongue and pressing it against the glass, rocking his head to and fro, inches from the unknowing Soapy. Maudie crinkles her eyes, her laughter lost to the sounds of the street, the barking of dogs wild with summer. Doesn't Wilmer see them? No, he's busy writing *Raccoon Ford* on his tablet, in big block letters learned from some schoolmistress back in, where is he from, he told her one time: Oregon.

"No charge for this, Emlee," Soapy whispers, "long as you keep it to ten words or less. It's on the house."

Now it's Maudie close to the window, crowding Frank Reid away from his spot, Maudie shooting Emlee a rude gesture with her fingers.

Soapy whirls: eyes in the back of his head. Frank and Maudie are gone, vanished.

"Who was there, Emlee?" Soapy says.

His face is quiet, his eyes level. He could pull his gun as fast as he snaps his fingers, and shoot her through the heart. He is said to know if one of his men has turned on him, knows it the instant it happens.

"Frank Reid was there," she says, "and Maudie."

Soapy frowns, and Wilmer claws his blemish.

Who were the other children back at Raccoon Ford who played crack the whip with her? Do they remember how it felt to spin away from the others? Where are they now? The day her mother cried about Big Jim and stirred the wash pot, the day she threw a gumdrop at the old man, why, that very day, she played crack the whip. It comes back to her now. That was the only thing to do after the old man's meanness and her mother's tears. She rounded up the neighbor children, and they joined hands while her mother hung clothes on the line and geese flurried in the grass. Big Jim fished till sunset.

"Tell my mother," Emlee says and pauses. "Tell her I'm fine."

Wilmer writes on his tablet.

"Tell her I love her. That's all. That's all I have to say."

"She will be so glad. Zada McCampbell," Soapy says as if he has tasted something fine, a sip of wine or a savory. "Off with you," he tells Wilmer, who races across the room to the telegraphers' platform. Wilmer hands Emlee's words up to them, reaching high, and the chief telegrapher, the most solemn one, bends to take the message, as if he is God.

"My lovely girl," Soapy says.

Someday maybe she can tell her mother: *I remembered to thank him, like it was real. And he said, "My lovely," in a way that, if I hadn't known about the wires, it might have made me feel something.*

"You're my girl for the next century," Soapy says. He speaks not infrequently of 1900, the year that will come roaring in like a tide. He is already planning a party for New Year's Day, 1900. "I can see it," he says now, "the dress I'll have made for you. Cranberry red. It'll match the punch."

"I should put Big Jim's name on there," she says, thinking of Big Jim's hair, black with gray in it, lifting as he cast his line into the river. Never mind that no telegram will go out, that God the telegrapher looks skeptical on His platform when Soapy snaps into action, shouting at him, striding toward him, leaving Emlee to climb back on the stool by the window with the sun streaming in, hot on her neck.

"Put the name Jim on there too," Soapy bellows to God. "Jay. Eye. Em."

God nods: it's done.

There's no easy way to get to the gold fields. Of all the stories the miners tell, that is the one that makes their voices rise to a pitch—how it was, getting there and getting back, over the mountains, cliffs of ice, packing their supplies on mules and horses and their own backs. The Canadian Mounties patrol the Yukon border, and they're strict. You've got to have a year's supply of food or they won't let you in. That's more food than Emlee can imagine.

Miners tell their stories at the house, where the women drink with them and invite them to their beds. How it was when the horse slipped and fell over the edge, so far down. *Of course he died, good old Paint, ol' Pardner.* How it was when a blizzard wiped out the world for two days and two nights, and men nearly died in camp. Your very fire would freeze in that weather. How it was to be set upon and robbed by a gang you'd believed friendly when they hailed you, when they accepted your bacon and coffee and asked the name of your dogs; you were just saying, *Lijah and Ben, and Minnie's my lead dog,* when they jumped you and was like to cut your throat.

Emlee knows most of the tales will be forgotten, as will the roll and tumble, the slap and tickle of the afternoons and nights in the house. The girls who listen to the men's big talk have themselves to think of. The stories only go so far with them. They will not have to struggle through snow or climb peaks or race down the other side on sleds with runners so razor-sharp you dare not touch them for fear of cutting your hand. It is a rare man who does not have a story of a dog, the heroism and courage of a Husky or a Newfoundland or even a mutt standing by him, braving avalanches, frostbite, wounds and death. Men weep about the selflessness of these creatures, whom they abandon in summertime. Now the streets are thronged with canines, thin and wretched, mating and fighting, scratching their ears, rife with fleas, mange, worms, distemper. Puppies are born in gutters. Soapy makes a show of his crusade. If he commands a man to give a critter a home or donate money to the Sled Dog Fund, the man obeys, as did Thaddeus Scott.

The girls make pets of the dogs, feed them scraps, harbor them in their rooms though it's against the rules. You can get kicked out if a dog pees on the carpet. "Filthy, to keep a dog inside," says Madame, who has a reputation to uphold. French Canucks, she tells the girls, know how to keep a house clean. "Animals aren't meant to live inside, they're dirty," she hisses, *"durrty,"* and the ugliness of her anger at the animals makes Emlee furious and ashamed as nothing else has done, this whole time. "Dirty," Madame declares, chasing a wolfish pup out the door with a broom. Madame's husband, Egide, is short and squatty like herself. Their arguments are fierce, driving the girls to stifled mirth. Egide wants to go to the gold fields. Madame says no: "You will die out there, you stupid man." Husband reels off the names of places he wants to see: Tagish, the Chilkoot Trail. "Why come so far to run a house of sin?" he asks his wife and spits tobacco. Spits so loud, you can hear him through the walls.

Emlee and other girls listen from hiding places. Emlee can pantomime the pause and the spit so perfectly that the girls clutch their middles and rock with laughter.

"You a priest?" Madame will say, and that shuts Egide up, for he is known to take a girl now and then. "You a priest, Egide?"

Pause and spit.

"I want to see Tagish," Egide insists. "You know they got a post office there? I seen a picture. They put all the letters on the ground and you go through and pay fifty cents for any that belong to you."

"Who'd write to you?" Madame screeches. "Not me. Go on then, Dummy."

On the other side of the kitchen wall, the girls can't hold their laughter any more. A Filipina lets out a long howl, "Eeeeyah," and a colored girl, choking, says, "Bless Jesus."

It can't go on much longer, this life. Any of it. Emlee, her back aching from hours on the three-legged stool, beckons to Wilmer. She gives him a coin, sends him out for a sandwich, and watches through the window as he hurries down Broadway, trailed by hungry, leaping dogs. Soapy could do more for them. Of course he could. How much would it take to build a kennel and staff it with loving hearts to tend the sick ones and pamper the well ones? Does Soapy steal even the Sled Dog Fund?

Wilmer returns with corned beef on rye bread, wrapped in waxed paper. Emlee devours it, the mayonnaise spurting from her mouth. She wipes her lips with a handkerchief given to her by a girl who left town last week, saying she was going home. The handkerchief was made from a pillowcase, Emlee guesses. That's the only way it could have grown so soft, from all the washings, all the dreams. "I've had enough, I'm a-going," the girl said, throwing her clothes out in the hallway for others to pick over and fight about. She shoved the handkerchief into Emlee's hands and departed at night, as if it mattered. The sun shines all the time.

What would the retreating girl take with her? Names. Dyea, Dawson City, Juneau. Her children and grandchildren will grow up hearing those dazzling names. "I was there," the girl can say. "I had me a lunch room." Or a laundry. Uh-huh. Won't tell about whoring. And leaving in the night? She'll forget that part, though it would be pretty to tell, would go with the names of the rough towns sprawling in the valleys of bones and ice.

The corned beef sandwich settles in Emlee's stomach, and the sun stops overhead. She is in the land where messages halt, in this office where all is a sham, where the wires go nowhere. Her mother will never get those words unless Emlee writes them in a letter. Soapy is there beside her, behind her, his hands on her shoulders, moving her body back and forth as if they are dancing. *I never see him come up.* "Are there raccoons at Raccoon Ford?" he asks. "Lots of 'em?"

"Oh yes," she says, "and there's a mill and a store."

Embracing her, Soapy rocks her so gently she might be in the river at home, not the rapids but the wide smooth run above the millrace. "Tell me about it," he says, and she knows he has forgotten about lunch. There will be no trip to Mort's today, no fried chicken, but that's all right; she had the sandwich. He's a whippet, going all day long on a crust, a crumb, whereas she needs her three squares a day. "Tell me," he says, leaning down to kiss her cheek. She closes her eyes.

"It's up on a hill," she says, "a bluff, with the river down below. The mill and the store belong to Mr. Beale. I worked at the store. It was how I made a little money. Not many people, really, live at the Ford. It's not a place that grows. There's bigger towns a few miles away, like Rapidan, where there's a bigger mill."

"The Ford." His hands slide down her back. His affection makes her nervous.

"That's the nickname of the place," she says. "Big Jim says in fifty years, won't be much left of it. Floods washed away the houses in the low places already."

Soapy's not listening. His attention wanders back to the office floor. He waves his hand like a showman. "Business is what it's all about, Emlee. Look what I done. I built this telegraph office. Built the Mascot Saloon. Got my pockets full of nuggets and dust, got money in the bank. Come on," he says, tugging her from the stool. He steers her toward the door, calling over his shoulder, "Mr. Prentiss, you're in charge," and Mr. Prentiss, a heavy old fellow, wags his dewlaps in assent.

Soapy did not list Emlee as part of his pride, she realizes. He spoke of the office and the saloon and the bank accounts.

The last time they slept together, he woke in the night with a gasp and said, "I can't get enough air." She had to rub his head until he fell asleep again.

"What kind of people do you think he's from?" her mother asked her once about Big Jim, and Emlee said, "I don't know."

"I think he's Scotch-Irish and English, like me," her mother said, "with his black hair and green eyes. I learn stuff about him in my dreams. Things come to me. I seen his mother, in my mind, and his daddy. And that gunshot or whatever it was that hurt his head? You know what I decided, Emlee?"

"What?" Emlee asked.

"I think it was something he needed. I think he might a-been sick before, with fits. That come to me in a dream. Sick with the fits, with trembles and such that kept people away from him. The shot to his head knocked the fits out of him."

"You got nothing to base that on, Mama," Emlee said.

"Don't matter," her mother said. "I saw in a dream, him and his parents by a fire, and his feet a-twitching and his mama and daddy not knowing what to do."

"But you made all that up, Mama. Dreams aren't real."

"Oh, they are," her mother said. "You're too young to know that," but Emlee was grown by then. Her mother had a flag of color on each cheek and crow's foot wrinkles by her eyes. She cried every day, out of Big Jim's sight, for joy.

How is it nobody knows about *no wires*? Emlee has never believed men are better than women at keeping secrets, but now she knows they are. The secret binds Soapy and his men together in a brotherhood. No wires. Didn't boys back at the Ford have a cave where they held meetings, where girls were not allowed? In that way, they made the world their own, keeping the yonder world at bay.

"What's in the cave?" she asked a boy once, and he said, "Indian bones. Bears." He raised his arms at her, growling. She wasn't scared.

Only Soapy scares her. If she were a miner, crouching by a fire, he would set his men upon her and seize her gold, her horse, and her dogs. The men would take off their boots, toast their feet by the fire, and drink the coffee in the pot, paying no attention to her, just another miner with bloody throat growing cold where they'd tossed her in a ravine. Soapy does that. He sends men into the snowy lands beyond the settlements, and woe to the loner in a lonely camp or the drunken braggart who flashes his gold in a tavern.

Soapy smells of pencil lead, of clean bullets, of speed itself. Every day, he is groomed at a barbershop. He leads Emlee there, where she will wait again, only in a more comfortable seat than the stool at the office, a high-backed sofa.

"Queen of hearts," the barber says to her as a greeting. Soapy folds himself into a luxurious chair, and the barber works up a bowl of lather with a badger-hair brush.

Soapy closes his eyes and says, "Sing to me."

The barber, an Irishman, takes a deep breath and launches into a song about a blackbird. Industriously, he brushes suds high on Soapy's cheeks.

Soapy has a full beard; the barber shaves only those few stray hairs above it.

Emlee should be feeling some excitement, she knows, at being with him. That must be love, but she has something else instead: her hands soft on demand; these long waits; her youth passing as slowly as the sun outside; the angle of sun on the barbershop floor; and the spicy smell of shaving lotion.

She sneezes.

"Bless you," says the barber, but Soapy doesn't stir.

She will hold out a finger to the monkey, who will take it in a leathery clasp, and she will turn her arm slowly so the creature revolves on the top of her dresser, its ringmaster's scarlet cape and tail sweeping in a waltz. Surely Soapy will tire of her in a few weeks, a few months, and she won't be sorry if he moves on to a new girl. At the house, girls want him, put their hands on him. She would gladly advise a new girl about the need for sleeping in gloves. She would not fight to keep the uncrowned king for herself. Soapy has cut his eyes at the Negress from Florida with her pretty face and lush lips, and at the Filipina whose braided hair is long enough to wrap around her body and who asks the men, "Want see my bosom?" Emlee has flashed her consent to these other girls, though they see themselves as her rivals.

Of the monkey, Soapy will say, "You love that thing more than me," and she doesn't deny it.

Emlee would kill anybody who would take the monkey or harm it. Sometimes when she is with Soapy at a dance hall, when a line of girls is high-kicking, when Soapy's arm lies across her shoulders and he lifts a glass of beer to his lips, her heart goes tight with terror, and she pats his cheek and says, "I'll be right back," loudly so he hears her over the stomping of girls' high heels and men's applause. He barely nods, as if she is going to the privy. She'll race to the house, to her room, and turn her key in the lock, so afraid the little creature will not be there, so relieved to find it asleep on her pillow or regarding itself balefully in the mirror that she cries out and enfolds it, her tears splashing on its cap. Beneath the red fabric of the elaborate costume, within the tiny ribcage, lies its beating heart.

Just for a little while, she will stay with the monkey and hold it. As long as she knows she can come back to her room, to the monkey and the basket of nuts to be cracked, she can bear to return to the dance hall, to Soapy, to her own glass of beer with its melting foam and to Soapy's hand exploring her neck as if mapping out her bones.

Maudie has claimed that the anonymous Indian woman out in the gold fields has a child by Soapy. Two children. "She's ugly as shit, I betcha," Maudie has said, mocking the face of a woman she admits she has never met, hooding her eyes and dropping her jaw open.

There they go again, out in the street, past the barbershop, Maudie and Frank Reid, Frank in a green checked shirt, Maudie hanging onto his arm, blowing bubbles with a wad of gum in her mouth, the jest among the girls being that's how Maudie stays in practice. Maudie's face twists in the sun; a purple balloon swells from her lips, and she snaps her teeth into it. Frank Reid embraces her. She does not seem steady on her feet. They are mad dogs, hyenas, stumbling down Broadway as if following the sun from one end of the muddy road to the other. Maudie holds something in her hand, a piece of paper. They vanish behind a knot of Indians selling moccasins and buckskin coats.

Emlee has heard of Indians who perish when they are locked away, who pine in their jail cells until they die, but they are Indians of Mexico, Aztecs she believes, not these people of far North and snow. She knows how that yearning would be, for she longs for her room when she is away from it, those times when Soapy keeps her by his side for a day and a night and part of the next day, at the saloon or the dance hall or the telegraph office. She's not allowed to leave him except for a little while. That is the bargain she has struck with him. She is glad such marathons are rare.

153

The barber wants to be her friend. As Soapy relaxes under the lather, the barber winks at her, meaning, I'll take good care of him; we want him to be happy, don't we, you and me?

She settles back in her chair while the barber trims Soapy's beard with sharp scissors. What happened to the Aztecs? They were conquered, and didn't they die? She is waiting, once more; that is her role, to loiter in this sunlit shop that smells of bay rum.

Soapy looks dead in the barber's chair, laid out for waking, cheeks hollow, eyes closed. She can't imagine him ever as a child. He was born thirty-seven, tough-skinned and crafty.

"Ah," says the barber, his face shining. "Hard as Mr. Smith works, he needs his rest."

She has not come to this place to find love. She did not expect to fall in love in Alaska. She wants to, though. She wishes she loved Soapy. His face looks bloodless, his lips a dark pulp amid the beard. She thinks of bees, of how they fly into dark spaces; that's why you have to keep your mouth shut around a hive.

She laughs, and the barber's head jerks up, his eyes full of terror, as if she'd fired a gun. He can't shush her, Soapy's girl. She might ask for anything here, and her wish would be granted: fresh strawberries, a dish of ice cream, her hair washed and arranged by the barber's expert hands. When the barber sees that she's content, he launches into another song.

Soapy, eyes still shut, says at the end, "You're right good, Ted. Come sing some night at my place."

Speechless, the barber gazes at Emlee and says at last, "I'd be honored."

Soapy's nickname comes from a gambling game. You wrap bars of soap with paper and hide a dollar in one or two of them. People pay to guess which bar's got the money. You clue in a friend so it looks easy to pick the right bar. Shuffle them around, play the rube. They'll be throwing their money at you, to play. A shell game, Soapy says, making two syllables of it: *shay-ull*. Emlee has made him play it with her, spreading bars of wrapped soap on the sheets of her bed when they are naked and Soapy is spent, though their exertions are never enough to tire Emlee. She always gets the right bar.

"It ain't hard," Soapy will say, and she wants to say, "You didn't fool me."

He boasts of winning a glass eye from a man in a poker game when he was twelve years old. He's been a whiz at faro ever since his boyhood in Noonan, Georgia. Bucking the Tiger, he calls the game. Went on cattle drives in Texas, Soapy did, and learned trick riding stunts which he used in a circus.

"When I was little," Emlee has said, propped on pillows in her beautiful bed, "I taught a goose to ride on a dog's back," but Soapy at her side didn't answer; he was far away on a cattle drive, charging through crimson dust with a thousand longhorn.

Somehow, she thinks he listened to Maudie, every word Maudie said.

"There's something else that might've happened to Jim," Emlee's mother once said, "and that is, God just sent him to me, so he fell right down from Heaven and hit his head."

"But so much time went by, from that battle till you met him," Emlee said.

"Don't make no difference," Zada said. "Time is God's, not ours. And that bad wound to his head, it ought not to healed, but it did. Whoever heard of brains showing, and the skull closing over again?"

Emlee was seventeen, and she'd been lying all morning in the woods with a boy she liked, their clothes peeled off, inventing glorious new things with their bodies. That was the first time she was ever with a man.

That afternoon, she helped her mother in the shed behind the house, putting eggs in water glass for storage. Her mother wiped six dozen eggs with clean flannel, placed them small-end down in a stone crock, and poured the water glass over them. The solution of soda and potash smelled sharp and clean. The eggs settled slowly, sending up a bubble or two.

"They'll stay good for months. It's like stopping time," Zada said. She put a board over the crock and directed Emlee to set a heavy stone on it. "There," she said. "That'll keep the weasels and varmints away." She wiped her hands on her apron.

"Mama," Emlee said, "what if I want to leave here?"

"You can go." Zada stepped out of the shed into the sunlight, and Emlee followed her. It was May, with bees in the linden trees, the sweetest time. "Don't you see what I'm saying, girl," Zada said, going back as always to her own life, her great love. "Jim don't have no past life. All those women hoping he was theirs, well, he wasn't even on this Earth till Cedar Mountain. God put him in a blue uniform and dumped him into battle."

"That's crazy talk, Mama," Emlee said, hoping her period would come soon, that she would not have to worry about a baby.

"You don't know what I been through," Zada said, "taking up with a Yankee soldier. There's people around here that want me shot."

"Nobody wants that, Mama," Emlee said, but into her mind flashed the face of the old man who'd insulted her at the store, the way he flinched when the gumdrop hit his nose. He was still among them, ancient by then, gimpy on the store of the porch, fussing at children.

"I used to lie awake trying to divine it," Zada said, "where Jim was from. For years, I did that. Now I've quit. He don't remember no childhood. Got no idea how old he is. Oh, someday I hope you're as happy as I am."

"Mama," Emlee said, squeezing her mother's hands.

"When you're ready to go, Emlee, go. I don't expect you to be a old woman, still living with Jim and me."

Zada's hands were rough as the pads on a cat's paws.

She gestured to the trees and said, "Listen," meaning the bees. "Ain't that pretty," she said. "Did you know Lafayette came through here, back in the Revolution? He crossed the river right here at the Ford. His men camped. Washed their clothes and cleaned their guns. Women and children that lived here, they knew the British was coming, the redcoats, so they hid in the swamp, lay down in the alder bushes."

"You talk like you saw it, Mama."

"I heard the old people tell it, when I was a child," her mother said.

Emlee cannot know that Zada will be overtaken late in life by the desire for adventure. The wanderlust Emlee feels will come to her mother too, the longing that occasionally strikes women of limited education and means, so that they leave their men at home ("Goodbye, I am off to the Nile") and set out for Israel and Australia, for Japan and Argentina, returning with souvenirs: dolls in the exotic costumes of a dozen countries. The house on the bluff at Raccoon Ford will fill up with Zada's dolls, blank and silent, with eyes of cross-stitch and buttons.

Zada McCampbell will live a long time, longer than her daughter. Zada will live to be a hundred in the house above the river bluffs, until the family name, borne by cousins, appears on a big sign in Culpeper: McCampbell's Harley-Davidson. If Emlee at twenty-one, in the sunlit Skagway barber shop, could know that, she would nod and say: *Oh. McCampbell's Harley. Of course,* she would say, if she could see the silver motorbikes stretching out in rows beneath the Virginia sun, with rippling plastic pennants to lure customers in.

Emlee is the link, or her mother is, from the French general Lafayette to the motorcycles that hug the curves on what becomes known as the Marquis Road.

III. Waterfall

Maudie bursts through the barbershop door with Frank Reid at her heels. Their arrival is a crash, a thunderclap. Soapy's eyes fly open; he leaps to his feet, hand on his gun. He has hurtled back from a far-off dream, Emlee sees, some boyhood picnic table in Georgia with sugared tomatoes on his plate. The barber freezes where he stands, arms in an arc. Emlee holds her breath.

Maudie is drunk, Frank Reid cold sober. Tears and bits of purple gum cling to Maudie's cheek. Her boast, a legend at the house, is that she once took on a whole party of miners at a camp and it didn't make her half as sore as riding horseback or chewing gum for too long.

Frank Reid raises empty hands. "You don't need a gun for this, Soap," he says. "The lady just wants to ask you a question." He shoots tobacco juice on the floor. The barber sets down the razor, reaches for a spittoon, and slides it toward him.

"Maudie," says Soapy softly, as if they are alone. "What has happened to you? Is he treating you bad?"

Maudie shakes a piece of paper in her hand, and Emlee recognizes it as a telegram. A war is going on in Maudie's face. Her purple lips work before words get out. At last, she says, "You tell me somethin', Soapy. This is from my brother who is dead. How d'you explain that? You playin' tricks on me, you sunna bitch?"

"We're wondering," says Frank Reid, "how her brother sent a message from Hell. She says that's where he is."

Maudie punches Frank. "Shut up."

Ignoring Frank Reid, Soapy extends his hand to Maudie. "May I read it?"

Maudie throws the telegram on the floor, and Soapy, all decorum, scoops it up and smoothes it out. Maudie says, "I think you know somethin' about this, Soapy. My brother died in the wintertime. My maw wrote me he got a fever and died. I got Maw's letter after you dumped me. Then today—*today*—I get this howdy-do from him."

"Would anybody like some sarsaparilla?" the barber asks with a winning smile. "I have some, nice and cold."

Emlee casts him a warning glance. Men have been shot for lesser sins than interrupting a conversation.

"You sent this, Soap. It's some gimmick, like your Petrified Man," Maudie says. She whirls on Emlee. "You put him up to it, dincha? You musta knowed my brother died. You and him cooked this up together."

"Maudie, listen to me," says Soapy, and Maudie's wet face fixes on his. "Sometimes messages get delayed. By accident. You been in Alaska for how long now?"

"A year," Maudie says in a whisper.

"Your brother Nathan," and Soapy's voice caresses the name. "Nathan might of sent this a full year ago, and it got stuck you might say in transit, the words not sped on their way till some telegraph operator in your brother's Idaho abode found the message he had took down on paper and forgot to send."

"Oh," says Maudie. "Well, shit." The fight goes out of her; she's a bitten bubble.

"I'm sorry to learn of Nathan's demise," Soapy says. "I remember you held him in right high esteem."

Maudie collapses against Frank Reid, tucking her head into his shoulder. Soapy's words make her brother's death a new catastrophe, and she wails until her gaze falls again on Emlee. She shakes herself away from Frank Reid, her eyes flashing like beetles' wings. "You," she says. "You'll never last here. Expecting everything done for you, like you're a queen." She advances toward Emlee.

Soapy steps between them and signals the barber. "We'd like that sarsaparilla after all."

"We don't need anything," Frank Reid says and drags Maudie out the door.

Soapy pauses before sinking again into the barber's chair and casting the telegram to the floor. He looks worn out, beat.

Emlee feels sweat on her cheeks. She lets her breath out slowly.

Soapy must know Maudie took it hard, his leaving her. So the telegrams are his way of softening it. Yes, he paid attention to all of Maudie's talk while he was with her, so he learned the names of her family and friends. That is why she gets a telegram every few days, even now.

Emlee reaches for a bottle of sarsaparilla on the tray the barber offers her. Very soon, maybe even tomorrow, she too can expect telegrams. Hers will be signed by her mother and Big Jim, though the messages will have been created, of course, by Soapy. Is there any harm in that, since he does it to cheer the women he loves?

Humming, the barber resumes his attentions to Soapy. "Haircut, Mr. Smith?"

"Just a little off the top," Soapy says. "You married?"

"No, sir. It always kinda scared me."

158

"Aww. It ain't so bad," Soapy says, and Emlee wants to ask: The Indian woman? The one in Spokane? "Look at my beauty here." Soapy gestures toward Emlee. "She'll make your eyes roll back in your head."

The barber's scissors snap over Soapy's temples.

"Left side first," Soapy growls: a superstition.

"Of course. Pardon me. I forgot," the barber says.

"Hey, you. How would you describe my face?" Maudie asked Emlee during the first hour Emlee spent at the house, when Maudie was still Soapy's girl. Maudie was rouging her cheeks and penciling her eyes at a mirror on the landing. She kept the eye pencil and the paint in her pockets. Emlee regarded Maudie's face.

"All mouth and stubbornness," said Emlee.

From the kitchen came the sound of drumbeats: Egide beating a tambourine made of caribou hide, the closest he'd ever get to camp and wilderness.

"Stubborn, yeah, that's me," said Maudie, rubbing lipstick off her crooked teeth. Emlee hoped she'd made a friend. "I'll never give him up, my guy."

That night, Maudie had a birthday party. She was always having birthday parties, always turning twenty-one. She loved cake. There were twenty-one different flavors of cake, with colored candles guttering on the tops, spilling drops of wax on the icing, and candles in holders on the mantelpiece and on the piano, because Maudie loved candles too. She could have birthday parties any time she wanted, because she was Soapy's girl. She was dressed as a shepherdess in a gown that showed off her breasts. She held a crook in her hand.

Drumbeats and a mournful harmonica: the sounds from the kitchen of a brothel in a town that clings to its fleeting summers. Emlee hears the drumbeats in her head while she waits in the barbershop. How many hours till she cracks nuts in her own room, till she pets the monkey, till she lies down to sleep with her hands in gloves? Maudie has bragged that Soapy once kept her busy for two whole days in bed.

Emlee can't imagine that, not for Soapy and herself. She felt more passion for the boy under the tree at home, whose name and face she can't remember.

Out in the street, Maudie as she hangs onto Frank Reid's arm must still have her rouge and eye pencil in her pocket. "Beard burn," she said that first day to Emlee, as they stood at the mirror. "That'll put the blood in your cheeks." One tooth crossed another, in Maudie's mouth, reminding Emlee of some wild critter that used its teeth for weapons. Maudie's purple lips looked rough enough to strike matches on, but never mind. Maudie was Soapy's girl, riding high. Twenty-one cakes, just because she wanted them, cakes on the mantel, on the piano, the house packed with men and girls. Egide in the kitchen, rapping on that drum: a French-Canadian, disconsolate and far from home, and the whorehouse was not his dream. Working at the shoe factory back home would have been good enough for him. That's what he used to do, Maudie explained: he sewed soles on boots, him and Madame both, working in a factory. It was Madame who had the itch to come out here, and now Egide had the gold-mining bug, only Madame wouldn't go no further. Maudie complained of the calluses on the heels of Egide's hands, from the drum. She liked to brag about her sensitive skin, showing off, letting the others know Madame's husband wanted her, "but I belong to Jeff now," she said, as if his real name were a plum in her mouth, "and no other man gets his hands on me." The days of drum and calluses were in the past, she proclaimed. She would marry Soapy, she declared to the other girls, with her mouth full of cake. "I understand him," she said. "He knows I got a head for business, just like him."

The girls and their guests ran out of forks and ate the frosted cakes with their fingers. Maudie got drunk and played the piano. Her breasts fell out of her white gauze shepherdess dress. She climbed on the piano bench, waved her crook, and hooked it in her bodice for laughs. She drew a nimble big toe up and down the piano keys, dark thunder to high twinkling tremolos, until she slipped. Soapy caught her in his arms as she fell, but gazing over her head, he found Emlee.

Emlee was full of her journey. She'd come so far. Her legs were a sailor's, bucking and quivering from the sway and pull of trains and ferries. Her bags were upstairs, not yet unpacked. She'd come here because Egide met the boats and offered rides to new girls. She'd marked Egide for what he was even as he called out to her from his wagon. She'd told herself she could stay at the house without doing what was expected of her.

Soapy set Maudie firmly on the piano bench. She passed out face-down with her nose on middle C.

Coconut icing, that's what was sticky on Emlee's hands and sweet in her mouth when Soapy approached with Egide's drumbeats in his steps and bowed to her. She still wore the brown suit she'd crossed the country in, her travel clothes. All the way over, on the train, she'd been asked was she a schoolteacher, and sometimes she said yes because it was what people wanted to hear. She had three marriage proposals and five offers of teaching jobs. She could be firing up a stove in some man's cabin or in a one-room school, and that would not feel any stranger than being at this house, amid this merry-making.

And there was Soapy, bowing to her.

The whole room went dead quiet. Maudie's reign was over. She was out cold at the piano, would wake up jilted, her cheeks creased from sharps and flats. Soapy's eyes were dark as tunnels, all conquest and claim, and Emlee's stomach flickered with a deep, slim pain.

And Soapy dropped Maudie that fast. "Like ol' Maud was a toad, peeing in his hand," sniggered the other girls, but they cleaved to her, because she'd been scorned.

Who could say what had made Emlee want to come here? For her, it started with a list in a newspaper back in Virginia, a list of the food you should take with you to the Yukon or to Alaska: beef jerky, oats, powdered eggs. Emlee hadn't known there were such things as powdered eggs. She'd read the list aloud to her mother, and her mother said, "Makes my mouth water." Even Big Jim spoke up: "Keep readin'." So Emlee went on: beans, ketchup, dried potatoes, chocolate powder, tea and coffee. Condensed milk. Dried fruit. Pemmican, what was pemmican? Her mother and Big Jim didn't know. "Sounds like some kinda bird," Big Jim said.

The whole time on the train, rolling across the big land, she'd thought of that list and it made a song in her head. Made her hungry every time she thought of it, not that she'd packed any such provisions. It was enough to know what she would need if she were a miner herself. Vaguely she pictured herself cracking rocks, extracting gold like nutmeats.

As Soapy bowed to her, as she stood beside the piano in her brown suit, she thought of the list, of reading it out loud in Raccoon Ford by firelight, her mother and Big Jim hungry from the words. She was hungry too. She would have it all, everything on the list.

The other girls whispered, *Maudie'll kill you,* even as Soapy took Emlee's hand and led her up the stairs. They wanted Soapy to hear. It was too exciting, him with the new girl and Maud passed out. The girls stayed up all night making popcorn and having a party among themselves, and never mind the men.

Emlee went with him because he was the biggest name in town. She'd heard of him even on the train and on the boat.

"You talk funny," Soapy said the first night to her, in bed. "Say house."

She said it. She was worn out, and the smell of popcorn made her hungry.

"You say *hoose,*" Soapy said. "Never heard anybody say it like that. Say mouse," and she did. "Moose," he said. "You say *moose.*"

"Oh, I do not," she said, but even then he was checking his pocket watch, for he had business to tend to, checking the time and reaching for his pants.

It seems to her she has heard the ticking of Soapy's watch ever since reaching Alaska. Maybe it takes longer than a few weeks to fall in love, though not for her mother. Soon as her mother climbed onto the poorhouse porch and saw Big Jim, that was it.

Soapy and the barber are talking about railroads: *There'll be one right through here soon. The aerial tramways that tote the miners and their outfits over the cliffs, why, that just ain't enough these days. Men will blast through rocks with dynamite to lay tracks and build tunnels.*

Emlee sips her sarsaparilla and leans her head back on the comfortable sofa. Soapy'll own the rail line and control everything about it, even the kind of food served in the dining cars.

"It's in the works," Soapy says as the barber dusts his neck with a chamois towel. "A buddy o' mine's getting a gang of Chinks together. They'll do the blasting."

"Really," the barber says. "That's wonderful, Mr. Smith. Why, everybody in town, in the whole Territory, will be in your debt. We want that railroad. Yes, sir."

Soapy examines his hands, holding them out for the nails to be buffed.

"Chinks, huh? Little yellow-skinned fellows, wearing pointy hats and eating rats?" the barber says, but Soapy's done talking, and the barber knows enough to shut up.

"On my tab," Soapy says when he's through. Rising from the chair, he presents his arm to Emlee.

Out on the street, he pauses, blinking as if he can't quite remember where he is. Emlee squeezes his elbow. A tremor runs through his arm. At last he announces they'll go to his saloon. Something's worrying him. She knows what it is: Maudie. He walks slowly, and she matches her pace to his.

She has heard that in springtime, Broadway runs like a river with urine, as great boulders of frozen waste, created all winter by peeing drunks, melt in the alleys. The Ford was so clean. When will she see her home again, and how will she ever get the monkey to Virginia? She might close her eyes and be back at Mr. Beale's store, weighing coffee and salt, measuring cloth for farmers' wives, slicing cheese, taking money and making change. Mr. Beale trusted her to do trades, too—fresh butter bartered for nails, a chicken for a jar of boot polish.

As Soapy nears his saloon, he walks faster. Emlee has been in this town mere weeks, yet she could walk its paths in her sleep. It's three in the afternoon by the big tavern clock when they make their entrance, king and queen. The smoke is dense, the air gummy with breath and liquor.

The piano is plunking, and men bow to her. Two pool tables are going; balls crack and rumble into pockets. The mirror behind the bar reflects Soapy and his men, and Emlee catches her breath for how handsome he looks. He's in his element. Her heart soars with the hope she can love him. She blinks, and the heads and faces in the mirror are eggs in a crock of water glass.

Men are singing:

Oh, what was your name in the States?
Was it Thompson or Johnson or Bates?
Did you murder your wife, and fly for your life?
Oh, what was your name in the States?

One of Soapy's men gives a sign. The man tugs on his ear and tilts his head toward a stranger. The music's too loud for talking, but the tug is enough. It means gold.

A few days ago, astride his white horse, Soapy led Skagway's Fourth of July parade. Emlee wanted to ride alongside him, but Soapy wouldn't allow it. "A lady don't make herself a public spectacle," he said as if hearing some voice in his head, a mother's instruction to some long-ago sister of his, and meekly Emlee said, "All right." She could look on, he said, from the balcony of the Mascot Saloon.

It was chilly and cloudy. She wore a new dress Soapy had given her, of light voile printed with violets. She shivered and wished she'd brought a shawl. Goose bumps rose on her arms. She could see all of Skagway. Broadway began at City Hall and ended at the foot of a mountain. Beyond the town stretched a forest, and a cemetery where the dead lay among stumps and fallen logs. The parade would begin at the wharf and proceed down the street. It wouldn't take long.

Bunting sagged humidly from the railings of the balcony and from the cupola of the Skagway National Bank. Emlee had her period; she felt hunted and shy.

A photographer sprinted alongside the parade, taking pictures of Soapy and the assorted buggies and wagons that comprised the show. A man on a bicycle claimed he'd pedaled all the way from New York City. Egide trudged along, beating his tambourine, accompanied by a makeshift band. Emlee recognized Wilmer playing a cornet and Mr. Prentiss, of the dewlaps, blowing a tuba.

Dressed as Cleopatra, Maudie rode in a dogcart pulled by Frank Reid. Maudie's dress was a draped sheet painted gold. Her eyes were heavily accented with a sooty mixture of her own concoction—lampblack and elderberry juice.

Her neck and shoulders were bare. Even from a distance, Emlee could see deep wrinkles on her chest, caused by the corsets she wore to push up her breasts. Light rain fell, and Maudie's gold paper headgear melted to paste. She lifted a bottle to her mouth till it was empty, then tossed it aside. Since Soapy left her, Maudie had lost weight, Emlee noticed. Her face looked haggard. She must be thirty, maybe older. Frank Reid's legs pumped until he pulled Maudie's dog-cart alongside Soapy's white horse. Maudie reached down, scooped a handful of mud from the street, and hurled it. The clod struck the white horse on the flank.

The photographer snapped a picture. Soapy looked straight ahead, but the horse turned and stumbled a little. The picture would not show the splotch of mud, for that was on the other side.

Later, at the saloon, Soapy said, "I knew Maudie done that. I just didn't let on."

A fine drizzle stung the cheap tables on the balcony and puddled on the canvas floor mats. Emlee was getting wet, but she couldn't go inside unless Soapy said so. She didn't dare ask.

"You oughta teach ol' Maud a lesson," said Soapy's men.

Soapy ignored them. To Emlee he said, "I don't hold it against her."

Emlee lowered her chin.

"But that horse," Soapy said, and Emlee saw with astonishment that he was on the verge of tears. "Betrayed me. Distracted by a dadgum ball of mud. Got less mind on him than a mule."

"He's a fine horse," Emlee said.

"I ain't gonna ride him no more," Soapy said. "Bad luck if I do."

"That horse coulda rared," said a man at the next table. "Riz up and killed you, Soap, ya know it? You had a narrow excape, and it's all that whore's fault."

"Shut the fuck up," Soapy snarled. He stood and shoved the man. Beer glasses went flying, and the man fell off his spindly stool against the flimsy railing.

Gasping, the man cried, "Your days of running this town is over. We-uns have had it with you." He crawled away.

The others scrambled inside. As the bunting flapped in the rain, Soapy sighed and put his feet up on a chair. Emlee dashed mist from her brow. Down in the street, Soapy's white charger nipped a roan mare tied beside him. Rain pelted his sides, washing away the stain of mud. Cleopatra, in tears, stumbled from her phaeton and pummeled Frank Reid, her shouts lost in the rain.

Emlee hunkered down in her chair, tugging her voile sleeves to her elbows. Cold and wet, yet skeeters hovered. One landed on her arm, and she slapped it, leaving a burst of blood.

Soapy looked at the mess grimly and said, "It is not unknown for people to get malaria up here. Don't think, because you're this far north, you can't get it. It's a dread thing."

Emlee swabbed at the blood with her handkerchief. Down below, Wilmer untied the white horse and led him around back to the stable. The roan mare stood dejectedly in the rain.

"You have got to stick with me, Emlee," Soapy said. "You do, and I might marry you. You don't, and you could end up in one of them cribs."

She took his hand. It was his pride and sorrow talking. The depraved women in the narrow cribs—just stalls where rutting went on, located on the town's outskirts and in alleys—were the most pathetic creatures she'd ever seen, opium users, scarred bruised throwaways unwelcome at even the lowest brothel.

"They're worse off than dogs," Soapy said.

She stroked his arm and laid her head against his shoulder. The comforts of cracking nuts and petting the monkey were hours away.

"Listen good," Soapy said. "I am married to a woman named Anna. Anna Nielsen, she was, a actress when I met her. We wed in Denver, and we have us three children. Been years, though, since we was together as man and wife. Differences sprung up between us. Anna's back with her folks in St. Louis, but I been good to her and the kids. She got her share of diamonds. For you, I would divorce her."

"What about Maudie?" Emlee said.

"I never told Maudie I'd marry her."

"But do you still love her?" Emlee pressed. "Seems to me you might."

"You think I'd have a woman who throws mud at me?" Soapy said. "You're prettier. I always get the prettiest one. Don't worry about her."

She didn't attempt to explain that she wasn't jealous of Maudie. She wanted to right something, to make him see how he felt, but the words weren't there.

When she didn't answer, he said, "You don't never say my name."

After a while, when Emlee was numb with chill, Wilmer brought a beaver robe and tucked it around her. She took it gratefully. Nothing had ever felt so warm and soft.

Back in her room, the monkey would eat the nuts she'd set out for it, gaze at itself in the mirror, and rearrange jars of cosmetics in ways it found pleasing. There were things it would do in its natural state, in the jungle, but Emlee could not imagine what those things were. She has checked its teeth, wondering how old it is. Because it's small, she thinks of it as young, but maybe it isn't.

The rain kept falling. She gazed over Skagway, thinking, *It's summer. It's the Fourth of July.* She wondered why the roofs of buildings were flat, not pitched, given all the snow that must fall in the winter. By September, certainly October, snow would be deep, if what she'd heard was true.

"My last horse died of the staggers," was all Soapy said, the whole afternoon.

She'd left the Ford in early March, on the first warm day. Young frogs sang in the swamp, their cries high and sweet. *Breath of spring,* she thought as she said goodbye to her mother in the yard, their feet crushing the purple crocuses and white snowdrops and yellow aconites that were the first flowers to bloom. The trees were still bare. Winter would come and go for a few weeks, before it was really spring.

Zada McCampbell couldn't say goodbye. She toed the blossoms and said to Emlee, "Aconite's good for toothache." And, "Warm weather brings cat scratch fever."

Breath of spring, Emlee thought as Big Jim drove her to the Culpeper train depot. Past the Female Institute they went. Past the beautiful Main Street home of Extra Billy Smith, the governor who had dominated the stage lines and railroads. In the side yard of the mansion, rugs hung on a line, and two colored women beat the dust out of them.

At the station, Big Jim unloaded her bags while she bought a ticket with money she'd made at Beale's store. When she reached the platform, he took some bills from his pocket and handed them to her.

"Thank you," she said, surprised, hugging him, careful not to touch the back of his head, which she imagined must still be sore. How could the brains be blasted out of a man, and he survive? In her embrace, he stood as still as a tree.

"Goodbye, Emlee, and good luck," he said. A long speech, for him.

"Marry my mama," she said. "Please marry her."

From the window of the train, she waved to him, but he'd already turned the horses around. The wagon flew up Davis Street, away.

On the long ride west, whenever she spotted a stampeding herd—of wild horses or elk, the buffalo being almost gone—it was Big Jim she saw instead, faster in his wagon than any prairie critters. Once she spied a lone, clumsy bear racing alongside the tracks, a comical sight. Passengers pointed and exclaimed. Wild horses running were beautiful. You could spot them from way off. You had to get your eyeful before the train spun past them. At night, she saw them in her dreams. She was too young to get stiff from sitting up to sleep.

In Seattle she bought a steamer ticket. It was the first time she'd seen water other than a river or lake or pond. The first time she'd seen the ocean.

"Coffee and brandy," Soapy says, "and two bowls of turtle soup."

The bartender says, "Coming up."

"And biscuits," Soapy says. "Put some ham in 'em."

"We got good venison pie today, Mr. Smith. You want some of that too?"

"I told you what I want."

"Yes, sir," the bartender says.

Soapy leads Emlee to a small table in a corner. When the meal arrives, she dips her spoon into the soup and lifts it to her lips. It's delicious, the squares of turtle meat tender, the broth rich. As is Soapy's habit, he takes out his pocket watch and lays it on the table.

At the bar, men are whooping and passing something among themselves—a burlap sack. One voice swells above the din, a stranger's, calling, "Hey. Give it back. I want that back now." Emlee has seen this trick before. It starts with a tug on the ear and ends with a newcomer losing his gold, and in between there's the handing around of a wallet or a sack.

Across from her, Soapy sips his brandy but leaves his food untouched. "'Scuse me," he says and rises from his chair.

It's like watching a play. The stranger's monotone sharpens with agitation: "Give that back now. It's mine. Give it here." Soapy approaches him, speaks, and shakes his hand. Then, to a man, the drinkers, card players, pool players, and revelers troop outside, Soapy leading his new chum by the arm. Emlee can see them through a window. They've gone out to look at the eagle suspended in its cage in the tree. Beneath the great bird, the men jostle in a way that does not look entirely friendly. Boys and dogs scurry around the edges of the crowd.

How silent the barroom is. The music has stopped. The piano player is outside with the others. She and the bartender are alone, with smoke lifting between them like a rising curtain.

"How's the soup, Miss Emlee?" the bartender asks.

"It's wonderful," she says, but she can't eat any more. She sets the spoon down. How must all of this look to the eagle with its rounded shoulders, leaning its proud head between the bars? She should be the one to free it, to make her way up into its tree at some dead hour when no one's around to see. She'll take an axe and hack through the cage, and the eagle will squeeze through the splintered boards, sluggish and cold, the memory of flight coming back to it. It will lift, soar, and disappear.

The bartender says, "A fool and his money." He wipes a rag down the counter. "Twenty-seven hundred dollars worth of gold in that poke. I seen it with my own eyes."

A man speaks from the shadows, startling them both. "It's time for the joke to be over," says Thaddeus Scott of Devon, Pennsylvania, rising from a bench beside the door, "and a poor joke it is." He's got a glass in his hand, and Emlee bets it's ginger ale.

"Oh, they'll give it back," the bartender says hastily. "It's all in fun. He oughta be a good sport."

Frank Reid strolls in. By himself, without Maudie, the city engineer in his green checked shirt is a dignified man. He nods to Thaddeus Scott, to Emlee. "Quiet in here," he says. "I hear a friend of mine's in town, back from the fields. Name of Stewart. You seen him?"

The bartender raises his hand and points to the window. "Out back," he says. "They're all out there looking at Mr. Smith's eagle. And you know what? It's feeding time. Here, Mr. Reid, take the eagle some of this sausage." The bartender offers a bowl of meat, but Frank Reid's hustling out the back door as fast as if somebody shouted *Fire*.

The bartender sets down the dish. For a long while, he and Emlee and Thaddeus Scott look at each other. From the backyard come shouts, and then shots ring out, high echoing blasts as if guns were fired skyward. Every man out there has a weapon or several. The bartender unties his apron, folds it, and stows it beneath the counter. "I'm a-take me a little break," he says, stepping from behind the bar. He goes out the front door and into the street.

Thaddeus Scott sets his glass on the counter and places some coins beside it.

"If you get a telegram tomorrow asking for money, don't pay it," Emlee says.

Another shot resounds. A billiard ball drops from the edge of a table, hits the floor, and rolls toward Emlee. She stops it with her foot.

"It looks as if you have the afternoon to yourself," says Thaddeus Scott. "Is there somewhere you would like to go? May I walk you there?"

He's faithful to his Ida, back home in Devon, Pennsylvania, and Emlee's glad. His face shows he'll escort her, and that's all. She could say, *Take me to the house where I stay, so I can pack,* and he would. She could say, *Take me to the steamer office. I want to buy a ticket.*

Soapy's watch ticks on the table. The hands show it's 3:28. She stands up. It is dangerous to linger here. She has never felt death so close at hand.

Men have sobbed in this room from exhaustion, from disappointment, as Soapy consoles them: "Fortune's a elusive thing." Men and women, drunk and sober, have wept at the beauty of piano music, for Soapy hires only the best. Emlee goes to the piano and presses a few keys.

She shed tears only once during her journey, and that was on the train, when she saw horses galloping, a small fierce herd hurtling, flying. For a long thunderous moment, they outran the locomotive. A woman across the aisle leaned over and said, "What's the matter, dear? They're all right. See, there they go." Only then did Emlee realize she was crying. The horses veered away from the train, and the woman reached up to close a window, saying, "This *dust.*"

If that wasn't heartbreak, what was?

Thaddeus Scott is holding the door for her.

Later it seems that even as she moved past him into the street, she saw the photographs that would run in the papers: Soapy being autopsied on a bloody sheet; Soapy in the morgue, eyes peeled wide open, the lids held with bits of wax; Frank Reid feverish, dying for twelve days in his hospital bed, attended by a nurse in a striped shirtwaist and a doctor who blinked the instant the shutter snapped.

"The public has a right to know," Thaddeus Scott says as he maneuvers Emlee past a man sleeping open-mouthed on the street. "To know if there are thieves among us."

"Have you changed your mind?" she asks. "About going to the gold fields?"

She can't hear his reply. The street's too noisy, but she believes he is saying no.

It's over: Soapy's rule, his very life. She senses it, knows it in her heart, though it's hours until the men meet each other down at the wharf, Frank Reid and Soapy. They'll shoot each other at close range in the lungs and in the hip, with motions like a dance. The sound she hears as she hurries along

Broadway with Thaddeus Scott is the sound of men closing in, of vigilantes gathering to plan revenge.

She has always known it would end fast.

Soapy has said he wants dogs at his funeral, in the cortege, all the dogs in town. It's Frank Reid who'll get the grand rites. Soapy Smith will be buried quick, dumped among the stumps in the graveyard by the angry and righteous, many of them his former friends, the same citizens who will erect an obelisk for Reid and will name the loveliest local site in his honor. Stewart, the newcomer, will even get his poke of gold back, minus six hundred dollars' worth, the sack being found in the vault of the Mascot Saloon.

"So where are we going?" Thaddeus Scott asks.

The day has turned warm and fine. There's a spot she has heard about ever since she came here, a place she wants to see. "The waterfall."

Reid Falls, it'll be called in future times.

"Do we need to hire a carriage?" he says.

"It's just up there." She points to the mountain at the end of the street. "We can walk."

She stops by the house for a hat and finds Egide alone in the parlor. The room is more silent and still than she has ever seen it before, stale and unkempt, as if Madame has stopped taking care of it entirely. The ottoman where Egide sits is tattered, with clots of stuffing erupting from the seams. Cigar butts litter the rug. The mantelpiece and the top of the piano bear globs of candle wax, spilled the night Emlee and Soapy met.

"Where is everybody?" Emlee asks Egide.

"Those crazy girls, they went swimming. They'll freeze their butts off." He holds a stack of postcards, thumbing them with thick, soiled fingers. The cards show photographs that must have been taken from high above, probably from the tramways: hundreds of packhorses trekking across the glaciers like a line of ants. "You think I can sell these?" he asks.

"I don't see why not." Emlee imagines Egide and Madame as shopkeepers in this very house, the two of them grown old, surrounded by racks of dusty postcards and dishes of flyspecked candy.

"Business is falling off," Egide says. "My wife and I got to branch out. So I got this idea. We'll sell stuff to tourists. As for you," he says as if seeing her for the first time in a long while. "You gonna marry Mr. Smith, drag him back to the States, be respectable? A little bird told me," and he waggles his finger at her. "Grab your chance. This'll be a ghost town one day. Boom, then bust."

"I'm going to stay a while," she says. "I don't think it's over yet."

"You don't know nothing," Egide says as if disagreeing with a child, "but

I hope you're right. I might go stake a claim. Just up and leave. My wife don't think I'd do it, but I will."

Emlee hurries up to her room, her heart pounding as always with fear the monkey will be gone or hurt. She unlocks her door, and there's the little creature asleep on the bed, its tail wrapped around its body.

"Fortune is a elusive thing," she whispers, and it stirs and yawns.

For a time she lies beside it, her head pillowed on her hands, knowing Thaddeus Scott, a solid man, a good man, is waiting outside the house. A sense of comfort, almost well-being, washes over her, never mind how temporary. Yet always there's that pain in her heart.

Big Jim, racing away from the Culpeper depot in the wagon: going where? She wants to believe he hurried home to marry her mother, but he might have gone anywhere.

She may never know.

Reaching the cascade involves a hike around the mountainside. Moving from shadow to brilliant light, Emlee and Thaddeus Scott navigate paths and ledges. Fronds and ferns brush the hem of her dress. He insists on leading the way. After a time, she hears shouts and recognizes the voices of girls she knows.

At the waterfall, the girls are laughing and screaming. Like dragonflies, they dart into the radiant water. The force of it, splashing down the mountain and striking the rocks below, is powerful enough to knock a person over, Emlee sees. Thaddeus Scott's face shows astonishment and pleasure at the height and power of the spill, and she feels a jolt of pride in having brought him here.

Yelling, the girls run about in scanties, hair plastered to their heads and down their backs. Dresses and shoes lie in careless heaps. Girls hover in the luminous spray that surrounds the cascade and gather the courage to dive into the torrent. Maudie's the boldest. With arms raised like a ballerina's, she hurls herself into the deluge, then prances out into sunshine. Children are playing too, Indians and whites, chasing each other and clamoring. Dogs yap and skirmish, shaking droplets from their coats. The cold is nothing to them.

The Filipina, wringing her long braid, cries out to Emlee, "Hey, where's all the men?"

"They're at the Mascot," Emlee calls back as if all is well. To Thaddeus Scott, she says, "There's a good place," and points at a grassy, level spot.

He wavers as if he might sit down and linger, but his loyalty to Ida wins out. "I must be going," he says. "Be careful. You don't really belong here."

"I'll be all right," she says.

After he departs, she removes her hat and kicks off her shoes. *Remember this*. She unfastens her jacket and skirt. She'll wait her turn, then leap into the water. The sun will shine forever, into those hours that should be night. She can stay here as long as she likes. She can be the last to leave.